Murder at the Folly

RINA MARTIN MYSTERIES

Murder
at the
Folly

JANE
ADAMS

JOFFE BOOKS

Joffe Books, London
www.joffebooks.com

First published in Great Britain in 2025

Cover art by Cherie Chapman

ISBN: 978-1-80573-387-4

PROLOGUE

July

There was a nursery rhyme Marcia remembered from childhood that stated boldly that while sticks and stones might break bones, words could never hurt. She had known the lie of that all her life; words, carelessly used, proclaimed in ill intent or just said thoughtlessly by someone who perhaps knew no better injured as surely as any beating, any hurled rocks, any broken bones. The difference of course was that when it came to injury inflicted by words, the breaks and bruises didn't show.

She had grown up knowing the pain that words could inflict and the additional hurt when those speaking them were meant to be those you loved and trusted. Those you were at least supposed to be able to love and trust. But she had left all of that behind her, hadn't she?

Hadn't she?

Twenty years married. Twenty years in which she had felt herself to be loved and cherished . . . in which she had been careful never to have put a foot wrong. She knew what he wanted — or thought she did — and was assiduous in supplying his needs, even when that meant neglecting her own.

But he was a good man, wasn't he? Never raised his voice to her, certainly never raised a hand. Helped around the house, encouraged her to go for promotions at work, to pursue her interests when he was working away. His work pattern of six weeks away and three weeks home had taken some getting used to, but she had, and it had made them both value his time at home even more.

Hadn't it?

Though, of course, those times when he was at home, she put her other interests aside and they did things together. Saw friends, visited relatives, indulged his love for ancient buildings and stately homes and theatre.

Saw *his* friends. Visited *his* relatives. Indulged *his* interests . . . and she told herself that was fair. She had all the free time when he wasn't there to see her friends, do as she pleased. She was happy.

They were happy. Or so she thought.

Then there was the morning she came downstairs and found the letter on the kitchen table, propped against the antique cut glass and silver condiment set with its multiple bottles for oils and vinegars and mustards that they never used. Her name, in his bold and scrawling hand, was written on the envelope.

Why wasn't he here? He'd said nothing about going out and he wasn't due to return to work for another week. Had he nipped out to the shops for something they had forgotten? If he wanted to leave a note to say he'd popped out, why hadn't he scribbled one on the chalkboard fixed to the fridge for just such a purpose, or even texted her?

No, she realized with sudden trepidation, this was something more.

She took a knife from the block on the kitchen counter, slit the letter open and withdrew the single sheet of paper, recognising it as the cheap printer paper he habitually bought for use with his old laser printer, the ageing machine having a tendency to eat paper with any substance to it.

Printed in the centre of the page were just a few lines, but the words punched her in the gut and then stabbed her so deeply she felt she'd never stop the bleeding.

I'm sorry. But I've been so bored I can't bear it anymore. I know it's not your fault and you can't help being who you are, but I've met someone who excites me and makes me feel alive again.

I've instructed my solicitor to start divorce proceedings. You can keep the house. I'll send someone for my things.

He had signed off with a familiar, handwritten scribble that approximated his name.

Afterwards she could not recall how long she had stood there, staring at the words. What she did remember was that sense of being suddenly untethered from herself, even though her body was aware of the coolness of the tiled floor beneath her feet and the scent of roses and sweet peas drifting in from the garden through the open kitchen window, the sun already warming the room at the beginning of another hot day. She was aware of all those things and of the feel of the paper between her hands and yet . . . and yet . . . it was as though she was somewhere else. Someone else. Someone she no longer recognized. For a few almost blissful moments this was happening to another person. Not to her. Definitely not to her.

And then, as though suddenly slammed back into her body, the whole force of his words hit her once again. With a little cry, half sorrow, half rage, she dropped the letter on to the wooden top of the kitchen table. For an instant, sorrow took control and the sobs rose in her throat. But the rage rose with them and, it seemed from nowhere, so did the scream.

She seized the knife she had used to open the letter, wanting to stab and shred, to destroy those words, to obliterate them. She slashed the blade across the page, drove its point into the wooden table and finally swiped letter, knife and glass-and-silver cruet on to the kitchen floor, where the cruet smashed into a dozen sharply faceted pieces.

Afterwards she thought that if her husband had been in range, she could — no, would — have stabbed him through the heart, just as he had stabbed her, and she would have felt all the better for it.

CHAPTER 1

April, nine months later

Although the once grand carved oak doors had long since been replaced by far less inspiring half-glazed, utilitarian affairs, once inside, Septon Hall hinted at the rather glorious residence it had once been. The oldest part of the hall was late Tudor and the tall, square space was still lined with original, age darkened linenfold panelling.

The central staircase was much later, a Regency addition from a time when the house had hosted some very grand balls, though as the past residents of Septon Hall seemed to have been reluctant ever to throw anything out, the bannisters rested, at intervals, on stiff carvings of ruffed ladies and gentlemen of the same vintage as the panelling.

The encaustic floor tiles were Victorian and would have looked quite at home in a suburban villa in their shades of red, white, black and pale blue. They had worn unevenly, some of the clays used in their construction being harder wearing than others. The mishmash of styles and ages might have jarred but Grace Sweetman took a moment, as she always did, to glance around. If you ignored the very unsympathetic doors that looked as though they'd been stolen from a nineteen seventies factory, the odd mix was actually quite charming. Septon Hall had been in the same family for hundreds of years and though it was now only a shadow of its former self, the impression was of a house that had been well loved. More to the point, a house that had actually been lived in and enjoyed and was not a mothballed museum.

She shrugged out of her coat and hung it on the stand beside the door. It had been her habit, while they had been filming here, to take a walk between breakfast and the start of the working day just to clear her head. A round table occupied the central space and Phil Perry stood beside it, one hand resting on the top, his skinny frame bent almost double as he removed his shoe. "Got a stone or something in it," he said by way of explanation.

Grace frowned. Phil was evidently loitering with some kind of intent. He had that look about him.

"You've got a letter." He pointed at a white envelope on the tabletop. "Who'd be writing to you here?"

Grace frowned. Who indeed? It wasn't unknown for cast and crew to have mail forwarded to where they were filming, but it was unusual and she'd certainly made no such arrangement.

Frowning, she picked it up. The name and address was printed on the front: *Miss Grace Sweetman, C/O Septon Hall.* There was no return address. Conscious of Phil's eyes on her, she slid a finger beneath the flap and tore open the envelope. Inside was a single sheet of printer paper, the cheap, thin kind, Grace noted absently. It was folded into thirds, top and bottom flaps over the centre. She opened it up to reveal two scant lines.

Bitches like you deserve all that comes to them. You'll get what you deserve and then we'll all laugh in your face.

"What is it?" Phil demanded. He came around the table and looked at it over her shoulder.

Impatient and irritated, she snatched the paper away. "None of your business." Her eyes narrowed with suspicion.

"Did you send this? Is this your idea of a joke? That would be just like you, wouldn't it?"

Phil looked shocked. Genuinely shocked, Grace thought.

"Nothing to do with me. I saw it there and I wondered . . . I wondered if . . . you know those letters people have been getting? There was a bit in one of the local papers the other day. Nasty letters, accusing people of stuff. And I heard Rina talking about it to Seth. Well, I saw it and I wondered. Rina said they all came in plain white envelopes, the name and address printed on the front. It looked like what she said."

"A lot of letters come in plain white envelopes," Grace retorted, "and no one handwrites names and addresses anymore, do they?"

"I do," Phil said. "If it's a birthday card or something."

"Well, this is obviously no birthday card."

A tall ceramic stick stand stood beside the coat rack. It was vivid blue and decorated with coiled, writhing dragons. Grace screwed up the letter and the envelope and tossed them inside. Immediately, she wished she hadn't. Phil would retrieve them, make a joke of it. And why not? she wondered briefly. It was a joke, wasn't it? It was an absurdity. But another part of her was hurt at the accusatory words. More than she would normally be, she realized. This was not a good time in Grace's life. Her most recent relationship had just imploded and work, here at Septon Hall, had been more stressful than she had expected. A few old wounds had already been opened these past few months and the additional stab in the back hurt more than she would usually have allowed it to.

She cast an impatient look at Phil, who was already eyeing the dragon vase and clearly willing her to leave.

"Oh, no," she said. "Oh no, I'm not having that."

Angrily, she reached into the vase and retrieved letter and envelope, stuffed them both in her cardigan pocket and stalked away. She was conscious of Phil watching her go. She glanced back once. He stood beside the table, an odd look on his narrow face. Anxious, she thought, and slightly pitying. Well, he didn't need to worry about her and she certainly didn't want his pity. Even so, she could feel tears pricking at her eyes.

* * *

Although it was only eleven in the morning, it was already turning out to be an unusually fractious day on set and Rina Martin wasn't exactly sure why. True, Grace Sweetman was being her usual demanding self, but everyone was used to that, and she was generally humoured and ignored in equal measure. Then there were what had become the routine technical glitches that had plagued filming from the very start and which everyone had come to accept as part and parcel of filming in an ageing location like Septon Hall.

Today, however, those daily irritations, both in terms of equipment and personnel were getting to everyone. Filming of this small but crucial scene between Lady Ellsworthy and her gamekeeper had been halted three times in the past half hour and everyone, cast and crew, were starting to look positively mutinous.

Rina sipped her tea and settled herself in a semi-comfortable seat at the end of a sagging settee, watching with resignation as Alison, the director, discussed the problems of a failed lighting circuit with the engineers.

"More old wiring at fault, I suppose?" Richard Cartmell, the screenwriter, flopped down beside her, tucking his long legs in. He was a tall, thin man and Rina got the feeling he was always worried about getting in the way.

"Not this time," Rina told him. "It's some of *our* equipment that's gone down this time. Something about a failed inverter." She shrugged.

"Oh, that sounds serious." He paused. "What does it do?"

"Well, I know inverters switch DC to AC electric. I only know that because we've got one from when we had solar panels fitted last year. The solar powers the batteries, the inverter converts battery power into mains."

"Well it's annoying, whatever it is. My lights all went out again last night, did yours?"

"Flickered a lot but I didn't lose them. This whole building needs rewiring, if you ask me. I don't wonder they leaped at the chance of having us film here. It's a pretty enough location but it must be a right liability trying to keep an old house like this going."

Reflectively, Rina sipped more of her tea. It wasn't good tea; the water in the portable urns never seemed quite hot enough and the tea was always scummy and pale. She craved a good hot potful back at home, with a slice of cake or even a decent biscuit. Septon Hall was, as she had said, a pretty place, or would be with the sun shining on it — April had been wet, the rain relentless these past ten days — but it was also cold and draughty and damp and, with cast and crew all camping out on location for most of the week, cramped. She was lucky; as star of the show she had her own room and en suite, such as it was. Getting sufficient hot water out of the shower in the morning was a daily challenge. She knew that Richard Cartmell was sharing his bathroom with two others. Some of the bedrooms in the main house had been refurbished to luxurious standards, ready for the guests who came to celebrate weddings and anniversaries, but neither cast nor crew qualified for luxury, Rina thought wryly, and they had been consigned to the largely unmodernized rooms in the servants' wing.

In its heyday, Septon Hall must have had a massive staff if the size of this wing and the number of narrow passageways, designed purely for service access, were anything to go by.

The room they were in was just off the main reception hall and looked out over the gravel drive and then a long lawn. At the end of the lawn the land rose steeply and a path led up a hill to the folly, a tall tower that had been put up in the eighteenth century and then remodelled in the nineteenth. Looking out through the large windows Rina could see about two thirds of it. The lower part of the tower was hidden from the house by a dip in the ground, the landscape flattening out just beyond the top of the hill. The builders had taken advantage of this geographical feature, though it puzzled Rina as to why, if they were spending so much on building a folly, the landowners at the time had not also paid for the top of the hill to be removed so the whole of the folly could be seen from the house.

She had walked up to it a few times with her friend Seth on days when they had been so frustrated with being cooped up for longer than they had expected and felt they had energy enough to burn.

"This is bloody awful tea." Rina set her cup aside.

"Coffee's no better," Richard commented. "The hot chocolate is at least drinkable, but I've got to be in the mood for that."

Rina nodded and shifted position on the old sofa. It really was old. It was what she thought might have been classed as a window seat at the time it had been made, which, if she was not much mistaken, was very early Victorian. It was carved wood, with scrolling arms and a padded back and seat. At some point it had been reupholstered or at least recovered in a not very sympathetic blue slub silk but she strongly suspected that whoever had done the job had restuffed the seat with the original horsehair.

"Looks as though we're off again," Richard said, and Rina noted that Alison was about to call for positions.

"Grace doesn't look happy," she said.

"When does she?"

"True." Grace Sweetman had been unknown to Rina before their sojourn at Septon Hall and Rina doubted she'd be maintaining the acquaintance. Grace was playing Lady Ruth Ellsworthy who, together with her husband, Lord Gilbert Ellsworthy, owned the fictional version of Septon Hall in which the original novel had been set. This was the seventh and last of the original Lydia Marchant novels to be filmed and Rina wondered if there would be any more. Not that it mattered in terms of content — Richard Cartmell had worked closely with the original creator of Lydia Marchant to produce additional storylines for the previous series of the long-running drama, which filled in the timeline between the existing narratives and would, all being well, extend the timeline beyond. The author of the novels, Judith Tavener, would be paying a visit to the set the following day. Rina hoped there would be fewer technical difficulties then.

"OK, looks like Grace is about to kick off," Richard said, bringing Rina's attention back to what was happening on set. "Poor old Phil's about to get it in the neck this time."

"You missed your cue!" Grace leaned in accusingly.

"I did not. You fluffed that last line. I assumed we would be going again. That line was completely wrong."

"It was not. Two words, I changed two words. And they meant exactly the same thing. Anyone else would simply have adapted and carried on. Talk about lack of professionalism!"

"My lack of professionalism? When you can't even be bothered to say the lines you're given. How do you expect anyone to play their role when you're feeding them the wrong line!"

"I changed two words. Anyone or their dog should be able to accommodate that." She leaned in closer to Phil. "Not that I blame you, particularly, of course. It's hardly your fault that you just don't have the experience to cope with a role like this, or the demands of a serious production.

"Ouch," Rina said softly.

"Enough." Alison had stepped in, and Rina could see that she was furious with the pair of them. She seemed to take a deep and steadying breath before saying, "Now take a break, we'll resume in five minutes." She spread both arms wide, pointing to opposite ends of the room, like a referee in a boxing match directing the fighters back to their respective corners.

Grace sailed off in one direction and Phil, red faced and clearly irritated, retreated to where the tea urn had been set up.

"I'll go and have a chat with him," Richard said. "It looks like Seth has stepped in to sort Grace out."

Rina glanced over to where Grace was now standing by the window, ferociously straightening her skirt and cardigan then pearl necklace as though any one of them might be to blame for her being out of sorts. Seth, aka Otis Finch, Lydia Marchant's faithful sidekick, laid a calming hand on her arm, his round face wrinkled with concern. At first it looked as though she might shake him off, but she seemed to relent.

Seth patted her arm and persuaded her into a deep armchair while he perched on the window seat. Rina was too far away to hear what he was saying, but it seemed to be doing the trick. "She's like a toddler having a tantrum," she commented to Richard. "She's even worse than usual today."

"Isn't she though? But Seth's balm seems to be working. I'll go and try to apply some to Phil. My guess is that Judith Tavener's visit tomorrow is winding her up. It's not going to be comfortable for either of them, I don't suppose."

"Oh? And why is that?"

"Oh, you know, after Grace stole Judith's husband. Anyway, I'd better see to Phil if any of us are going to get through this morning."

But I want to know about the husband, Rina wanted to say. She sighed, supposing it would have to wait until lunchtime. Seth was bound to know the full story and would be happy to have a gossip.

Alison had been talking to Phil, nodding her dark head sympathetically, her pale, long fingered hand resting on his shoulder. Phil, in full gamekeeper getup of tweeds and leather patches was calming down, the high colour fading from his face. Alison smiled at Richard when he arrived and retreated gratefully, Rina thought. She watched idly as Alison crossed to speak to the lighting director and then glanced at her watch. More than five minutes had passed, to Rina's count. Alison took in the room, pale blue eyes keenly analysing the mood and demeanour of actors and crew before deciding that everyone had settled down enough to continue. At her nod, the floor manager called for "positions, please" and cast and crew moved to obey, Grace just a little slower to her mark than everyone else, letting them all know that she was still miffed.

Here we go again, Rina thought, watching keenly as the scene unfolded and Phil, in his role as Fitzsimons the game-keeper, reported that poachers had been out again and that Professor Stenson, who was leading the fictional dig, sent word he had more finds to show her ladyship later on. It was an insignificant-seeming exchange, one that ended with Lady Ellsworthy glancing at her wristwatch and then shaking it impatiently and asking Fitzsimons for the time, thus setting up an alibi. Then, Rina knew, there would be an overcompli-cated plot twist regarding broken watches and times of death that ultimately proved to be just a shoal of red herrings. As Lydia Marchant would demonstrate.

Dead on cue, Rina, as Lydia Marchant, strode across the Grand Salon, interrupting the conversation and asking where on earth Lord Ellsworthy might be. He was supposed to have met her half an hour before.

"How should I know?" Lady Ellsworthy questioned. "I don't keep him on a lead."

"Well, perhaps you should," Lydia Marchant told her tartly. "At least then he might manage to be on time."

* * *

"Is it true Grace stole Judith Tavener's husband?" Rina asked as she and Seth took their trays off to their favourite corner table.

Seth's round face seemed to grow even rounder with surprise, his mouth an O. "Who told you that? Oh, it's no real secret, I suppose, but a lot of water has passed under a lot of bridges since then. It must have been, what, getting on for twenty years ago. And I'm not sure I'd describe it as theft. Tony wasn't so much stolen as a willing participant in the kidnapping, if you see what I mean. Grace can be compelling when she wants to be."

Rina's expression must have told Seth she found that hard to believe because he laughed. "Oh, you didn't know

13

her back then. She was magnificent in her younger days and, truth be told, a much nicer person." He added this a touch sadly.

"You knew her well?"

"I'd not seen her for some time when the Judith Tavener incident was going on, but I did indeed know her well when we were both fresh-faced young thespians trying to make a living. For a time we were good friends. But we drifted apart, you know what it's like. And then time takes its toll on the body and on the mind. Makes the body softer and the mind harder in some cases and I'm afraid our Gracie was one of them."

"What happened?" Rina asked.

"Oh, I don't know, not one thing I don't think. This isn't an easy business to be in, you know that. Some people handle disappointments badly. They get resentful and angry, I suppose."

He turned his attention to his food and they ate in silence for a moment. It was clear that Seth either didn't want or was unable to give a simple answer to the Grace Sweetman conundrum. Glancing at the woman, now holding court on the other side of the room and for the moment charm itself, Rina fancied she could still see traces of the younger iteration of Grace. The softer, perhaps more vulnerable young woman she might have been. Or was she, Rina wondered, just trying to see those traits because Seth had assured her they had been there?

"Is she still with this Tony . . ."

"Emmerson. Lord no. He hung around for a few months and then must have decided she was too much like hard work. Tried to go back to Judith, I believe, but that wasn't about to happen."

"No?"

"No. What he did practically broke the poor woman. Judith was never what you'd call robust. She took it very badly and who can blame her? Grace swept in, broke up her marriage and in truth she didn't even want Tony once she'd got him."

"Did Grace make a habit of that kind of thing?"

Seth seemed reluctant to answer. Finally, he said, "The Grace I first knew wasn't like that. As I said, I lost touch with her for a while and by the time I met up with her again, around the time all this was kicking off with Tony, well, all I can say is that she'd definitely changed."

How old was Grace Sweetman? Rina wondered. Mid-fifties now? So, in her thirties when she persuaded Tony Emmerson to jump ship. Something occurred to her. "Judith must have been writing *Murder at the Folly* when all that was going on."

Seth looked startled for a moment, then nodded. "I believe so, yes. *Folly* was the third book written?"

"Yes. The first two had done all right but from what I've heard a new editor came on board that wasn't too keen. I believe *Murder at the Folly* had already been commissioned and scheduled, so it was going ahead but was meant to be the last Lydia Marchant, and Judith Tavener was going to move on to something else. So, in what she thought would be the final book, she wrote an older version of Lydia Marchant. Then it became a massive success and of course everything changed and she went back and wrote another four books that happened earlier in the timeline. So *Folly* was the third written but the seventh in Lydia's timeline. If I recall, someone had suggested to her that she put some references into *Folly* about possible earlier cases, just in case she eventually got the opportunity to pick the series up again."

"Well that was clever of someone," Seth approved. "Turned out to be very good advice."

Didn't it? Rina thought. She wondered if that someone had been Richard Cartmell, seeing as the screenwriter had worked so closely with Judith Tavener on adapting the original books and creating additional plots for the TV series. Had they known each other back then? She was about to ask when Seth glanced at his watch.

"Well, better love you and leave you for a while. I've a couple of phone calls to make before the afternoon session."

He rose, bent to kiss Rina on the cheek. "See you later, my dear."

Rina, watching him go, moved on to her dessert. Sticky toffee pudding. Not a patch on what the Montmorencys made at home, but it would do. She really did need something warming and unctuous. She thought again about the spat between Grace and Phil that morning. Was the woman really feeling unsettled at the idea of Judith Tavener's visit? As Seth had commented, a lot of water had flowed under bridges since then and presumably Judith had made no objection to her one-time love rival being cast in the production of *Murder at the Folly*. She had, Rina guessed, enough clout that she could have protested, had she felt the need.

Maybe the fact that she hadn't was in itself interesting. In her position Rina suspected she'd have raised Cain and insisted on a change of actor. But then, what did she know? She'd had no real experience of that kind of emotional turmoil first hand. She had fallen in love and been married only once. Been widowed far too early and never seriously wanted anyone else. There *had* been brief relationships. She had known that her beloved Fred would not have wanted her to be lonely and so she'd genuinely tried to get back on that particular horse. But nothing had stuck. Some of these brief forays had drifted into comfortable friendships, others had been so brief and insignificant she doubted she'd recognize the men if she passed them in the street. Not that there had been many. A half-dozen, maybe, across however many years.

Still, it did seem curious that Judith Tavener had not objected to Grace Sweetman being in the production. Curious too that the author had asked to come and watch the filming of this particular book — with this particular cast — when Rina could not recall her wanting to be present for any of the others. Or perhaps that was because it was the last book in the original set?

Rina knew that outlines had been submitted for the next series and that Judith was involved in that process, but, she supposed, that wasn't the same thing. *Folly* had been the breakthrough book, the one that had cemented her reputation and catapulted her from midlist to bestseller. She was bound to have an affection for the novel, just because of that.

But still, Rina being Rina, she wondered about motives. It would be interesting to observe events the following morning when Judith Tavener was due to arrive. Very interesting indeed.

She sat back, sipping the last of her tea and absently watching the chattering groups at the various tables. The tea served with meals was at least a decent brew and the catering staff made sure Rina had a proper pot, with extra hot water should it need topping up. Rina was very grateful for the extra consideration. The room they used as a refectory could get a little crowded at mealtimes. It reminded Rina of a school lunch hall, with the floor-to-ceiling dividing panels that could be folded back out of the way to make the room larger. The modern kitchen was used for catering events, with its cafeteria-style counters used as passes for more formal occasions. This section was then used for additional preparation and for storage. It was quite utilitarian with stackable chairs and tables and a washable floor covering and little clue as to the grandeur that had been restored to the function room behind those folding panels, apart from the ceiling. That was something else, Rina thought. Ornate plasterwork ran in deep friezes around the perimeter and the top of the walls. Massive roses that would have set off the sumptuous glass drops of chandeliers now supported brushed steel, industrial lighting.

Beyond those folding panels it was a different story.

On the function room side the panels were disguised by draped fabric and swags of flowers. There were actual chandeliers hanging from hefty chains and the tables and chairs swathed in white — and whatever other colour guests might choose. One bride had apparently declared a love of purple, which Rina speculated might have been quite overpowering. But she was glad the house was being used. Old places like this should get a new lease of life, and those parts that had been dressed up for public consumption had, on the whole, been nicely done, keeping the character of the place and creating what she imagined would be a lovely backdrop to a special day. Though she didn't like to think what it would cost.

People were starting to move now, taking trays back to the counter, drifting off to get ready for the afternoon. Cast and crew didn't mix much, Rina noted, but that wasn't particularly unusual. In any workspace people liked to discuss their concerns with those who would best understand them. Phil Perry was the exception to that rule though, Rina thought, as he got up from where he had been sitting with the lighting techs and, after depositing his tray, made his way over to her.

"Have you got a minute?" Phil asked.

"Well, we've both got to be getting back. If we talk on the way?"

Phil nodded. "OK. Look, it's about Grace."

Rina got up and started towards the door. "What about Grace? Look, she gets impatient with everyone, you shouldn't take it to heart."

"No, it's not about that. I know the way she is and it's all water off a duck's back to me, it really is. No, you know those letters people have been getting. The nasty ones?"

"The poison pen letters? I didn't realize you knew about them. It's mostly been a Frantham problem."

Phil looked slightly embarrassed. "I overheard you talking to Seth about it the other day and I'd read something about it in one of the local papers anyway. I mean, it's a really nasty thing to be happening, but anyway—" They had reached the hallway now and Phil paused, glanced around as though to see if anyone else was listening. "I think Grace got one this morning."

"Grace got one?"

"Yes. I say I think but actually I know. I was there when she came back from her walk. I was standing by the table in the hall and I told her about the letter. It was addressed to her. It had come in the post. Well, I thought that was a bit odd, you know?"

Rina nodded. "Though people do sometimes get their mail forwarded, if it's something important."

"True. Yes, that's true, but this was . . . well, there was a picture in the local paper, with that article I told you about, of the kind of envelope and font that was used."

Rina nodded again. "Yes, I saw that." She scrutinized Phil carefully, noting the air of supressed excitement alongside what she was generous enough to mark as genuine concern. "So, what happened? Presumably she opened it."

"Oh, she opened it all right and she went deathly pale. I was worried, I can tell you, so I went over to her to get a look at what had upset her. She, of course, didn't want any of *my* sympathy and she snatched the letter away before I could read it properly. I just saw the bit that accused her of being a bitch."

Rina raised an eyebrow and Phil laughed uneasily. "I mean, anyone who's ever met her knows that she really can be. But I think she was genuinely upset too. I think that's why she was extra sharp today."

"Perhaps," Rina agreed, though she wasn't sure she'd have described Grace's mood as extra anything. Grace was generally acerbic, even when she was being relatively cheerful. "Phil, why are you telling me this?"

He looked hurt. "I'm worried about her, Rina. I really do think she was upset. I know she won't tell me anything or even accept sympathy, but you can have a word with her. I mean, everyone listens to you."

Rina sighed. "We're going to be late," she said, ushering Phil across the hall and towards the Grand Salon. All right, Phil, if the opportunity arises then I'll talk to her."

Not that she'll welcome it, Rina thought. Still, it was interesting that Grace had received one of the letters. That's if she had and it wasn't just Phil . . . No, Phil wouldn't have sent it — that would take too much effort. He had never struck Rina as someone who'd expend energy if he didn't have to. And, besides, it was in no one's interest to upset Grace Sweetman. She was enough of a diva as it was.

"I'll try and catch her when we finish for the day," she told him as she pushed open the door and they both slipped inside.

Something not to look forward to, Rina thought.

CHAPTER 2

Twenty miles away in Frantham on Sea, Rina's friend, Inspector MacGregor was not having the best of days either. The morning had brought him three locals requesting a moment of his time, each of which had turned into more than an hour. Sergeant Baker, a lifetime local who knew everyone and had just the right kind of touch for emotional crises, whatever their cause, had unfortunately booked a day of his annual leave and Constable Andy Nevins, currently manning the front desk, was clearly not old enough to have sufficient gravitas or experience.

Mac had known what the problems would be as soon as each arrived — the rash of nasty and, to Mac's mind, anachronistic letters that had been doing the rounds in the past few months. He was more used to hearing about online stalking and social media bullying than someone actually putting pen to paper. Poison pen letters, Rina had called them when she had first heard about their existence, and Mac had to agree that they were definitely poisonous and definitely causing distress.

So far there had been seventeen that he knew about, all sent within the last six months, and he had encouraged anyone unfortunate enough to get such a letter to bring it to the police. This morning brought the total up to twenty. Some recipients, like the three who had arrived that day, had brought them along. Others had just been left anonymously, pushed through the police station letterbox or, on one occasion, stuffed beneath the windscreen wiper of Mac's car. But this was the first time there had been three arrive, along with their recipients, in a single day. In general, they had averaged about one a week though sometimes a month had passed in between the next letter being written. That was, of course, unless other recipients had thrown them in the bin and not told anyone.

Mac's first visitor of the day was Trixie Burns, a local hairdresser, young and blonde with an immaculate retro pixie cut that reminded Mac of a young Mia Farrow. Trixie shared the salon with her mother, Marge. Mac had gained the impression that Trix, as most people called her, was more excited than concerned.

"It came to the salon," she'd said. "Well, we knew what it was, soon as we saw it. I mean, no one sends us letters. It's all just bills and junk mail. If it's birthday cards or suchlike, then they come to the house, don't they?"

Mac had agreed they probably did. The letter she'd placed carefully on his desk was unopened. It was addressed to Miss T Burns.

"Mum said to bring it straight here. Not to open it first in case of fingerprints. Of course, there'll be loads on the envelope, but you might get something from inside."

She had sat down in the chair opposite Mac and looked at him expectantly. "Well, go on. Open it. I've got to get back for my ten thirty lady."

Mac had searched in his desk drawer and removed a pair of thin blue latex gloves and an evidence bag. He'd donned the gloves then taken his Swiss army knife from his pocket and slit the envelope, noting the anticipation on Trixie's face. She hadn't seemed the least bit concerned as to what the letter might say. Inside was a single sheet of standard white printer paper, just like all the rest. He'd slipped the envelope into the evidence bag and, with Trixie's permission, unfolded the letter, read it and turned it so that Trixie might read.

"Ooh, the bitch!" Trixie had said.

"You think the sender is a woman?"

"Well, isn't it usually? Me and Mum, we've read up on these things. It's almost always a woman. Women are better at spite, Mum always says. Men just overthink it."

An interesting assessment, Mac had thought. "And the man referred to in the letter, any idea who it might be?"

"Unlucky," Trixie had told him, laughing. "I've got a long-term girlfriend. We're moving in together next month."

Mac had laughed with her. "So the sender is—?"

"Someone who doesn't know me," Trixie had finished for him. "Kirsty and I have been together best part of two years and we've not exactly hidden the fact. Mum keeps on at us about getting married. I think she just wants an excuse to buy a posh frock." Trixie had shrugged. "I think it's safe to say whoever sent this, she's not a customer and she doesn't know anyone who is, so you can discount maybe twenty per cent of women in Frantham straight off."

"Would that it was that easy," Mac had said. "Of course, it might be a bluff. She might be pretending not to know — that's if it is a she."

"It's a woman all right," Trixie had told him, standing up. "Right, I've got to be off or I'll be late."

Mac had thanked her and slid the letter into the evidence bag, looking at it for a moment. About half of the letters had been like this. Short, vague, spiteful. This one read:

What will happen when I tell his wife what you've been doing with her husband every Thursday?

They reminded Mac of the random cold calls he sometimes got, suggesting the caller help him claim for compensation for an accident he hadn't actually had. Call enough people and some would definitely have been involved in an accident. Some of those would indeed be keen to claim compensation. It was entirely possible that the sender might have struck lucky with this particular missive and caused someone to become very worried indeed. And yes, those vague, unspecific letters did have the feel of messages sent to random people, just on the off-chance they might score a hit.

Others had been much more specific and suggested that the sender actually knew or at least knew something about the intended recipient. They had often been much more upsetting.

Trixie Burns had definitely been unimpressed, and Mac had no doubt as to what the main topic of conversation in the salon that morning would be. Thinking about it, he was pretty sure that it was Trixie who did Rina's hair and that of the Peters sisters. He could imagine Rina and the younger woman getting on.

He had been about to get up and fetch coffee for himself and Andy when he'd heard voices in the reception area and then Andy had stuck his head around the door.

"We've got two more," he'd said and Mac could hear the surprise in his voice. "And, boss—" he'd lowered his voice — "both ladies are very upset. Can they come in together?"

"Of course. Andy maybe some tea might be in order? I'll go and fetch coffee when we're done."

Andy had nodded and ducked out, returning a moment later with two women Mac knew by sight. Both had looked distressed. Andy had brought another chair and set it down, settling both women with a gentleness and care that, Mac thought, Sergeant Baker would have been proud of. "Mrs Bluett and Mrs Majors," he'd told Mac. "I'll go and make that tea."

It had taken half an hour and a pot of Andy's tea for Mac to coax the full story from the two women. Mrs Bluett was in her eighties and a lifelong resident of Frantham. Mrs Majors, around the same age, Mac guessed, had moved down with her husband forty years before and was now widowed. The two of them were long-time neighbours.

"This is still a lovely place to live," Mrs Bluett had told him. "Even in the winter, when it can get bitter cold. But we've got our weekly groups we go to together and we help each other out. Some nights I go to Esme and we watch the telly together, other times she comes to me. We've neither of us got family close by."

Mac, who had not yet seen the letters they had received, had wondered if the sender had hinted at something more in their relationship. It had turned out he was way off.

"When Esme came round this morning with her letter, I'd not opened my post, but I soon realized I'd had one as well. Esme was most upset and so was I. You should be doing something about this. I know we aren't the only ones, but people should just not be allowed to make accusations like this. You should be doing something."

Mac had been about to reassure her that they were trying but Mrs Bluett had dug in her capacious black handbag. She'd taken out two envelopes and placed them down on Mac's desk, regarding them with unalloyed disgust.

Mac had picked them up.

"To suggest such a thing," Mrs Bluett had said. "Everyone knows that Mr Majors, Christopher, died of a heart attack. His third. He collapsed in the kitchen and we called the ambulance, but it was very clear to both of us that this time he'd not be coming back from it. That this was the big one. Everyone knew it was just a matter of time. His doctors had all told him the same, he'd had so many different treatments over the years and there was so much else wrong with him, with the cancer and everything, but it was the heart attack that killed him in the end.

"Almost sixty years Christopher and Esme had been together. Everyone knew how devoted they were. And then for her to be sent this! I wouldn't be worried for myself," she had added angrily. "I'd have burned the thing in the fire, but to accuse poor Esme! I just won't have it."

Mrs Majors had sat with downcast eyes, trembling. Mrs Bluett had put a comforting arm around her friend's shoulders.

For the second time that morning, Mac had donned gloves and retrieved evidence bags from his desk drawer, aware of Mrs Bluett's eyes on him.

The letters accused Mrs Majors of poisoning her husband and stated that Mrs Bluett had colluded. He'd slid the letters into evidence bags and said gently, "I can see why this was so upsetting. And you've no idea—"

"Who could be so cruel? No, Inspector, no idea at all. It's your job to find that out."

"And neither of you has—"

"Argued with anyone recently? Again, no. At our ages we're grateful to still have friends around us. Arguments are for those who have time for them. We do not."

He had paused, wondering how to phrase the next question. "On the day Mr Majors died, you were both there when it happened?"

Mrs Bluett's eyes had narrowed. "Just what are you suggesting, Inspector? You can't possibly be taking this seriously."

"No, of course I'm not," Mac had told her. "But whoever wrote this letter knows the two of you are good friends and perhaps also know something about the day Mr Majors died."

Mrs Majors had raised her head and looked at him in alarm. Mrs Bluett had sat back and glared, but he'd had the feeling she had already considered the possibility.

"You're suggesting that whoever wrote this trash might be someone we know," she'd said flatly. "Might be someone we regard as a friend."

"Or a friend of a friend. Someone who might have heard about what happened and be using their knowledge from that relationship to write hurtful things."

"Oh, Sheila." Mrs Majors had reached for her friend's hand.

"It's the detail, isn't it?" Mrs Bluett had said. "About him lying on the kitchen floor. That's quite specific."

Mac had nodded.

Mrs Bluett had seemed to gather herself. She had clasped Mrs Majors' hand tightly and then said, "Esme, you and I have some work to do. Inspector, we will compile a list of all the people we see regularly in our weekly groups, and we will ask them if they happen to have spoken about Christopher's death to anyone else."

"It would be quite a natural thing to do," Mac had said soothingly. "I doubt anyone meant any harm."

"No, but it meant the information was out there. I'll drop the lists and an account of anything else that might be said into the police station in the next few days," Mrs Bluett had told him. "Then you can cross-reference our names with others you may already have." She narrowed her eyes at him again. "You have been collating names and contacts, I suppose."

Mac had assured her that he had.

"We photographed the letters on our phones before we came here." Mrs Majors had seemed to recover her composure. "And we'll be sharing that information with our friends. If they have received any such nastiness, we'll be urging them to share it to. Hiding away isn't going to do anyone any good, is it?"

"No," Mac had agreed. "It's really not."

Mac had watched as Mrs Bluett patted her friend's hand. Sheila Bluett, he'd decided, was in some ways just an older version of Rina Martin, but he suspected Mrs Majors was not naturally nearly as brave. It had taken her a great deal of courage to come and be so open about these accusations.

He had walked them out, more in need of a decent cup of coffee now than he had been an hour before but had felt he should allow Mrs Bluett and Mrs Majors to remove themselves from the area first. Diving straight out to the coffee shop felt a little frivolous in the wake of such obvious distress — and he had no doubt that Mrs Bluett, as well as being indignant, was also deeply upset.

As he'd watched the two women make their way down the promenade Andy had asked about the letters. Mac had told him.

"That's one of the nastiest so far, isn't it? You don't suppose there's anything in it?"

Mac had glanced at him.

"We have to ask, don't we?"

Mac had nodded. "But we can be discreet. We can get a copy of the death certificate and find out who certified. However, I doubt there's any more to it than any of the others."

What a morning. Mac fetched his jacket from where it hung on the back of his chair, checked what Andy wanted and at last went to fetch their coffee. The accusations had been a real mixed bag. Random shots in the dark about people having affairs, having shoplifted, stolen a cat (that was an odd one), lied, it wasn't always clear what about. And that was the thing too — whoever was sending these letters seemed to lack imagination. There had, to Mac's knowledge, been two accusations of cat poisoning, one of cat shaving, four of having affairs and two of shoplifting. Two more of having lied to their boss on their CV about their qualifications. Of those two, Mac remembered, one had been sent to a man so long retired that his last boss was himself in sheltered housing and the second to a fourteen-year-old who didn't even have a Saturday job. She had, so far, been the youngest recipient.

Others had been more specific. One of the accused cat poisoners was, quite possibly, guilty as charged. She certainly hadn't liked her neighbour's cat and had made several complaints about it 'messing' in her garden. The cat had indeed gone missing, but Mac wondered if she had actually resorted to poison. There was a busy road nearby and it was more likely it had been hit by a car but not reported. However, just in case there might be more to it, the letter was now in their 'follow up' file.

The remaining six, before today's recipients, had made direct accusations. In two the married men accused of having affairs had been named. The most serious accusation had related to a hit and run in which a teenager had been badly hurt — that was being seriously examined and, it turned out, may have some truth behind it. Another contained an accusation of embezzlement from a workplace and the company concerned had, at the request of their employee, investigated and identified no actual theft. The last two concerned allegations of domestic abuse, one of which did not seem to check out. The other had spurred the woman involved to seek help and she was now in safe accommodation, miles from Frantham. Her husband had been charged.

Score one and possibly two, for the author of the letters, Mac thought. Two, if the hit and run accusation led anywhere. Though if they knew these things, why not act on them in a more straightforward way? If the writer of the letters didn't want to be directly involved, then there were numbers they could have called to make an anonymous statement — or even, as had often happened, have left a note in the letterbox at Frantham's tiny police station. Mac liked to think that the locals knew himself and his team well enough to be certain action would be taken.

Mulling all of this over to himself, Mac collected their coffee and returned to the station. He would take another look at everything, see if something leaped out at him that he'd missed before.

* * *

True to her word, Rina caught up with Grace as she swept from the set late afternoon and asked if she was all right.

"Why wouldn't I be?" Grace sounded genuinely surprised.

"You seemed upset this morning," Rina said. "Perhaps with more than just Phil fluffing his lines?"

Rina waited, hoping Grace would take the hint and open up to her.

Grace scowled. "Phil should learn to keep his mouth shut. Not everyone requires the Rina Martin agony aunt treatment." She glanced at her phone. "Anyway, I have a dinner date. Seth and I are going out. I must get ready." She marched off before Rina could say more.

Seth himself was just crossing the hall and Rina hurried to catch up with him.

"You're taking Grace out to dinner?"

He laughed. "We're just heading down to the local pub. They do perfectly nice evening meals and I thought it might cheer her up. She's seemed off today, even for Grace. I thought she might be persuaded to talk to me."

"She might," Rina said. "I've had no luck."

Swiftly, she filled Seth in about the letter and what Phil had told her it had said.

"Ah," he said, "well that can't have helped. I'll see if I can get her in a better mood, ready for Judith's visit tomorrow."

"I'm sure we'd all be grateful if you could," Rina told him.

CHAPTER 3

Rina had hoped to have a word with Seth, to ask how his evening with Grace had gone, but she did not see him until she arrived in the Grand Salon ready for Judith Tavener's visit.

Judith Tavener cut something of a birdlike figure, Rina thought. She was one of those women who looked as though a breath of wind might blow her away. Rina, who had always been of more solid construction, had envied such figures in her youth, when they had always seemed to be the ones who attracted the attention both of eligible young men and of casting directors, but now, in her mature and more sanguine years, she just got the urge to feed them cake. There was, however, something about the demeanour of Judith Tavener that caused Rina to think that even the dense deliciousness of one of Matthew's chocolate fudge confections would not be enough to weigh her down. She had the look of someone preparing to take flight at any moment, ping away in the manner of a goldcrest or a wren, which to Rina's mind seemed always to teleport into another dimension rather than fly.

Or perhaps she might more accurately be compared to a moth, hands fluttering, constantly in motion, like little wings. What, Rina wondered, was she so nervous about?

Everyone on set adored her books and, more to the point, adored the fact that her creation had been revived and several careers resurrected to boot.

There was also something oddly anachronistic about the woman. She could imagine Judith in Regency dress, dancing with some version of Mr Darcy, or even in silk and lace and crinoline, as opposed to the tailored grey trousers and cowl neck red sweater she was currently wearing.

Seth sidled up to her. "Have you met her before?"

Rina shook her head. "No, though apparently Richard has known her for a long time."

They both turned their gaze on Richard Cartmell, screenwriter for the *Lydia Marchant Investigates* series. It was interesting, Rina thought, just how closely he'd worked with the novelist to bring her creation to the small screen. In fact, far more closely than was commonplace — it was more usual for writers to hand over their stories, close their eyes and hope for the best as someone else revamped and generally reorganized plot and character into something more suited to the visual medium.

Richard, suddenly aware of their scrutiny, raised a questioning eyebrow. Rina smiled at him and then turned her attention back to Judith Tavener and her escort. Thinking about it, Rina could only think of three occasions when she'd met David Scott-Lawrence before today. The producer was a bear of a man, looming affably over the moth-like Judith. Rina quite liked him, but two lunches and a script meeting early on in the series relaunch did not, she felt, qualify her to pass more accurate judgement on him.

Alison Pool, the director, was in contrast very hands on, extremely efficient and knew just how to get the best out of her cast and crew. Alison stood aside now — she also knew when to get out of the way — watching indulgently as her producer made effusive introductions. Rina saw her glance at her watch, no doubt wondering how late they would have to work to make up for the interruptions this morning. They were nearing the end of filming on this latest series, and everyone was feeling the strain. Filming in an old house in the middle of nowhere might sound romantic, but unseasonal torrential rain, a burst pipe that had put one of the main areas off limits for a week, the ongoing electrical problems and the inconvenience of working in an effective rabbit warren of small rooms and dimly lit chilly corridors had tried everyone's patience.

True, the larger and more impressive ballroom, library and salon that had been used for most of the actual location shots were wonderful but wardrobe, makeup, dressing areas and everything more utilitarian had been housed in what Rina assumed had been servants' quarters and storage rooms, linked to the main house by a narrow, dimly lit underground passageway and very far from convenient both in terms of moving equipment about or trekking back and forth between scenes.

Today, in readiness for the next scene to be shot, cast and crew were once more assembled in the Grand Salon. The rather Baroque confection, all cherubs, nymphs and swags and velvet drapes, seemed to Rina to be at odds with the more austere late Tudor panels and with the stiffer and more formal stone carvings around the opening of the fireplace, of men and women in ruffs, doublets and farthingales. She gathered that it had been remodelled several times. Most extensively in the eighteenth century, when the cherubs had taken up residence and then again in the nineteenth, when some wealthy Victorian ancestor of the current owner had taken it upon themselves to quite literally gild the lily — and the cherubs, floral motifs and swags. It might, Rina thought, glancing up at the brassy nymphs cavorting above the fireplace, have looked quite effective by candlelight but mid-morning gloom cast by lowering grey clouds outside coupled with the harshness of electric light inside did nothing to soften the brashness and the bling. The whole room looked slightly tacky.

Shivering slightly, she moved closer to the fire. Seth followed her. "You'd have thought when they were going all out on the curlicues, they'd have spent a little more money on a decent-sized fireplace," he commented. He was wearing a jumper under a heavy tweed jacket and had a bright red cashmere scarf wrapped around his neck. He still looked pinched and chilled.

Rina nodded. The fire surround might have been impressive, but the hearth itself would be hard pressed to heat a room half this size — even if it had been made up with sufficient logs and coal. It was, she thought, a mean little fire.

"I won't be sorry to get back home," Seth added. "It's been a tough old run, this one."

"It has," Rina agreed. Filming had not been either smooth or easy. Technical difficulties had dogged the production, recurrent illness among both cast and crew — nothing serious, just a series of sniffles and coughs and colds that didn't want to go away — had made everyone miserable. And it had been impossible to keep warm. The house was chilly, no getting away from that, and both cast and crew had taken to wearing their outdoor clothes inside. Rina had bought a heated throw for her bed and huddled under it gratefully at the end of the working day.

The only good thing about filming at Septon Hall was that it was close enough to home that she could go back to Frantham whenever she was not required. The little car she had bought a few months before had seen intensive use as Matthew Montmorency drove the twenty miles back and forth to pick her up and drop her off. Rina could have driven herself, but she preferred to leave the car in Frantham so the household had easy transport. That, after all, had been the point of getting it in the first place.

"Right. Here we go," Seth said. Judith and the producer were now heading their way.

"And this, of course," David Scott-Lawrence was saying, "is Rina Martin, or, should I say, Lydia Marchant."

The smile that suddenly lit Judith Tavener's face warmed Rina. "I'm so happy to finally meet you," Judith said. She extended a hand and Rina shook it gently. The hand was skeletal, bone beneath a thin covering of skin, definitely bird-like, though she was also very pretty, Rina decided. She had soft blonde hair, now streaked with grey, brushed back from an almost heart-shaped face and large grey eyes that presently danced with enthusiasm and genuine pleasure. Rina smiled back at her.

"You've really brought her to life," Judith declared. "How on earth have you done that? You've made Lydia so solid, so real."

"I had good material to work with," Rina told her.

Judith opened her mouth to say something more, but the producer was gently moving her on. "And this, of course, is Seth Collis, aka Otis Finch, Lydia's loyal sidekick."

Obediently, Judith shook Seth's hand but as she walked away she glanced back at Rina and just for an instant Rina caught something less than happy in the woman's gaze. Something troubled, something . . . lonely? Then it was gone and Judith was greeting Richard Cartmell with a kiss and a familiar hug. "*My* loyal sidekick," Judith said, echoing David Scott-Lawrence's words and Richard laughed.

"And very happy we are about that," the producer said. "Now I know Alison is keen to be getting on, so if we make you comfortable over here . . ."

David settled Judith in a chair beside the inadequate radiator, cast iron and impressive looking but reliant on a furnace down in the cellar that was never fuelled with sufficient coal to do the job. It probably still cost a fortune to run, Rina thought absently. The producer was now making his excuses. Duty done, he no doubt had meetings with more important people to attend.

Alison was marshalling the troops and Seth was in position for a small pickup scene from earlier in the story, where he and Lord Ellsworthy discussed an archaeological dig that had taken place in the grounds a few years before. Originally the scene had been scheduled for filming outdoors, up close to the folly that gave its name to the book and where an actual dig, eighteen years ago, had uncovered bits of Roman and Saxon remains. Unfortunately, the weather had been so bad that Alison had finally made the executive decision to shoot the scene inside. They really could not afford to wait for the weather to get its act together.

She'll freeze sitting there, Rina thought, looking over at Judith. In the alcove next to the fireplace was a small table on which lay a stack of blankets the cast had left for wrapping people up between scenes. Several of the scenes that took place in the Grand Salon and the ballroom called for flimsy and filmy evening dress. Rina suspected that even in its heyday this house would have been too cold for anything but thermals.

She collected a blanket and crossed to where Judith sat. "You'll be cold, sitting there," she said softly, aware that Alison was about to call for silence as filming recommenced.

Judith took it gratefully, mouthing her thanks and wrapped it around herself, up to her shoulders. Not wishing to cause a distraction, Rina remained where she was, leaning against the lukewarm radiator as Seth declared his admiration for the boxful of Roman finds that Lord Ellsworthy was showing him and that had been found close by the folly. Lord Ellsworthy waxed lyrical about the empire. Rina was not quite certain if he was referring to the Roman one or the last throes of the British. Either would apply, she supposed.

"And then they found this," Lord Ellsworthy declared, taking an item from the box and holding it out for Seth/Otis to see.

"Goodness, what is it? Some kind of brooch?"

"Indeed, indeed. First century they reckon, by the design of it. It's called a fibula, don't you know. Bronze. Made for holding a woman's dress together, so they tell me. Or maybe a cloak. I had a replica made for Lady Ellsworthy. I'll get her to show it to you later, if you've an interest in this sort of thing. Only difference being the pin on this original one is hammered bronze. Jeweller chap that made the replica suggested we replace that with a steel pin. Reckoned it would be stronger and smoother and thinner, better for modern clothing, don't you know. Wouldn't want to make holes in a woman's coat now. That wouldn't do at all."

Otis agreed that it would not.

Rina glanced at Judith, interested in her reaction to seeing a part of her story in the process of being brought to life. The look on the woman's face gave her pause. She had grown pale, her jaw clenched and her mouth now a thin, compressed line. It was as though the scene was causing her actual pain. Concerned, Rina touched her gently on the shoulder and Judith flinched. Rina drew back as the younger woman collected herself, flushed as though suddenly embarrassed and then her smile returned as Alison cut the scene and crossed to chat to Otis and Lord Ellsworthy.

"I was here when it was found," Judith said.

"The brooch?"

"Yes, it was an actual dig. Very exciting. We got to see and even handle the pieces as they came out of the ground. Of course, I just had to include it in the book."

"I imagine you did." Rina said, echoing Judith's sudden show of enthusiasm. The . . . distress — Rina could think of no better word — that she had shown only moments before now seemed forgotten. "It makes for a very unusual murder weapon," she added.

"I thought so." Judith nodded. "A little different from your usual blunt bludgeoning or simple stabbing with a kitchen knife."

"They'll be using the replica for the murder scene, of course. A pity — it would have been interesting to have had access to the original."

Rina had not noticed Grace Sweetman coming over. She stood now at Rina's shoulder, looking not at her or Judith but instead observing the conversation between Otis and Alison. Her nonchalance seemed forced, Rina thought.

Judith leaned forward and peered round Rina to observe Grace. "I suppose they're worried it might get damaged," she said mildly. "Besides, it's the replica that's used for the murder in the book, so that's accurate."

Grace snorted. "It's still a mistake, if you ask me. It would have been far more dramatic to have used the original object. And anyway, the book and a television series are quite different animals. They need a totally different approach." She turned her gaze on Judith for the first time, also leaning slightly to peer around Rina.

Irritated now, Rina moved to the other side of Judith's chair. "There," she said. "Now the two of you can talk without me getting in the way."

Grace scowled at her and opened her mouth as if to speak but the floor manager's call for "positions" silenced whatever it was she had been about to say. The scene between Otis and Lord Ellsworthy was rerun. Once more Otis admired the finds but this time he took the fibula in his hand and held it out, playing with the pin, studying it closely. There would be a closeup, Rina assumed, to ensure the viewer got the point.

The thought amused her. The bronze replica fibula that Seth was holding and that had been created to stand in for the original found at the dig, certainly had one hell of a point and, when opened fully, looked almost like a stiletto with the curve of the brooch back forming a useful handle. The replica with the steel pin that Lady Ellsworthy would wear on her coat in a later scene looked the same, until you examined the pin. Longer, thinner and hardened steel. Definitely stiletto like. She was reminded of her great aunt's stories about the use of hat pins as an improvised weapon against young men who got 'fresh' on the trolleybus and wondered whether Roman ladies had made use of their brooches as improvised self-defence weapons as her suffragette great aunt had done.

Though perhaps not, if that was what held their dresses together. She realized she didn't really understand how Roman costume worked and made a mental note to google the question later on.

This time the scene ran on, the two men parting to dress for dinner. Rina glanced at her watch and noted that it was time for lunch. Alison came over to collect their special guest and Grace, with a final disdainful look that took in Judith, Rina and the Grand Salon, drifted off.

"Hope to see you later," Judith said with what Rina could see was a genuine smile.

"I'll look forward to it," she told her. Judith intrigued her. Judith and Grace's shared past piqued her curiosity. But right now she was hungry and that could wait.

"I'm definitely ready for a feed," Seth said. "I think it all went well, don't you?"

"Of course it did." Rina took his arm. "And yes, I'm hungry too. All this tension is giving me an appetite. Now, tell me how it went with Grace last night."

Seth laughed. "You sound like the mother of teenagers asking about a first date."

"If I was the mother of teenagers, I hope I'd realize that I'd not get an answer," Rina told him. "Whereas you and I are too old to play games. Did she admit to receiving the letter?"

Seth nodded. "Actually, she showed it to me. After a couple of glasses of wine and over a surprisingly nice brandy with our coffee. Rina, it's something and nothing, no actual accusations, apart from the fact that she can be a bitch, and the writer's wish that she be cut down to size, so she can laugh at Grace. And I'm assuming it's a she. It sounds like a woman writing it, somehow."

"I suppose the odds are going to be in favour of that," Rina agreed. "And was she upset?"

"Surprisingly, yes. I think the letter came at a bad time. I think she's had a recent breakup, but I don't know the details. It's always been hard to keep track of Grace's dating habits, but I got the feeling this one was more serious than most."

"Well, I can understand her upset," Rina said. "It's not a nice thing to happen. I really need to tell Mac about it."

"Do you have to? Isn't this a private matter?"

"I suppose it is," Rina agreed reluctantly. "But it is strange. Most of the recipients have been people living in Frantham, or close by. Grace is an outsider."

"Well, there you're wrong," Seth told her. "Didn't you know she bought a house down here a while back? Maybe three, four years or so, I think. It's apparently only a few miles from your neck of the woods, just along the coast."

Rina hadn't known that. "Do you know where?"

"Not exactly, no. But I can ask, I suppose. However, maybe it's more significant that the writer sent the letter here, where she knew Grace would get it. That makes me think the sender wanted her to get it now, while we're still filming. We talked about this a bit last night. Grace is convinced someone wants to put her off her stride, make her look unprofessional."

"That feels like a stretch," Rina said.

"Maybe so, but it's what she thinks. For Grace, work and identity are closely tied up. She's worked pretty consistently. I can think of only a couple of times when she's been completely out of contract, and I don't imagine she was happy either time."

Rina considered this for a moment. "It didn't cross her mind that Phil might have sent it?"

"For a moment, it did. But she said the idea was too sophisticated for Phil to have thought of. She reckons he's not that smart."

"Ouch," Rina said.

"Ouch indeed," Seth agreed.

* * *

It was close to 7 p.m. before Rina chanced to have another conversation with Judith. It happened only because Richard Cartmell had taken it upon himself to give Judith the grand tour and they had ended up in the wardrobe department. Rina had caught her jacket sleeve on a raised nail on one of the doorframes and was showing Theresa Barnett, the wardrobe supervisor, what she had done when they came in.

"It's an easy fix," Rina was reassured. "I'll get on to it as soon as I've seen to Miss Sweetman's coat lining."

Rina nodded her thanks and glanced over at Grace, who had a camel hair coat laid out on one of the rickety tables Theresa had commandeered, and was fiddling with a large rip in the lining.

"What happened there?" Rina asked.

"What happened is that the lining is far too small for the coat. I put it on and the damned thing ripped! Just look at it."

Rina went over. The lining had torn on the centre back seam. It looked bad, but it could be mended. The fabric either side of the seam would need reinforcing, but then it would not be too hard to do. The coat, she noted, was a vintage piece. "It's bound to be a bit fragile, given the age," she said. "It's amazing it's survived in such good condition, considering."

"Well I need it for the morning," Grace announced loudly.

Rina glanced at Theresa, who was sorting through a box of what Rina recognized as fine webbing used for repairs of this kind. "And I'm sure it will be," she said in a soothing a tone as possible. "Theresa always gets things ready for us on time."

Theresa Barnett was used to the tirades, Rina knew, but she smiled gratefully at Rina anyway. She was only in her thirties but already had a wealth of experience, particularly with period drama, everything from Jane Austen to a film about gangsters and sixties nightclubs in Soho. Theresa was small, with brown, cropped hair and strong, slender hands, a ring thimble seemingly a permanent fixture. "You won't know it was ever torn, by the time I'm done," she said.

"Well it shouldn't have bloody torn in the first place."

Grace seemed set to begin her next rant, but the door opened and Judith came in with Richard Cartmell.

"And finally," he was saying, "our rather wonderful wardrobe department, run by the equally wonderful . . ." His voice trailed off as he caught sight of Grace Sweetman. Or, Rina thought, as he caught sight of her expression.

"Oh, feel free to look around," Theresa said warmly.

"Thank you. Oh look, there's Lydia Marchant's cape!"

Judith sounded so delighted to have spotted Lydia's signature piece that Rina went over and took it off the hanger. "It is rather splendid," she said. "And it's very warm. Theresa found it just before we shot the first series and, you know, it was like finding an old friend. It just really helped me to get into the character."

"Is it original? Oh yes, look at the labels. May I try it on?"

"Of course you can," Theresa told her. "It's from about 1946, but it's the kind of garment people would have hung on to and it felt just right for Lydia Marchant. I had to reline it, the original was in tatters, but once that was done it was all fine."

"Harris Tweed does last," Rina said.

Judith swung the cape around her shoulders. It was far too big for her, too wide for the narrow shoulders, too long for her slender frame. Rina thought she looked rather like a child playing dress-up, but she could see that Judith was delighted.

"The right clothes help, of course, but they're not the be all and end all of it. Costume is not something one should rely upon." Grace's curt tone cut through their merriment and Rina found herself turning towards the woman, noting with irritation that the others had too and no doubt this was exactly what Grace had wanted. She had taken the coat from the table and put it on, had taken one of the replica fibulae from the tray in which it had been stored together with other small props and was fitting it into the lapel of the camel coat. It was the one with the steel pin. The one that Lady Ellsworthy would be given by her husband.

"They should definitely have allowed us to use the original that they found at the dig," she declared.

"I doubt the pin would have gone through the fabric," Judith said. "I was able to take another look at it in the museum a few days ago—"

"Oh, were you indeed?"

"Yes, and the pin is very blunt. In fact, there's a little bit missing from the tip. I'd forgotten that. No wonder, though, after so long in the ground. But it would ruin the fabric if you tried to use it. Besides, as I said earlier, in the book it's the replica with the steel pin that Lady Ellsworthy wears."

Grace scowled at her and turned her attention back to fiddling with the brooch, repositioning it on the lapel. "There," she said. "Now that's all ready for tomorrow." She shrugged out of the coat and dropped it back on the table. Then she left.

"Tomorrow?" Theresa questioned. "Have they changed the shooting schedule and not told me? I didn't think Lady Ellsworthy got her brooch until the scene they're shooting on Friday."

"She doesn't," Richard Cartmell confirmed. "Grace is just being her usual self and trying to wrong-foot everyone. I'm just going to take Judith for a coffee," he added, looking at Rina. "Will you join us? Theresa?"

Theresa shook her head. "Too much to do, but if someone could organize some tea and a sandwich, that would be great."

Rina promised that she would and left with Richard and Judith.

* * *

Later that evening, hot chocolate on her bedside cabinet and the heated throw pulled up cosily around her shoulders, Rina thought about the day and what Grace had said about the television series and the book being such different animals.

She was right, of course. What might take a writer many words to describe could be shown in a single image or a pan of the camera across a room. And screenwriting was a different discipline to being a novelist. There were writers who could do both, of course, but a screenplay would frequently portray scenes in a totally different order from those which appeared in a novel, and Rina could think of two instances in the Lydia Marchant universe when characters had been conflated or cut altogether because they perhaps only had a minor role to play or because what they brought to the screen could be indicated by another character or even by a bit of clever camerawork.

Intrigued by her train of thought Rina took both her hot chocolate and her copy of Judith's original novel from her nightstand and found the scene that depicted the finding of the butler's body, the fibula sticking out of his neck and a pool of blood on the carpeted floor of the library. What was it, she wondered, about butlers and bodies in libraries that was so appealing in fiction? She supposed she should blame Agatha Christie.

That thought in mind, Rina settled down for sleep.

CHAPTER 4

Twenty miles away in Frantham, Mac had made his way to have dinner in the Martin household. His partner, Miriam Hastings, with whom he shared a small flat above a boathouse in Old Frantham village, just around the headland from Victorian Frantham, was away on a course and he had been grateful for the invitation.

Not, Mac reflected, that he ever needed one. He could turn up at any time and feel welcome, be fed cake or lunch or dinner — Matthew and Steven always cooking a little extra for the freezer or for anyone in sudden need of an additional portion.

Tonight, there had been lasagne and a spongy chocolate pudding that Matthew had not made before, but which Mac was certain would be making further appearances. It had gone down very well with vanilla ice cream. The Martin household always ate well — a combination, Mac guessed, not just of Rina being comfortably off but also that everyone living in the same house was able to pool resources and look after one another. It was an enviable position to be in, he thought, remembering the two elderly women who had come to see him that morning. At the moment Mrs Majors and Mrs Bluett had the support of each other but what would happen if one of them died? Mac found himself recoiling from their potential loneliness with a horror born of the knowledge that once upon a time that had been something he'd had to endure.

"I hear you had more of those horrid letters brought to you today," Bethany said to him as they idled over coffee.

He smiled. It was as though she had read his thoughts. "And where did you hear that?" he asked.

"Oh, we ran into Trixie Burns's mother," Bethany told him. "Didn't we, Eliza? Fuming, she was, though she said Trixie was just amused by it all. But then Trixie would be. Nothing ever seems to upset that girl."

"She is a little ray of sunshine," Steven said. "So, what was she accused of?"

Mac was about to say that he really couldn't reveal that but Eliza was ahead of him. "The writer accused her of having an affair with a married *man*." She laughed contemptuously at the idea.

"Well, clearly they don't know Trixie Burns," Steven agreed. "And the other two were from Mrs Bluett and her friend, Mrs Majors, I believe."

"I couldn't possibly say." Mac smiled.

"Oh, no need to, we already know." Matthew poured Mac more coffee and nudged the sugar bowl in his direction. "I spotted them on the way to see you yesterday morning. Furious, Sheila Bluett was, told me all about it. Mrs Majors, Esme, she's mortified by it all. And anyone that knew her and Christopher would be too. I rarely met a more devoted couple. He was a lovely man, very kind, would do anything for anyone and she's the same."

"You know them well, then?" Mac asked.

"The ladies both come to the tea dances at the marina and Mrs Majors usually runs the tombola on gala days," Eliza told him. "Of course, she didn't do it last year. Christopher was barely cold in his grave, and the poor dear was in no fit state to be at a gala. But they've been back at the tea dances these past few weeks. I think Sheila dragged her there the first time, but she had a nice time and no one bothered her when she just wanted to sit and watch. I mean, Steven does that all the time, so why would they?"

"No reason at all," Steven told her. "They're a nice lot there and it's perfectly pleasant just watching everyone have fun." He cast an affectionate look at Matthew, who loved to dance and cut a fine figure with his long legs. Steven and Matthew, like those others in the Martin household, had been entertainers for most of their lives. The Montmorency Twins had started as a comedy song and dance act, their dissimilar builds and looks adding to the ridiculousness of their claim to be twins. Matthew was still tall and slim, now with a thick mane of grey hair, Steven much shorter in stature, a little thin in the hair department now — something no one would ever dream of mentioning — and his knees were too sore and arthritic to let him dance. They had been together since they were both sixteen.

The Peters sisters, Eliza and Bethany, were actually sisters. A little older than the Montmorencys, they had done everything from chorus line to magicians' assistants and even been part of a knife throwing act. They had also done some acting along the way, mostly with touring companies, even a little television. They were now elegantly retired and tucked safely into Rina's fold.

Mac smiled. He loved these people and Rina. Especially Rina, who had drawn him into her little circle when he'd been a broken mess and helped him heal. When he had first got to know them all a young magician called Tim Brandon had also been living at Peverill Lodge and trying to make a name for himself. He now performed three times a week at the Palisades, a local Art Deco-style hotel, worked as a consultant for a computer games company and lived with his fiancée, Joy, just a few miles away. They were currently visiting Bridie, Joy's mother, though Tim was expected back for his usual Sunday performance.

"Anything from Rina today?" he asked.

"Only a text saying she'd met Judith Tavener and that she seemed very nice. I think she's looking forward to getting home," Bethany said.

Matthew nodded. "She says this tranche of filming has felt like a real slog. You know how much she usually enjoys it? Well not this time."

"She mentioned she didn't much like the house and that everyone was struggling with the rain," Mac said. "I don't remember a wetter spring."

"No, the garden's sodden, not a chance of getting on it yet," Bethany agreed. "Rina won't get back on Saturday, or at least not until late, but she'll be here on Sunday. You'll come to lunch?"

Mac told her that he'd love to and prepared to take his leave.

CHAPTER 5

On the Thursday morning Rina joined the rest of the cast and crew for breakfast and then walked with Theresa Barnett back to her domain to collect the jacket Theresa had mended for her.

"Did you manage to get Grace's lining done?" Rina asked.

"Oh yes, eventually."

Rina picked up on the irritated tone. "Problems?"

Theresa glanced around as though worried someone might overhear. "Well, I can't prove it, of course, but I'll swear the original tear was just a tiny hole. The fabric was all stretched out of shape around the tear. It was like she'd wormed her fingers into it and ripped right down the back seam. Old thread does give way, but I've not often seen it go like that, not just by putting it on. I mean, she'd been wearing the coat all week, if she'd noticed the seam starting to go, she should have said something. But, Rina, I checked it over the evening before, like I always do when costume comes back at the end of the day, and it was all fine. Why would she do that? I was at it till after ten, reinforcing the edges and restitching. You'd not know it was ever damaged now," she added, with a touch of what Rina thought was entirely justified pride.

"You'll have to show me," she said. "And show me how you fixed it."

Would Grace have done something so spiteful? Rina wondered. Possibly, though that didn't necessarily mean that Theresa had been her target. Grace could sometimes behave like an irritable toddler, chucking things around just because she was miffed. She could be totally professional when working, but could also be randomly petty. It wasn't the first time she'd deliberately caused more work for someone or made a fuss when none was necessary. Rina could hear the frustration in Theresa's voice. Theresa was normally very even tempered but Grace was pushing even her limits.

They had reached the door to the wardrobe department now. There were two rooms, one for costume and one for props. The larger had once been the servants' dining room and the second, smaller room the housekeeper's parlour in the days when Septon Hall had a full staff.

Theresa opened the door and they went inside.

"Oh." Theresa paused on the threshold, wrinkling her nose. "It smells odd in here. I'll bet the drains are playing up again, though funny we didn't smell it in the hall."

That's not drains, Rina thought. She stepped past Theresa and walked to the back of the room, glancing right and left between the rows of hanging rails, pausing when she reached the tables set against the back wall and was then able to look through into the second room.

"Oh," she said. "Oh, that's not good."

"What is it?" Theresa asked, hurrying to join her before Rina could warn her off. She followed Rina's gaze and let out a little yelp of shock. Phil Perry lay sprawled on his back in the doorway to the props room. His pallor and the blood-soaked rug beneath his head told Rina that the man was dead, a very familiar object protruding from his neck.

"We need to help him." Theresa's voice was shrill.

"I think he's beyond that."

"But you can't be certain!" She started towards the dead man.

Gently but firmly, Rina held her back. "Go back to the dining room. Keep everyone there, call the police, I'll check that he's definitely dead."

Theresa nodded but shock had frozen her, and she did not move until Rina nudged her towards the door. "Go, call the police," she said. "I'll be right behind you."

Theresa moved then, almost running for the door. Rina waited until she was gone and then took a step towards to Phil's body. He lay on his back, head tilted to one side, the murder weapon protruding brutally from his neck. Rina could not immediately tell if the bronze replica had been used or the one with the steel pin that Grace had pinned to her jacket the previous evening. It didn't matter, she supposed. Whichever it was it had done its job.

She went no further; there was no need. She had unfortunately seen a fair few bodies, enough for her to know that Phil was dead and, judging by the faint green-tinged pallor around the mouth, had been so for quite some time. She left the wardrobe and turned back towards the dining room. She was perhaps only half a minute behind Theresa but already the news had been announced and was causing the inevitable shock. The door to the dining room opened before Rina could reach it and Alison emerged, Seth on her heels and Grace not far behind.

"Is it true?" Alison gasped.

"I'm afraid it is. Have the police been called?"

"Theresa's on it. My God, this is dreadful. How was he killed?"

Rina hesitated. She knew from experience with such things that the police would want to reserve as much information as possible and only reveal it when it had an operational purpose. But she had to tell them something and, besides, Theresa had also been there and would not be likely to be discreet.

"He was stabbed," she said.

"Oh my God," Alison said again.

"We should all go back inside until the police get here," Rina said and ushered everyone into the dining hall. She wondered if Theresa had seen what the murder weapon was. She wasn't sure what the younger woman had taken in. Theresa, leaning against one of the serving tables a few feet away, mobile to her ear was nodding furiously and saying yes, yes, she understood. She looked dazed and Rina guessed that the call handler might have had to repeat their instructions several times before they finally got through.

Theresa got off the phone and Rina guided her to a chair. "They're on the way?"

The younger woman nodded. "And an ambulance. I thought . . . maybe?" She looked hopefully at Rina, who shook her head sadly.

"I'm sorry, Theresa, it looks as though he's been dead for quite a while."

"And how on earth would you be able to tell?" Grace's voice was sharp and accusatory.

"I've encountered dead bodies before," Rina said quietly. Far too many, she thought. She wanted desperately to speak to Mac but knew this was not in his domain. Another officer would be in charge of the case. She wondered if it would be DI Anning, who had run an investigation only a few miles from the hall around Christmastime. Mac and Anning had a less than amicable past, but seemed to have come to some kind of truce. Rina knew Anning was not exactly her biggest fan, not having the same tolerance for civilian interference in police matters as her beloved Mac.

"What happens now?" Alison was asking.

"The police will have to take statements from everyone," Rina said. "The house, or parts of it anyway, will be designated as a crime scene and the forensic team will take over first, then the investigation proper will begin. We'd best all stay here until they turn up. Oh, though someone had better warn the house staff what's going on. They won't know, will they?" Rina had not given this much thought until now. The production had its own catering crew and the house itself was lightly staffed, just the estate manager and three or four others, based across the rear courtyard in the old stable block.

"I'll see to that," Seth told her. "I'll go round by the drive, just in case the rest of the house . . ." He paused, harrumphed and took off.

In case the rest of the house becomes part of the crime scene, Rina finished silently.

A few months before, as part of a pre-Christmas celebration weekend, she and Seth and a third cast member, Jess Winteringham, who played Adelaide, Lydia Marchant's niece, had been caught up in a murder at the Palisades Hotel near Frantham. Jess was not here this time, Adelaide's main scenes having been filmed early in the production run, but Seth would well remember the tension and the boredom that would soon prevail at Septon Hall.

At least, she thought, everyone had already been fed and there was still plenty of tea and coffee on tap.

Theresa was staring at her, a look of revelation on her pale face. She leaned close to Rina and whispered, "I've just realized I don't think I took it in at the time. He was stabbed with the brooch, wasn't he? With that fibula?"

Rina nodded and said softly, "Best we keep that to ourselves until the police get here." But she could see that Alison, still standing close by, had overheard, her hand fluttering to her mouth.

And Grace had heard too. The colour drained from her face and she grimaced as the implication settled in. "Someone's setting me up!" she announced loudly. "Some bastard is trying to frame me."

So much for keeping that quiet, Rina thought.

CHAPTER 6

Rina had been right about the boredom. Right too about DI Anning being the officer in charge. The SOCOs had arrived — Rina had watched eagerly out of the dining room window but there was no one she knew. Mac's partner, Miriam, was a SOCO but Rina remembered she was away on some kind of management training course and would have been unlikely to turn up here anyway. This was not her usual shift.

She fetched herself another cup of tea and, once settled, took her mobile from her pocket to see if Mac had replied to her message. She had left him a voicemail telling him about Phil Perry and how she had been there when his body was found. She'd mentioned also that she suspected a clumsy attempt at implicating Grace Sweetman in the crime. She wished she could have spoken to him in person, but just leaving the message had somehow made her feel better. The shock of finding Phil's body was slowly sinking in, made worse by the necessary inaction of waiting to be interviewed. Rina hated inactivity. She wasn't made to sit around. It made her feel useless and helpless.

She'd been slightly surprised that Anning had not asked everyone to hand over their devices, but he had simply told them to be sensible adults and reminded them all that there would be strict penalties for anyone interfering with an investigation by contacting the press.

Still nothing from Mac. Frowning, she shoved the phone back in her pocket.

"I thought I was done with real-life crimes after that business at Christmas," Seth grumbled.

"You'd have hoped so," Rina agreed, though the truth was her life for the past few years had involved rather a lot of 'real-life' stuff. Since Mac had arrived in Frantham the murder rate had skyrocketed, something the Martin household regularly teased him about.

"Do you think Grace had anything to do with Phil's death?" Seth asked her.

"Do you? You know her better than I do."

Seth looked away for a moment and Rina understood that the thought had crossed his mind. He shook his head. "No, not really. She's got a temper, but I can't really see her going that far."

"I can't see it being any of the cast or the crew," she said. Or was that just that she didn't want to? These people were her friends and colleagues, and she had come to like them all.

"No," Seth agreed, "but that's going to be an obvious conclusion for the police to come to. Anyone here could have had the opportunity. Though I don't see why anyone would have reason. Phil could be annoying at times, but so can we all. I liked the man."

Rina nodded. "I liked him too. I think we all did, but you're right, anyone in this room would have had the opportunity. But what would be the motive?"

"There you have me at a loss. I mean, it's not impossible that someone came in from outside. The security in this place is laughable, isn't it?"

"It's not great," Rina agreed. There were cameras on the front and back door and one at the end of the drive and some security lights set around the house but nothing else that she was aware of and both cast and crew tended to come and go as and when they liked. It wasn't much of a stretch to think that other people might be able to do the same.

"We had that nasty little incident with the souvenir hunters back in series three," Seth went on.

"I remember." Someone had broken into one of the trailers and stolen a few small items that had then ended up on eBay. It had caused a kerfuffle at the time and the police had been involved. "They were just kids though," she said. "And opportunists at that. I don't think they were even fans, just kids chancing their arm."

"But what if it's something like that again?" Seth said. "Someone comes in, Phil spots them and there's a confrontation?"

"It's possible, I suppose," Rina said. Just now it seemed as possible as anything else.

She looked around the room at the anxious faces, the tears. Everyone would be terribly shaken by this, she thought. They would be looking at one another as possible suspects, as possible murderers, and that was a horrible thing to contemplate.

Presently, they sat alone at a small table. Rina was not surprised. Everyone in the cast knew that they had been through something like this before and, though there had been a lot of initial questions about what they should expect, as the first rush of shock and excitement died down and the police arrived, that previous experience began to set them apart. As everyone settled in for the inevitable waiting, people had gravitated towards those with whom they felt most comfortable or at least those they felt they knew best.

The lighting crew and the sparkies and the sound guys had pulled two long tables together and were playing cards. Theresa had been drawn into a huddle with her assistants, Kylie and May, and the trio, Ben, Gill and Ebony, who took care of hair and makeup.

The rest of the cast and crew had settled into friendship groups, taking solace in one another's company. Apart from herself and Seth, the only people who seemed to have been isolated — or who had isolated themselves, were Grace and Richard Cartmell. Cartmell looked uncomfortable but resigned. Grace was unusually pale and did look genuinely upset. Perhaps, Rina thought, more because she felt she had been implicated in the murder than because of Phil's death.

No, she told herself, that was unfair. Unnatural death shocked everyone, even those equipped with such a practised carapace of unconcern as Grace Sweetman.

Rina was glad that Judith Tavener had not stayed on overnight but had returned to her hotel. She had been due to, in Alison's words, "pop back for a while" that afternoon, but that no longer seemed likely. Rina wondered if she had heard the news, who might have told her? Had she been alone when she heard? That would not have been pleasant.

The main door opened and Alison came through. She had been the first to be called to interview and Rina guessed that was so she could give DI Anning an overview of the setup at Septon Hall in regard to the filming. She had overheard two officers stating that that the estate manager and his team would be spoken to separately and probably sent home. Their office was about as far from the wardrobe department as it was possible to get and all apart from the estate manager lived off-site. They would have been arriving for work around the time that Rina and Theresa discovered Phil's body.

"Alison," Seth called to her. "Come and sit." He pulled out a chair.

Alison looked questioningly at the police officer who had escorted her back, then came over to join them.

Rina was unsurprised when the officer went to fetch Theresa. No doubt she would be next. It was interesting, Rina thought, that they had been left to their own devices in a way that differed greatly from their experience at the Palisades. Seth must have thought the same thing because he said to Alison, "At least they're letting us talk to one another this time."

"This time? Oh, of course. You've done this before."

"Probably depends on circumstances and resources," Rina said vaguely but she was thinking, Anning wants to see how much our stories vary. He wants to judge how much we've been discussing this and what theories are coming out. He understands we all work closely with one another, know each other well and he's wants to get a sense of the gossip and any infighting or friction, and by allowing us all to say what we like to one another now, he's hoping we'll be more open with him. When the murder happened at the hotel, just before Christmas, the guests had mostly been relative strangers to one another, not friends and colleagues as they were now.

"How did it go?" Seth was asking Alison.

"Oh, it was all perfectly polite and straightforward," she said, but she sounded tense and Rina could tell that she was close to tears.

"There were two of them. This Inspector called Anning. Not that he did much. It was a woman asking the questions. Detective Sergeant Hurst. I mean, she seemed nice enough, wanted to know how everything worked here, who had access to the wardrobe and props rooms. If Phil had upset anyone or had any enemies. How easy I thought it would be for someone to get in from outside. I told them I'd never even thought about that. I really didn't know."

She lifted her hand and wiped impatiently at the tears that Rina had known would flow. Alison would not be the only one in tears this morning. And for those who didn't feel they could cry, there would be irritation and even outright anger. It was not going to be a comfortable experience for anyone.

Seth put an arm around Alison and offered to get her some coffee. Briefly, she leaned into him and allowed herself to be comforted. Then she pulled away gently. "I'd love some coffee," she said, raking in her pocket for a tissue and wiping her eyes and nose. "How could something like that happen here?" she demanded suddenly. "We've always been such a happy crew and everyone liked Phil. I can't believe he had an enemy in the world."

Well, he must have had one, Rina thought. For him to have wound up dead.

* * *

Back in Frantham, Mac had picked up Rina's message. He listened to it twice before making some calls to try and clarify what was going on. A dead actor, a body found in the wardrobe — Mac could not get the image out of his head of a large, wooden armoire, even though he knew that was absurd — sounded too fictional to be fact.

"Well," he said to Andy Nevins, as the latter stuck his head around the door to offer tea, "it looks as though our friend Rina has stumbled upon yet another fatality."

"Who's been murdered this time?" Andy asked.

"Did I mention the word murder?"

"No, but . . . dead body, Mrs Martin . . . odds are."

Mac nodded, taking Andy's point. Odds certainly were. "It's an actor, name of Phillip Perry, part of the cast of the latest Lydia Marchant," he said. "DI Anning is SIO, I just spoke to one of his sergeants and they're still interviewing cast and crew. Rina mentioned that someone may be trying to implicate one of the other cast members, a woman called Grace Sweetman. Thing is, I know that name. I remember her from a good few years back and if I remember right she was charged with criminal damage."

"You investigated?" Andy asked.

"I did. It was a good long while ago, just before I was made up to DS, in fact. I'd have to check back, but I don't remember it being a complicated business. I think her boyfriend had left her and she'd gone round and damaged his car and some of his other property. She didn't really even deny doing it, I don't think. What I do remember is her being very angry and very loud." Mac smiled at the rather fragmentary memory of a tall, blonde woman insisting that she knew her rights and was saying nothing until she had a lawyer.

"So, what happened?"

"I assume her lawyer was summoned and she was interviewed. I handed the case off to someone else and I also vaguely recollect that it never came to court. I think she paid for the damage and her ex dropped the charges, but without tracking down the paperwork I don't really remember. The name's unusual, which is probably what stuck in my mind and I knew she was an actor, so when Rina mentioned her . . . I'm assuming it's the same woman, anyway."

"Probably is," Andy said. "I don't think Equity allows there to be two actors with the same name. I think one of them would have to change it."

Mac nodded. He'd heard something to that effect too. "Anyway, I left a message for Anning mentioning the Sweetman business, or what I could recall of it."

He saw Andy cock an inquisitorial eyebrow. "Want to be involved, do you, boss?"

Mac laughed at him. "Get off and make that tea," he said. But he considered the question. Did he want to be involved? Well, he thought, seeing as how Rina was, he probably did.

* * *

Rina's phone buzzed in her cardigan pocket as she followed the constable down the long corridor to the Grand Salon. She wondered if it was Mac.

The constable glanced at her but said nothing. He opened the heavy oak door and ushered her inside, taking up position beside it as though afraid she might make a run for it.

Was it only yesterday, Rina thought, that they'd all been shooting that scene in here, with Judith watching on, wrapped up in a blanket?

The room was chilly and Anning and the woman who must be DS Hurst had sensibly set up a table close to the fire. It was burning more brightly than it usually did, Rina noted, and logs and a full scuttle of smokeless briquettes had been set on the hearth, a juxtaposition that amused her. The position of the table did mean that anyone coming to be interviewed had to walk halfway down the length of the room to get to the table at which the police officers sat. She recalled auditions where theatre managers had employed a similar tactic — though that had usually been so they could get a good eyeful of the young women desperate to be in the chorus line.

Pulling her attention back to the present, she eyed DI Anning and his colleague. Anning was a solid-looking man. He looked older than Mac and his salt-and-pepper hair receded in a classic widow's peak. It was still thick though and with a slight wave to it that must have been attractive when he was younger. He was at that stage in life when some men seem to get slightly jowly and when a lot of men in Rina's profession either contemplated surgery or sought to hide the fact by always keeping their chins lifted just a tad too high.

Anning was not such a man. He seemed to have fully embraced the bulldog look and he watched her approach with his chin tucked down and his steely grey eyes fixed firmly upon her.

He's trying to intimidate me, Rina thought. She'd have no truck with that.

She paused as she reached the fire and stretched out her hands. They genuinely were cold and she rubbed them briskly while she shifted her attention to Anning's DS. Even seated, Hurst looked tall. In her thirties, Rina guessed. Dark brown eyes regarded Rina with a degree of amusement and Rina decided she was inclined to like her.

"You've got more fuel out of Robbie than we ever manage," Rina said, indicating the logs and the coal scuttle. "Mean as old Scrooge he is, usually. But then, I suppose murder does shift the goalposts."

She sensed Anning wince and she fancied it was at her mixed imagery and that intrigued and impressed her, far more than the bulldog expression or the stern gaze.

"Well, you would know," Anning said. "You seem to have encountered more dead bodies than that woman in *Murder, She Wrote*."

He pointed to the chair set in front of the desk and Rina sat down.

"I'm DI Anning, and you probably think you know all about me. This is DS Hurst. She'll be conducting the interview."

Interview? Rina thought. She was about to question the terminology but thought better of it. No doubt it was a word that Anning found unsettled people. Most people. Politely, Rina turned her attention to DS Hurst.

"So, tell me what happened this morning," the sergeant said.

Slowly and carefully, Rina recounted the events of the morning. Going with Theresa to wardrobe, the odd smell, Rina knowing that it wasn't the drains, the finding of Phil's body. Recognising the murder weapon.

"I couldn't tell, of course, if it was the fully bronze replica or the one with the modern steel pin," she finished. "Whoever had killed Phil had rammed that thing too deeply into his neck."

She was aware of Anning eyeing her thoughtfully.

"There are two of those brooches?" Hurst asked.

"Technically, there are four, but the fourth, the Roman original, is on loan to the Bridport museum. The family who own this place, the Meachers, had a replica made just after the original was found and I suppose the family still have that one. I've never seen it. That was, I think, about eighteen years ago. Then, for this production, two others were made, one in bronze for those scenes when the whole brooch would be on show and the other, the one to be worn, with a steel pin. It's a bit gentler on modern fabrics."

Though whichever had been used hadn't been very gentle on Phil Perry's throat, she thought.

"When did you last see Mr Perry?" Hurst asked.

Rina had already thought about this. "In the canteen at around seven thirty," she said. "At about six thirty I'd dropped off my jacket for Theresa to do some running repairs. I went with Richard Cartmell and Judith Tavener for a cup of tea. Richard took tea and sandwiches back to Theresa, who still had work to finish, and then came back to join us. That was at around six fifty."

"Ms Barnett was going to be working on Miss Sweetman's jacket lining," Hurst said.

"Yes. Then Richard came back, we chatted for a while. Seth joined us. Phil popped in to get himself a coffee probably around half past seven. He came over and spent a few minutes chatting, asking Judith how she'd enjoyed her day, that sort of thing. He said that he and some of the sound crew were going to be playing pool in the old billiards room. They do that most evenings, I think. Judith left around eight and I went to my room shortly after."

"And after you went to your room?"

"I phoned home, chatted for a while, then read my book and fell asleep."

"Apparently Mr Perry had an argument with Miss Sweetman, on set."

"He did. But it's not particularly unusual for Grace to have a disagreement with someone. She can be prickly."

"And the disagreement was about?"

"Grace claimed that Phil had made her miss her cue. Phil countered that she had fed him the wrong line and so how could he hope to give her the right cue if he didn't have the right line. It was the kind of quibble they had all the time. Alison had words with them and things carried on."

"And did Miss Sweetman and Mr Perry generally get on?"

Rina considered for a moment. "Generally speaking, Phil got on with everybody, even Grace. She was in a particularly awkward mood when she had her spat with him. Seth, who knows her better than I do, suggested it might be because Judith Tavener was going to be visiting. You probably know that they have history. Grace was responsible for breaking up Judith's marriage, or rather—" she corrected herself quickly — "Judith's husband went off with Grace, so I suppose he should share the responsibility."

Although DS Hurst was doing her best to hide her surprise it was clear to Rina that she had not known. "That was getting on for eighteen years ago, I believe. The husband, Tony Emmerson, didn't stay with Grace for very long but the marriage never recovered. He didn't go back. I understand that Judith was very distressed about the situation so perhaps Grace was unhappy that she was on set and wondered if she might make a scene."

"Which might have made her extra prickly," Anning suggested, his tone wry.

"Seth and I did wonder about that," Rina acknowledged. She did not bother telling Anning that she had known nothing about the marriage breakup until Seth had told her.

"And how did the rest of the cast and crew get on with Phil?" DS Hurst asked. "It's been suggested that Phil Perry was something of a gossip, that perhaps he upset people from time to time."

Rina was surprised at the sudden change of direction. "And where did you hear that?" she asked. "I didn't consider Phil any more of a gossip than other people. This is a close community, people talk about one another, people get bored and speculate, but on the whole there's no malice in it and I don't believe that Phil had a malicious bone in his body."

Was that true? she asked herself. Actually, Phil was capable of being as snide and sneaky as anyone else but for the most part he just collected fragments of speculation and information, like a small child might collect pebbles on the beach. He might cherish them and polish them and then at an opportune moment scatter them with as much care as a bored child might scatter those same pebbles. "I don't think anyone took Phil seriously," she said thoughtfully. "He loved to read the tabloids, and the celebrity magazines, always knew the latest rubbish about who was dating who, or what they were wearing on the red carpet. I don't believe he ever set out to upset anyone."

"But he gossiped about members of the cast and crew?"

Rina shook her head. "Not the crew, definitely not. He had friends among the crew, but . . ." How could she explain? "The thing is, the cast are your peers, your equals, you get to know everybody quite intimately and it is a very closed and closeted world in some ways, quite incestuous. Especially a cast like this, which for the most part continues series to series."

"Except that Mr Perry was not part of that inner circle, any more than Miss Sweetman is," DS Hurst said. "I think this is the only series that they both appear in, is that right?"

Rina nodded thoughtfully. That was true. "I suppose we've all been together for longer than would be normal," she said. "The filming has been interrupted several times and so the overall time has been extended and that's put stress on everybody. It's made it easy to forget that Phil and Grace are not part of the normal team. Phil in particular has fitted in very well, and it feels as though he's been around for ever. Sometimes when people come in as guest artists, just for a series, or even an episode, they can be . . . They can feel like outsiders, even when everybody sets out to make them comfortable it's inevitable that particular friendship groups form and they might seem difficult to break into. Phil never seemed to feel uncomfortable. He was friendly and confident but without being pushy and I think everybody just responded to him."

"Did he form any particular friendships?"

Rina shook her head. "I'm not sure that he did, though, thinking about it, he spent more time with the crew than he did with the cast. He just seemed generally friendly. As I say, he liked to gossip about celebrities, but generally he was easy to be around." She was feeling her way now, thinking intently about her actual relationship with Phil. The general relationship Phil had with cast and crew. It was true that everybody got on with him but now she considered it she wasn't sure that he was close to anyone or that anybody really encouraged closeness. Phil was pleasant and well liked and amused everybody by reading out the gossip columns. He wasn't above speculating about the cast, teasing people if they paid too much attention to somebody, dressed up for the evening, made some remark that could, with a bit of a stretch, be misinterpreted, but it never felt malicious. It was just Phil, slightly childish at times, but *seemingly* harmless. Rina realized suddenly how little real attention she had actually paid him. Phil's chatter was like background noise, lift music, in a way. You were conscious of it but, to her at least, it was uninteresting and repetitive enough that it was easy to tune it out.

Grace on the other hand rarely seemed to say anything that wasn't double-edged but people ignored her too. Whereas Phil was always just prattling, Grace could be unpleasant in such a generalized way, equally dismissive of and picky with everybody — except perhaps Seth — that after a few days her attitude failed to have much impact. It was acknowledged as being just Grace. In reality, quite graceless. It was only when things boiled over, as they had with Phil the day before, that anyone felt the need to intervene or even to take notice.

She tried to explain this to DS Hurst but wasn't sure she made a very good job of it.

"What I can't understand," she said, "is what he was doing in wardrobe in the first place. He had no reason to be there. Of course anybody can get in, the door doesn't lock properly. We kept asking Robbie to put a keypad on it or sort the lock out but he hasn't done that yet. The only thing I can think of is that perhaps he was meeting somebody. It's pretty much out of the way, so for anybody that did want a private place to meet, they're unlikely to be disturbed."

"And is it likely Phil would have been meeting someone?" DS Hurst asked her.

Rina shrugged. "Well, that's kind of the question, isn't it? Did he meet someone, and did that someone kill him? Grace of course is upset because she believes she is being framed for it because of her character's association with the brooch."

"And is that what you think?" Anning asked her.

"Well, it would be a very clumsy attempt, wouldn't it? Anyone can get into that room, and into the props room beyond. Yes, Grace was being very silly and possessive about the brooch — she pinned it on to her coat last night and made pronouncements about it being a pity that it wasn't the original or at least the other copy. But anyone would have had access to either of the reproductions. Just because Grace happened to have handled one or the other, not just last night but at various other times, just because her character uses it as a murder weapon in the original book, that's hardly a reason to accuse Grace Sweetman of being a murderer."

"Of course, you've had extensive experience of such things," Anning said wryly.

Rina refused to rise to that. "Unfortunately, yes," she said. "But what was he doing there, and who was he with? It's unlikely to have been Grace. And it is such a tucked away location and it *would* be good for a clandestine meeting. Of course, this is a big house and full of nooks and crannies if privacy is what you're looking for, but the wardrobe at least has a portable heater. This is a cold old place."

Anning laughed. "Perhaps you have too much imagination," he said. But Rina got the feeling that he agreed with her, that it was more likely Phil had agreed to meet someone than that someone could have stumbled upon him by chance.

"The other thing is, why use the fibula? It's not the most obvious of weapons. It's not like a knife or a hat pin, and there would have been plenty of things in the props store within very easy reach to have either stabbed Phil or bashed him over the head. So, I'm asking myself, if it's not an attempt to implicate Grace, does it have some significance for the killer?"

Anning raised an eyebrow. "Mrs Martin, I know that certain of my colleagues have given you a degree of latitude in the past, even involved you or allowed you to become involved in investigations. Now I know you mean well, but perhaps you should leave the speculation to the professionals. And I would ask that you perhaps desist from speculating publicly, at least until we have completed all of the interviews."

"I will," she promised him and noted Anning's look of surprise. He had clearly expected some belligerence on her part. "But there's one more thing you should know. It's probably not connected but the coincidence is something I don't like at all."

She filled him in on Grace's receipt of the poison pen letter and that Phil had been there when she had opened it.

"It certainly didn't help her mood," Rina said. "She was very upset. Seth took her out to dinner the evening before last to try and cheer her up and get her to talk about it but I think it really rankled."

Anning was watching her intently. Rina shrugged. "As I say, it may be nothing but I thought you should know."

Shortly after this Rina had her fingerprints scanned and was told she could return to the canteen. She had barely got through the door before Grace Sweetman was bearing down on her, clearly incandescent.

"So, do they think I did it, do they think I'd be even capable of doing this? This is a dreadful thing, a dreadful state of affairs, I am the victim here, you hear me? Someone wants me implicated."

Rina blinked at her and said calmly, "Grace, you are not the victim here. Phil is dead, he is the victim."

Grace glared at her but the constable who had brought Rina back was now asking for Ms Sweetman to follow him. Grace left in high dudgeon but Rina could see that she was genuinely distraught.

I don't blame her, Rina thought, noting that all eyes were on Grace as she sailed from the room. There would be quite a few individuals in that group who believed that Grace was indeed capable of, might even have been responsible for, Phil's death.

Did Rina think so? Truthfully, she really wasn't sure.

CHAPTER 7

"So, how are you?" Mac asked when they spoke on the phone later. "I can't imagine you want to go through anything like this again."

"Indeed not. Everyone's been interviewed now, and of course the production is going to be closed down until the police and SOCO are finished with the place, so Matthew is coming to pick me up. I wouldn't mind a chat later if you've got time."

"I've already been invited round for supper tonight," Mac told her, so I'll see you around seven."

Rina, watching from her bedroom window, saw Matthew pull into the drive and stop beside the large front door. "That will be nice," she said. "Matthew's just arrived so I'll just get my bags together."

Earlier, two young officers had gone room by room to make a quick inspection of bags and belongings before everyone left. Rina had watched as one riffled through an already packed suitcase while the other opened drawers and checked under the bed. She had wondered what they might specifically be looking for. She had wondered if they even knew.

Rina took the servants' stairs down. It was no quicker or easier than the main staircase down to the lobby — slightly more inconvenient, in fact, when carrying a wheelie suitcase and another bag down the narrower space — but it meant she could possibly take a quick glance towards the end of the corridor that led to the wardrobe department and other utility areas beyond. She paused at the foot of the stairs, opposite what had once been the entrance to the old kitchen and was now a large storage room. The end of the corridor led off into what had been the service wing. She could hear the murmur of voices coming from one of the rooms. As she stood there, a young, uniformed officer leaned around a door and asked if he could help her.

Rina shook her head. She turned away, interested that Anning was not yet treating this side of the house as a crime scene but had segregated only that corridor and the rooms off it. Did he have other witness statements that tracked Phil's movements after she had seen him?

Probably, Rina decided. Phil had intended to play pool with some of the crew, so had probably been in company until what, ten o'clock, or possibly much later if they'd kept to their usual habits.

The snooker room was in the main body of the house. It still bore vestiges of former glories — if you could call deep red chenille curtains and overstuffed leather sofas and armchairs former glories. She supposed you could, for that emulation of what she assumed an Edwardian gentleman's club might have looked like, if you believed the Sherlock Holmes films, even if it wasn't exactly to her taste.

The wheels of her suitcase trundled noisily along the uneven flagstones leading from the kitchen towards the dining room, then quietened as Rina turned a corner into a carpeted hallway. Passing the formal dining room and finding the doors open, Rina glanced inside. The long table had been set up for the next scene in the shooting schedule and gleamed with silver and glass. Equipment was ready. It was the odd, personal reminders that caused Rina's throat to tighten. The cardigan left on the back of a chair. A half-drunk cup of tea and a few biscuits on a plate on the sideboard. A coffee-stained shooting script, covered in scribbled diagrams and indecipherable notes.

We'll be back in a few days, she told herself sternly, but she felt oddly bereft, as though this was the end of something and not merely an interruption. She knew, even if and when they resumed filming, this series of Lydia Marchant would not be the same. A man they all knew had been killed and it was possible that someone she had been working with, living with, laughing with, was responsible for his death and that would be the case for everyone involved. Something every single member of cast and crew would have to come to terms with. That would change everything.

Of course, it was perfectly possible for someone to have come in from the outside. The front and back doors were locked at night, the catering staff leaving by the back door at around nine and making sure everything was secured when they did. After that, anyone wanting to come and go would do so through a small side entrance, leading into what had been the drying area for the laundry. Spare keys had been cut and hung in the dining room and theoretically anyone taking one was meant to sign a sheet pinned to the wall and then sign the key back in.

Theoretically.

Rina knew that no one really bothered and also that the door was frequently left closed but not locked when people went out, especially if other people had forgotten to return the keys to their proper place. A keypad would have made more sense, she thought, but that would have cost money and the Septon Hall management didn't seem keen on spending on areas that those attending events weren't likely to see.

It was a small door and Rina supposed you'd have to know it was there, but the number of people who did know it was there was likely to be considerable. Cast and crew, catering staff, anyone who'd worked at Septon Hall or who had mentioned its existence to someone else.

She wondered if she should have mentioned this to Anning but presumed the house manager would tell him, or he'd find out for himself.

Seth was in the hall, waiting for a taxi. She had offered him a lift but they were going in opposite directions and so he had elected to call a cab to take him to the train station.

"Goodbye for now, my dear," Seth told her, kissing her on the cheek. "I'm sure we'll be back in no time."

Practically, she thought, it could be several days or even a couple of weeks before they came back to Septon Hall and continued with the filming. Rina was not sorry to be leaving. She had needed a break even before the murder, but she was simultaneously frustrated with all the delays. Ultimately these cost money, and she worried that this threatened the future of *Lydia Marchant Investigates*. What would the public think about a real-life murder intruding into their fictional death and mayhem? It could go either way she supposed — it could put people off or it could draw a whole new audience into the fold. But it all felt tainted now. It felt like something precious had ended.

Seth's taxi drew up and he plucked his cases from the floor and hurried out, pausing to shout a greeting to Matthew, who was leaning against their small blue hatchback.

Seeing Rina, Matthew came forward to take her bag and she leaned into his very welcome hug. She would be glad to be home. To her surprise, she felt tears pricking her eyes. Impatiently, she blinked them away, a little shocked at the sudden rise of emotion.

Glancing back at the house as she was getting into the car, she spotted Anning standing by the window of the Grand Salon watching her thoughtfully. She thought about waving, decided against, got into the car and slumped wearily in the passenger seat.

"I need a decent cup of tea," Rina said. She closed her eyes for a moment and when she opened them again they were at the end of the drive, Matthew pausing while a car passed before pulling out on to the main road.

"So," she said, "what's happening at home? Mac tells me he's coming to dinner tonight."

"He is. Steven is baking bread and there'll be chicken and ham pie and apple crumble for dessert. I don't suppose you've been eating properly," he added, turning his leonine head to look her way. "And Mac certainly hasn't been. He only cooks when Miriam's there."

Rina settled back in the seat and sighed contentedly, happy to be fussed over and cosseted for a while. "And what about the poison pen letters? Have there been more of those?"

"Ooh, yes," Matthew told her. "There have indeed. But I think our mysterious sender is beginning to show how little they really know about the recipients and that's what will catch them out in the end, I'm sure of it."

By the time Frantham came into view, Rina and Matthew had brought each other up to speed. She knew she would be going through this discussion and discovery again when she reached home and probably a third time in the evening when Mac had come over and they'd all spent time picking events apart over coffee. Mac, of course, would not discuss any ongoing investigation, but so much was common knowledge that there would still be plenty to talk about. It was a rule in the Martin household that 'business' discussions did not take place until after dinner, but from coffee onwards anything was fair game. Anyone encountering the folk at Peverill Lodge for the first time might come to the conclusion that they were somewhat obsessed with food, dinner time being particularly important and everyone gathering for a substantial meal. Rina, thinking now about dinner and looking forward to her lunch, supposed that was partly true. But for the members of her little family, who had spent their working lives in the most transient and unsettled of occupations and for whom security had seemed like something only other people got to experience, the act of cooking for one another, for eating together, for sharing time and attention and love, had become almost a sacred thing.

She was so incredibly lucky, Rina thought.

* * *

From the window of the Grand Salon DI Anning watched Rina leave. She was an interesting woman, he thought, and he could understand how she might have got under DI MacGregor's skin. Anning considered himself cast in a tougher mould. Civilians should know their place.

She had given him some interesting information, though, about the Sweetman woman and the poison pen letter and that had got him thinking. It would be useful to get Mac on board with the investigation, just on the off-chance that there might be a link between the murder and this letter-writing campaign. Mac and that bright young PC of his would have more of a grasp on that angle. Anning had heard that Andy Nevins was studying for his DC examinations, and he knew that Andy had effectively 'acted up' on a couple of occasions. It wouldn't hurt for the lad to get a bit more experience in the field to help back up his studies.

It was unlikely, Anning thought, that the writer of the letters had taken a giant leap for criminal kind and got into the business of murder, but stranger things had happened. Besides, although a man was dead, it didn't necessarily follow that there had originally been intent to kill in the assailant's mind. People lashed out with terrible consequences on so many occasions. The thought rolled around in his mind like a die cast on to a roulette wheel, and if he was indeed asked to place a bet, he'd put his money on murder. There were indeed more ready and obvious weapons in the wardrobe, to have been grabbed and wielded in a fit of temper.

He had spoken to Grace Sweetman again and, very reluctantly, she had first admitted to receiving the letter and then, with even more reluctance, showed it to him. He got the feeling that the woman was actually embarrassed by it, that all her bluster and show was cover for someone who was not nearly as confident and secure.

But wasn't that often the way?

He had been particularly interested in Phil Perry's behaviour that morning, if Ms Sweetman had had any sense that he knew more about the letters than he had suggested. She hadn't thought so. It was remotely possible, Anning thought, that Phil Perry had an inkling regarding who the letter writer was, had perhaps arranged to meet with them.

Anning dismissed the thought as far-fetched even while it was forming. Though, on the other hand, fact often was stranger than fiction. Though why meet someone here when more public, neutral ground would have been safer?

Anning gave up on that particular set of questions for the moment. He'd get Mac and PC Andy Nevins on board and see if anything from that angle emerged.

Anning left the Grand Salon and took the back stairs to the top of the house. Phil Perry's room was in the process of being searched but there was nothing relevant so far. He'd been sharing this shoe cupboard of a room with two other actors who had been told to take only essential items with them — these had been checked before they left.

Along this same corridor were three other rooms, all very similar. Basic furnishings, one with an ensuite shower. There was a shared bathroom at the end of the hallway. A similar arrangement of rooms led off the stairway to the right.

It was chilly up here, chilly and dark, Anning thought. Weak sun filtered in through skylights that were green with moss and algae, so it felt as though the rooms and the corridor were underwater.

One floor down and the rooms were larger but still basic and the layout was similar, corridors off central stairs. Looking at the plan one of his officers had drawn up for him he found Rina's room at the end of the right-hand hallway. Theresa from the wardrobe and one of her assistants shared the next room. The writer, Richard Cartmell was down at the far end.

A small door at the end of the hallway opened into another stairwell and Anning followed it down. The stairway was very narrow. He was not a big man but his shoulders brushed both walls. Light filtered in through more glass, narrow windows, reminiscent of arrow slits this time, supplemented by motion-activated battery lamps attached to the low ceiling. The batteries needed replacing. The light was dim. He guessed this passageway was little used these days but the lights suggested that it was not entirely off limits.

He came to a door partway down the stairs. It opened on to a broad landing and he recognized the corridor that led to fully refurbished guest rooms and eventually to the broad staircase down into the entrance hall.

Eventually being the operative word. It was a long corridor and he could see a half-dozen doors opening off it, their spacing suggestive of substantial rooms or even suites. He guessed that he was on the second floor.

Leaving the corridor for later examination, he ducked back inside the narrow stairwell and followed it down. A second door gave access to the first-floor landing. Down again and the door at the bottom of the staircase opened on to a far less luxurious view. He found himself in a narrow, white-washed corridor and for a moment couldn't place where he was. He heard voices to his right and followed the sound through a half-glazed door. Now he recognised the location. He was standing outside what he had been told was the butler's pantry, a room he had commandeered, along with a couple of portable gas heaters and some folding tables and chairs, to use as his centre of operations. The Grand Salon might be fine for doing initial interviews, but it was hardly suitable for running an investigation.

Further along this corridor was the wardrobe. The crime scene. A little further than that and you'd come to the back stairs down which Rina Martin, obviously trying to get a glimpse of what was going on, had come earlier, according to one of his officers.

He didn't really blame her — he'd have been curious too.

He turned the other way and followed the passageway past storerooms and what looked like an old scullery, into a large room. A quick nose about suggested this might have been a laundry room. He recognized the big copper boilers that would have had fires lit beneath them for heating the water and there were two massive sinks with mangles set against one wall.

A small door led out into an area walled on only three sides, open to the elements on the other. It caught the wind, which channelled along the side of the house. The remnants of drying racks and pulleys were still fixed to the tall ceiling. The door hinges, he noted, were well oiled, as was the newish lock, set in place above the old cast iron affair complete with keyhole and large, impressively sized brass handle. A brief examination told him that the old lock was also in good working order.

This, he realized, was the door that was used after the front and back entrances had been locked up for the night. He realized also that the new lock meant nothing, so far as security was concerned. Currently, the sneck had been pulled back and the latch was down, holding it in place. The handle on the old lock could be used to open and close the door and give direct access to and from the outside.

The door had already been examined for prints — he'd ordered that as soon as he'd found out from the estate manager that it existed. The world and his wife had probably touched it, Anning thought, so he didn't hold out much hope.

Now, he ensured that the door was properly secured and then stood in the old laundry thinking about the route he had just taken.

Yes, anyone could have got inside. Equally, or perhaps more importantly, it would have been easy for anyone to have moved from the basement of the house up to any floor without being heard or seen.

How many more of these blasted access stairs and passageways were there? And what did the CCTV cameras cover? Surely there would be some coverage of that little back door.

Anning already had people looking at the CCTV recordings. Hopefully, something that simplified his life might turn up.

CHAPTER 8

Dinner was a comfortable affair, a time to catch up on news and just enjoy the company of her dearest friends. Inevitably, after the table had been cleared and dishes stacked, the conversation turned to the poison pen letters and to events that had stopped the Lydia Marchant filming dead in its tracks.

"Horrible that you found him," Eliza said. "Do you think he'd been dead long?"

"I think it was more horrible for Theresa," Rina said. "She was terribly shaken up. As to how long he'd been there, I'm really not sure. I didn't touch him, but he looked cold and like the blood had drained and left that kind of greenish pallor you get when a body has been lying in the same place for a good while. I managed to have a chat with Alison this afternoon and she says that no one seems to have been with him after around eleven. He'd been playing pool for most of the evening and then said he was going to bed. A few of the others stayed on in the billiard room for about another half hour but no one admits to seeing Phil when they went up to bed, even though a couple of them would have passed the wardrobe department on their way upstairs. They were sleeping in what was the old servants' quarters."

"No one noticed anything, and no one remembers there being any unusual noises or anything else?" Bethany said.

"No light under the door?" Steven asked.

"No, but it's a very heavy old door with a draft excluder brush fitted to the bottom, so I wouldn't have expected any. The light was off when we went in," Rina remembered. "Theresa switched it on. It's not the brightest of rooms. There are windows, but they're quite high up and that frosted glass like you get in bathrooms. Anyway, it looks as though no one's bothered cleaning them in years."

"So, where in relation to the wardrobe department was the victim staying?" Mac asked.

"Along the corridor and up the back stairs, one floor above where my room was. I'd not seen his room, but Phil said it was like a broom cupboard up in what had been attic bedrooms. He was in on his own, the room next to him had I think three people sharing and there's a bathroom along the corridor. There are so many staircases in that place and these little linking corridors so the servants could move about and not disturb the family. It's like a rabbit warren. The first week I was there I was constantly getting lost. It's an interesting old building but all the holes and hollows will make the investigation more complicated."

Matthew got up from the table. "I'll go and make you some coffee," he said, "and you and Mac can go off and have a proper conflab while we do the clearing up. Go," he said, over Rina's half-hearted protests, "you both know you want to."

Gratefully, Rina retreated to her small sitting room at the front of the house. A fire had been made up and the two easy chairs placed either side looked inviting. This was Rina's space, strictly invitation only, a place to gather her thoughts, work at her computer or have the sort of private conversations even the closest of families sometimes require. The curtains were already drawn but Rina parted them for a moment and looked out on to the familiar street. It was already dark. The street lights would still be lit for — she glanced at her wall clock — about another hour. Due to cost-saving measures by the local council, the lights in the side roads went off at eleven. She let the curtains fall back and went to sit down in her favourite wingback chair.

Matthew came in with the coffee tray and set it down on a small table beside Rina's chair and then left them to it.

"I didn't think I'd be involved in another murder," Rina said heavily as Mac settled more comfortably in the opposite chair. "It's a bad business and, I don't know, it feels full of spite, somehow."

"Murders often are."

"Oh, I know that, Mac, but there's something about this one that feels petty. Febrile, even. As though the murderer wanted to make some kind of a point. Why use the brooch?"

"Maybe they just grabbed the nearest object," Mac suggested.

Rina shook her head. She got up and fetched a pad and pen from the drawer in the computer desk and drew a quick sketch plan of the murder scene. "Look," she said. "The door is here, leading into what was the servants' dining room. That's the main wardrobe section with a couple of racks of overspill clothing through here—" she pointed to the smaller room — "which is used for the props. This was the housekeeper's parlour, apparently. Originally there was a door from that room out into the corridor but that's blocked off by a large set of shelves."

"Definitely no way in or out?"

"Definitely not. It's solid oak and weighs a ton. I'm told it originally stood against this wall in the servants' hall." She indicated the back wall under the windows. "The estate manager mentioned that they moved it out of the way to deal with a damp problem about ten years ago, got it into the other room and then left it there. Anyway, it means the only way in or out is through that one door. I have to say, Theresa wasn't happy about that. She was worried about fire. I suppose, with that much fabric and other flammable stuff around, you have to be conscious of these things, but—" she shrugged — "apparently it was all within fire regs, so . . .

Anyway, there are hanging racks here, here and here in the first room and another in here, against the bookshelves. A big table and two smaller ones at the back of the wardrobe area. I suspect the big table was the original dining table. It's a massive, scrubbed pine affair. There's a lot of racking in the props department, stacked with boxes and trays and loose props, all logged and labelled. The tray with the brooches and other smaller objects on is kept on this rack here." She pointed at the end closest to where the two rooms converged.

"The body was lying here, in the doorway, so, yes, if the killer had been in the props room, the tray would have been close to hand, but so would a policeman's truncheon, a very heavy church candlestick and a set of real carving knives, with a sharpening steel in a fitted box. They would then have had to step over the body on the way out. But . . ."

"At what angle was the body lying?" Mac asked, anticipating where this was leading.

"Head over here in the props room, feet this end, in the wardrobe area. So, I'm thinking he was attacked in here." She jabbed a finger at the wardrobe side. "Stuck in the neck, fell backwards."

"So, whoever killed him would have had to get the fibula, then go into the other room and stab him while he was standing about here." He pointed to her plan. "That would have afforded sufficient space for him to fall backwards into the opening."

Rina nodded. "Which suggests they took the brooch with the intention of doing exactly that. It wasn't the impulse of a moment. It was, well, maybe not planned, but they had some thinking time between taking it, leaving the room and deciding to stab Phil in the throat."

"It certainly sounds like a possible scenario. You're sure the brooch had been returned to the tray? Didn't you say the Sweetman woman had pinned it to her coat?"

Rina nodded. "Though I don't know if that was the same one used to kill Phil. In any case, Theresa told me she returned that brooch to the tray after Grace Sweetman had left. The police asked her that and she's certain that's what she did. It becomes second nature, after a while, just to make sure everything is put back in place at the end of the day."

"Wouldn't there usually be a props person?" Mac asked.

"There is. Ebony Brooksby. She's part of Theresa's team. She's been acting as properties supervisor. She's assisted Roberta Plessis on the last three shoots. Roberta had to have surgery on her knee, so Ebony's taken over temporarily."

Mac sipped his coffee, a thoughtful look on his face. "And Phil Perry was popular?"

"Generally speaking, yes. He was a bit of a gossip but never seemed deliberately malicious. Sometimes his teasing could be heavy handed but if he was called out on it, he'd apologize and back off."

"Heavy handed in what way?"

"Oh, in a playground sort of way. Immature. Earlier in the filming of this series a couple of the techies started a relationship. They wanted to keep it quiet as one of them had an ex still working for the show and had no wish to cause problems while everyone still had to work together. Phil got wind of this new relationship and kept making silly remarks. Childish remarks, not to the couple particularly but along the lines of 'Rick and Kev have been seeing a lot of each other, haven't they, wink wink?' And I mean, he actually said the 'wink wink'. Anyway, a couple of us had a word with him and he stopped it straight away."

She paused. "The trouble with Phil was, he opened his mouth and let the words fall out, the brain was rarely consulted first. It was an unfortunate trait, but surely not enough to get him killed."

"People have been killed for all sorts of reasons," Mac said. "I was once called to a domestic that started because a couple was arguing about whose turn it was to put the bins out. Somehow it escalated and they both started chucking things at each other. It got so loud the neighbours called the police. Just before the police arrived, she lost it big time and stabbed him with a kitchen knife. And that was that, things escalate."

Rina nodded. "That's tragic," she said. "But the point was, that got loud. People heard the argument. There *was*, theoretically at any rate, room for intervention. Whoever killed Phil seems to have given no warning of violence. I saw the body, Mac. Phil was unaware of what was going to happen until it did, I'm sure of that. He was taken totally by surprise, didn't get the chance to defend himself and certainly didn't even have time to cry out."

When Mac had gone, Rina felt too restless to sleep. She sat in her little room listening to the sounds of the Peverill Lodge residents retiring for the night, wishing sweet dreams to the heads that popped round her door to wish her the same, or check she didn't want a last cuppa before settling down.

She reassured Matthew that she was fine, just feeling fidgety and unsettled and as that was often the case when she returned home either mid-filming or at the end, Matthew accepted that with only mild expressions of concern. Slowly the house grew quiet. She got up and looked out of the window on to the quiet road of tall Victorian terraces. The street lamps had turned off, leaving the street silver-grey where the moon lit the pavement and soot black where the houses cast deeper shadows. The street was empty, apart from a cat slinking between parked cars. Glancing at her clock, Rina noted that it was almost 2 a.m.

She was tired, but knew she'd be unable to get her brain to shut up and let her sleep. She let the curtain fall, leaving the cat to its prowling and the night to its silence and then crossed to her desk and fired up her laptop. What did she actually know about Phil Perry or Grace Sweetman, or indeed any of her colleagues? With a few exceptions — she had received Seth's life story in at least triplicate — very little indeed. Well, that could soon be mended.

An hour of searching produced a lot of information but was any of it actually relevant? She learned that Phil had started as a child actor on the set of a now defunct soap opera set in a holiday resort. He'd had his first big break at eighteen, as the love interest for the main character in a teen werewolf comedy that Rina could not recall. It had only run for one series but it had got him noticed. Out of curiosity she'd looked for episodes online and, after finding a few clips, decided she might have enjoyed it. The series was not streaming anywhere and neither were DVDs available, which seemed a pity. It didn't even seem to have achieved cult status as these short-lived programmes sometimes did.

Phil had taken an entirely predictable, safe, if unspectacular, route via TV, a little theatre and the odd voiceover. He seemed to have worked consistently though, which was a rare attribute in itself.

No marriages, no significant others, no children. No scandals . . . Rina sighed.

Grace Sweetman, on the other hand, had plenty of history. Three marriages, all short-lived, a few other relationships that had been recorded more because of their noisy endings than their long-term significance. This included a spot of criminal damage on Grace's part, which had briefly brought her to the attention of the authorities.

Rina was intrigued by images of Grace in her youth. Pretty, blonde, unremarkable, though there was something in the eyes, even then, that spoke of a grim determination to succeed. She thought about Seth's memories of her as a much more likeable person and wondered how much of that was true, how much rose-tinted lenses. Nostalgia tended to soften memory. She even found one picture of Grace with a very young Seth. They made an attractive couple and she wondered if they had ever been more than friends. If Seth would admit to that. It might have hurt his pride to have been just one more of Grace Sweetman's exes.

She noted the time and decided it was time to go to bed. Nothing to be gained from looking at old photos and credits on IMDb. Tomorrow might well bring more news.

CHAPTER 9

The following morning Rina was first down, as usual. She was surprised to see an envelope already on the mat by the front door. Surely it was too early for the post.

Picking it up on her way to the kitchen, Rina glanced at it curiously. The letter was addressed to her, Mrs R Martin, but had clearly been hand delivered, and Rina knew immediately what it was. She had now become the recipient of one of *those* letters.

She set it on the scrubbed pine table while she filled the kettle and then made herself a pot of tea and some toast before opening the envelope. Rina wasn't quite sure what made her delay, what accounted for the odd reticence she suddenly felt. She decided it was because the letter was intrusive. It had been sent to her home, was designed to disturb her peace, invade her sanctuary. That, Rina felt, was unforgivable, aside from any accusations the letter might contain.

Eventually, having poured her second cup of tea, Rina picked up the envelope and examined it. The name was printed on the front. No full address. Most of the letters, so far as she understood, had been sent through the postal system. Had someone heard that she was back and wanted to get this missive to her as soon as possible?

She opened it with a knife, some vague thoughts about DNA on the flap momentarily occurring until she noted that this was one of those self-seal jobs. Rina wasn't keen. In her experience the sticky wore off and made them unreliable. Then you had to secure the flap with a piece of tape, which kind of defeated the object and certainly detracted from any notion of convenience.

Inside was a single sheet of standard printer paper with just a few lines of print. Times New Roman, she thought.

It should have been you that was killed. You had it coming. Always sticking your nose into other people's business. Your time will come and it'll be you with the knife stuck in your back.

It was interesting that whenever it was reported that someone was stabbed to death, it was assumed that they had been stabbed in the back. The opposite was usually more accurate — and it was also the case that knife wounds were as often caused by slashing as they were stabbing, which involved getting up closer and more personal with your victim.

Rina stared at the black words on the white paper. Centred on the page so that the top and bottom thirds folded neatly and precisely over them, they looked sparse and oddly stark. Harsh. She was suddenly aware that all of these random thoughts, all of these little reflections occupying her mind were only her attempts to push away the instant response she had experienced on seeing this letter.

Rina had been shaken by it. Upset far more than she would have reckoned on being. It was the very fact that someone had taken the trouble not only to write these few lines with the intent to cause hurt and distress but that they had then taken the trouble to post the letter through Rina's own front door. Up until this moment the letters had been a known issue, but they had also been at one remove and, occasionally, as with the one sent to young Trixie, even the source of some amusement. Disdain, even, that anyone could take them seriously.

She was knocked off balance by the understanding that she was, in fact, taking this very seriously indeed. Not, she thought, as she got up and took her cup, saucer and toast plate over to the sink and washed them carefully before setting them to drain, that she seriously believed the anonymous sender was out to do her actual physical harm. More that she was suddenly horrified by the intrusion and, by extension, the realisation that such a letter might be sent to those in her household who were more vulnerable and easily upset.

That thought in itself caused her to pause. It needed some unpicking.

She walked down her garden path and emptied the dregs from her teapot into the compost bin, returned to the house and gave the pot a quick wash.

What if such a letter was sent to Matthew or to Steven, Bethany or Eliza instead of to her? That was just the problem. Matthew or Bethany would shrug it off, she felt. They would take the attitude that such a person as the sender of these letters should be ignored if possible and eventually brought to book for causing such distress and inconvenience as they had.

But what about Steven and Eliza?

Steven was becoming fragile. He could not walk so far, he was finding the stairs hard, he now used a perching stool in the kitchen when he and Matthew cooked. All solvable problems, but all somewhat undermining of his sense of self. Such a poisonous letter might well be upsetting.

But it was Eliza she worried most about. Though older than Steven, Eliza was still physically robust but lately had been showing occasional signs that her mental acuity was not what it was. Rina was horrified by the idea that Eliza might receive such an accusatory missive and be so distressed that it disturbed what was becoming a more delicate balance.

Taking her coat from the stand in the hall, shoving her purse in one pocket, phone and letter in the other, Rina left the house and made her way down on to the promenade, where a glance at her watch informed her that it was after nine. The tiny police station would now be open.

She would take this problem to Mac. Confide, later, in Matthew and Steven and, yes, she would tell the Peters sisters but only when she was confident she could laugh the matter off.

Something would have to be done, and now that Rina was unexpectedly back in Frantham, she would be making certain that it was.

CHAPTER 10

Early on the Friday morning Detective Inspector Anning sat behind a table in the Grand Salon and surveyed his domain. Sergeant Hurst had not yet arrived and so he was alone in the room, his brain exploring the conundrum of Phil Perry's murder.

What had emerged from the interviews the previous day was a remarkable consistency — a remarkable consistency of non-information. Phil, it seemed, was well liked, could be a gossip, could be a bit of a tease, perhaps even a mischief maker, but everybody was eager to emphasize that Phil was not malicious. That Phil could be a little tone deaf at times but that no one really took offence or if they did that he was quick to apologize.

Nothing got Anning's suspicions aroused more than when a person was consistently either praised for being harmless, conspicuous for being quiet and inoffensive, or he was told that everyone liked them and they were universally popular. He was particularly suspicious of this latter description as, in his experience, it was almost always followed by a qualification.

The qualifications varied from, "Oh, he could be a bit of a lad," to "He had a bit of a thing for women, never seem to hold down a relationship." Or "Everybody liked him, though sometimes he could go a bit too far with the odd comment, or the wife got offended because he could be a bit off colour or he could be too loud, especially when he'd had a drink."

It was his experience that no initial description of a victim or a suspect escaped these qualifications — and why would they? People are complex and the relationship that one person had with a colleague would be different from the relationship they had with their mother or their sister or their friend or their neighbour. But rarely had he come across a description so consistent, even down to the word, as he had when it came to Phil Perry. Glancing through the statements Anning ticked off a bingo card of *"popular"*, *"nice enough"*, *"gossipy"*, *"liked to read scandal magazines"*, *"could sometimes go a bit too far"*, *"always apologized"*.

It made for interesting if slightly tedious reading, but Anning found it intriguing and it also made him suspicious — of two things. The first was that no one really knew Phil Perry in anything like depth, the second that there was far more to Phil Perry than met the eye.

The other interesting thing that had somewhat brightened Anning's morning was discovering that not only did Grace Sweetman have a record, albeit one that only warranted a caution, but that a certain Inspector MacGregor had been involved in her initial arrest some fifteen years before and that same Inspector MacGregor, Mac to his friends, had done some ringing around the previous day, having a little nose into the Phil Perry murder.

No doubt, Anning thought, at the behest of a certain Rina Martin.

Anning had a bit of history with Mac, not all of it good. Mac, he felt, had made a bad judgement call that had led to the killer of a little girl temporarily getting away. Mac had run to the wounded child, thinking erroneously that he might be able to save her, instead of — and Anning told himself repeatedly that this is what he would have done — chasing down the suspect. In his more reflective moments, he was not as certain that he would have behaved in any way differently to Mac. But Anning's judgement was compounded by the fact that Inspector MacGregor had gone on to have a nervous breakdown and Anning was convinced that would never have happened to him. It was a weakness he was incapable of submitting to.

For a long time Anning had been deeply critical of Mac, but more recently they had worked together on a case and he had come to accept that the inspector was at least his equal in terms of investigative ability and did not look likely to fall apart again in the near future.

And then there was that young constable, Andy Nevins. He was, Anning thought, wasted on a place like Frantham on Sea and Anning felt he owed it to the profession to bring on young talent when he saw it. This last was motivated by two disparate impulses. One was genuinely to give the young officer a chance to get proper promotion, which he'd never get in that dead-end place, and the other, perhaps less admirable, was that it would annoy Mac.

He was willing to acknowledge he might be wrong about Mac on some level but the man still wound him up. Sensitivity incarnate was not on Anning's immediate lists of admirable qualities.

However, he did feel that Mac and Nevins might have something to bring to the party and so, still waiting for his sergeant to finish whatever it was she was doing, he picked up the phone. Looking at his watch and deciding that the inspector would not be at work yet, he dialled Mac's private number.

CHAPTER 11

Rina arrived at the little police station and was disappointed to find that neither Mac nor Andy was there, though, she consoled herself, Sergeant Baker was always a good listener.

At this time of the morning there was little demand for the sergeant's services so they both retreated to Mac's office with big mugs of tea and some biscuits that Rina had bought on the way.

"Mac called in to say that Inspector Anning had rung him about an hour ago suggesting he pick up Andy Nevins and they both go over to Septon Hall and see what they can contribute to the enquiry," Baker told her. "I believe Mac had some dealings with one of the actors involved at some point."

"That would be Grace Sweetman," Rina told him, drawing on the research she had done the night before. She had been slightly surprised that Mac had not mentioned it but then she reminded herself that he did have his professional standards to uphold, even though he frequently stretched the point with her.

"I take it from your tone you're not keen on the lady," Baker suggested.

"I shall have to be more careful of my tone," Rina said.

"Some of us have known you long enough to register these things," he told her. "I doubt most people would notice."

"I would hope not. But no, I'm not keen. However, I don't believe she killed anyone, well not Phil, anyway. Though it seems there's someone who might like us to think so."

"Oh? So, are you going to fill me in?"

Rina smiled at the comfortable tone, the note of laughter in Baker's voice. For the next few minutes, while he dunked biscuits and refilled his mug twice from the large brown pot, Rina brought him up to speed with what she knew about the murder of Phil Perry, which, she quickly realized, was not really a great deal.

"But that's not what brings you here this morning," he guessed.

"No, it's not. When I got up this morning, this was on the front doormat." Rina drew the letter from her pocket and laid it on the table.

"Ah," Frank Baker said. "So you've finally got one. Young Andy and me, we reckoned it was only a matter of time. And what does this one accuse you of?"

As Mac had done the previous day, he dug in the drawer for an evidence bag and a glove, opened the letter flat on the table and slipped that and the envelope away, sealing and dating the flap of the bag. "Not that it will likely do any good," he said. "Unless something drastic happens, likely this will get nowhere near the fingerprint techs, but best be prepared." She felt his keen gaze rest upon her. "This has got you rattled, hasn't it?" he said, sounding surprised.

"It has a bit," Rina confessed. "To be truthful, Frank, I always assumed I'd just laugh it off if I got one of these blasted things. But it's different when it lands on your doormat. When it's actually in your home. I've been put in some tight corners, you know that, and on occasion been genuinely frightened. I wouldn't say I feel anything like that, but I'll admit this has unsettled me. I mean, what if it had been addressed to one of the others. To Eliza or . . ."

He nodded sympathetically. "I got talking to Matthew a few weeks back, reckons Eliza has her off days."

"Occasionally, yes." Rina frowned. "What made you and Andy think I was bound to get one?"

"Because the one thing most of the recipients have in common, or at least the ones we know about, is that they're visible. They are known in the community."

"Like young Trixie, at the hair salon. Or Mrs Majors and Mrs Bluett. They're both active at the marina, at the social club there."

Frank Baker nodded. "Or the recipients are people that have been brought to people's notice by something they did that got a ripple of publicity. Like being accused of poisoning the neighbour's cat."

"Mr Machin," Rina said. "Flora Castell stood on his doorstep yelling at him to come out and face her. She swore he'd killed her cat."

"There are those think he did, but nothing's provable so far. But, yes, a bit of street scandal brought him to the notice of a wider public and he gets accused by the letter writer too. I'm not revealing anything that isn't common knowledge here, but you get my drift."

Rina nodded, taking the point. Not only did her acting career raise her profile but she was also active on several committees and a couple of charitable trusts. She was very much in the public eye.

And, of course, now there was a murder . . . but that begged the question: why now? She had been present at the Palisades Hotel just before Christmas, when a body had been found dumped in the library. The story had made the national and even, briefly, the international news. The letters had started to arrive in people's letterboxes long before this. The earliest, so far as Rina was aware, had been back in the previous September. Why had she not received one before now?

She put this to Frank Baker, who shrugged.

"Who knows? Perhaps whoever sent the letters is working through a list and it's just interesting timing that they've got to you just when you've found another body."

"*Another* is a little cruel, Frank. I try not to make a habit of it."

He smiled at her. "All I can say, Rina, is that the letters have been sent more recently to people who are much more in the public eye, for whatever reason. Trixie and her mum are very well known anyway, but Trix got in the paper a couple of weeks ago when she won some big competition or other. For cutting hair," he added, as though she might suddenly have been winning awards for mountaineering or ballroom dancing. "Mrs Majors was in the marina newsletter last week when they put out some pictures of the spring fair. They posted a 'welcome back to a beloved member', or some such caption, below the picture of her manning the tombola for the first time since her husband passed."

"And I found a body." Rina nodded. "Or, rather, I was there when a body was found." Somehow that differentiation mattered, though she wasn't sure why. "And that was on last evening's news, together with the journalist commenting that filming had been halted. The sender must have realized I'd be home, it must have seemed like an opportunity too good to miss. They couldn't wait for the post, so they hand delivered it."

"Which at least might mean fewer fingerprints to deal with, should it come to that," Frank Baker said hopefully.

"Perhaps, but we both know this is not going to be anyone's priority. No one's actually been hurt, so far as I'm aware. Nothing's been broken into, nothing's been stolen. It's hard enough getting Forensics out for burglaries, isn't it, what with the cost cutting and the — what do they call it — budgetary constraints. It's a wonder Frantham has a police presence at all."

"Hush, Rina, someone might hear you and decide to see if we're value for money," Sergeant Baker said.

Looking at his face Rina realized that he was only half joking.

"Well," she said, getting to her feet. "Thank you for the tea and the chat, I'd best be off home."

"I'll let Mac know you called in and why. That's if you don't catch up to him first."

She thanked him again and went on her way, slow steps carrying her back to Peverill Lodge. Suddenly, Rina felt weary. Not surprising considering she'd only had a couple of hours sleep, absorbed in her research it had been well after three when she had finally noticed the time and taken herself off to bed.

She checked her watch. It was ten minutes past ten. She could have a nap before lunch, and perhaps one after as well, then she'd try and catch Mac. Anning might even have finished with him by then. It was now Friday morning, and she'd be seeing Mac and Miriam on Sunday anyway. They could have a proper chat about events. Not, she told herself, that anything was likely to happen in the next couple of days. The murder investigation would plod along, detailed police work would be the order of the day rather than anything flamboyant or exciting. The poison pen writer would probably busy themselves finding other victims. Life at Peverill Lodge would settle into its usual, comforting pattern. Yes, a nap would be a good idea.

She turned the key in the front door and, on entering, stood in the quiet space for a while noting the clink and clatter from the kitchen as someone — probably Matthew — busied themselves with pots and pans. The creak of a floorboard on the landing upstairs. The smell of lemon and beeswax polish, slightly reminiscent of cough syrup and the sharper fragrance of the flowers in the hall vase. Home, Rina thought.

The kitchen door opened and Matthew smiled at her. "I thought I heard the door." He tilted his head quizzically. "Your expression tells me you need tea with maybe a little brandy in it." He opened the door wider and waved her inside.

Home, she thought again, where everyone knows you far too well and you can't hide a damn thing, and she realized suddenly just how grateful she was for that.

CHAPTER 12

Mac and Andy arrived at Septon Hall just after 10 a.m. Andy had quickly been scooped up by a woman who introduced herself as DS Hurst and who stated her intention to bring PC Nevins up to speed. Andy looked bewildered but followed the woman as she set off at a quick pace down one of the corridors that led off the main entrance hall. This, Mac thought, was the first he had heard about Andy doing anything of the kind and looked forward to hearing Anning's excuses, first for summoning them in the first place and secondly for purloining a valued member of Mac's crew.

Mac shrugged. Andy was well capable of looking after himself and from what he had heard of DS Hurst he would find the experience valuable. The woman had a reputation for briskness and certainly didn't suffer fools either gladly or otherwise, but she also had a reputation, from what Mac had heard, for nurturing talent and Andy was certainly a talented officer. As he stood there waiting for someone to come and collect him, he was struck by the growing realization that perhaps the days of Andy calling him 'boss' were numbered, and that number was a very small one.

Well, Mac thought to himself, Andy had accrued a great deal of experience with himself and Sergeant Baker, experience that a young constable would not usually have had and that officers much longer in the job would have been envious of. It was time for Andy to leave the comfortable nest of Frantham on Sea and head out into the big wide world.

Footsteps made him turn and he saw Anning standing in a doorway off to his left.

"Mac, come on through. I take it Hurst has taken possession of young Nevins."

"It would appear so."

He followed Anning into a large room and glanced around with interest. A long run of windows looked out on to the driveway and the park beyond and a tall building on the hill that he assumed was the famous folly. It was visible from several miles away and reminded Mac slightly of the tower on Glastonbury Tor, though only at a distance. St Michael's Tower stood four square; the Folly was more like a lighthouse with a flat top and military-style crenelations around the rim.

The room in which they now both stood was decorated in what Mac thought was probably some kind of Baroque style. There were cherubs and swags and semi-naked women dancing above the fireplace, all quite heavily gilded. The fireplace itself looked older and the surround he took to be more Jacobean than Baroque, the carving simpler with stiff figures in Tudor dress, who looked distinctly disinclined to dance naked covered in gold leaf and very little else.

"Apparently it's called the Grand Salon," Anning told him. "Whatever it's called, it's bloody cold and getting the estate manager to supply us with enough coal and wood to keep the fire going is a job and a half. I set up here in the first place because I was told it was the only room available at short notice, but I've now got us moved into a butler's pantry and part of the old kitchen and at least there's a decent stove and tea-making facilities. If you care to give me a hand with carrying the last of the paperwork, we can go and get ourselves warm and find a decent cuppa."

Max scooped up the rest of the folders that Anning had indicated. "So you've summoned us here," he said, "but I'm not clear why."

"You're not? I thought you were a detective."

"Grace Sweetman?"

"She's one of the reasons. You know she's now living down on the coast, only about ten miles from you?"

"I didn't, but I still don't see—"

"You've had dealings with theatrical types, I figured that might come in useful. I also figured we might continue to improve our relationship, shall we say. Last time we collaborated it worked out fine. I thought, seeing as you're likely to be staying down here for a while, we may as well cooperate again."

Mac regarded Anning cautiously. "I suppose I just come as a package deal with Constable Nevins," he said. "And I suppose this means we've been officially seconded and I'll get notification of that at some point."

"I've put in the request, yes. I don't imagine it will be turned down. Fact is, I'm short of experienced officers. You and the lad have experience in spades and I have too many raw, unseasoned recruits with not enough nous on the team. I've recently lost three senior officers to promotion and have another off on sick leave. So, I assumed you'd be happy enough to step into the breach. And seeing as you've got experience of the Sweetman woman and other—"

"Theatrical types?"

"Exactly." Anning grinned at him. "And I fancy young Nevins will enjoy getting a bit more experience and responsibility. Working in a larger team than you can offer will give him that."

Mac thought about reminding Anning that PC Andy Nevins had already had plenty of experience being involved in major crimes, including a number of murder investigations, but he didn't bother. He straightened the stack of folders resignedly and nodded. "Lead on."

"Sure you can be spared from that hotbed of crime that is Frantham on Sea?" Anning asked as he led Mac down the corridor along which Andy and DS Hurst had previously disappeared.

"As long as you get me back by the summer season," Mac told him, matching Anning's tone. "All those families ready for a week away and a spot of organized crime. Spring, of course, just brings out the vicious gossips."

"Yes, I've heard about your spate of nasty letters," Anning said. "Bit unusual, that, even for a place as lodged in the past as Frantham."

Mac bristled at the description but then told himself not to rise to Anning's bait. Anning would just enjoy his discomfort.

They had passed two heavy wooden doors and now reached a third. Anning swung it wide and the noise spilled out into the corridor. A dozen people sat in a large room that Mac guessed had once been a kitchen. There were windows set high up in one wall, reminding him of Rina's description of the wardrobe and props room, and a few copper pans still hanging from hooks beneath slatted shelves. Computers had been set out on a long refectory table, stacks of files and papers lay on a long, low cupboard that ran the length of the room. The floor was flagstone but still patchily covered in worn brown lino that could well be late Victorian.

Dust motes floated in the slanting light struggling through the frosted glass, stirred up by the purposeful progress of officers crossing the room, shifting papers, pausing to speak to colleagues, rattling computer keyboards. Mac sneezed.

"Gesundheit," Anning said. "It's certainly a dusty old place, this. I've allocated space for you over there." He pointed at a table on the far side of the room on one side of which Andy Nevins sat, tapping away on a laptop. A second computer was open on the other side.

"And, as I promised, there's a kettle over there and the makings of tea and coffee and, I believe, some herbal and fruity blends. Don't tell me I'm not progressive."

Anning laughed at Mac's expression. "Welcome aboard. There'll be a briefing in ten minutes. I expect the lowdown from you on our Miss Sweetman and anything else you think we should be aware of when dealing with these actor types, seeing as you're our resident expert. And you can bring us up to speed on these nasty letters folk on your patch have been getting lately. It would seem Miss Sweetman got one too."

CHAPTER 13

After lunch, Rina told the rest of the household about the letter. She made light of it and reiterated what Sergeant Baker had theorized about the letter writer just targeting people who happened to be in the public eye, albeit briefly. Rina, of course, had a higher profile than most, but it was probably the murder at Septon Hall that had incited the action on this occasion.

"It was probably just too good an opportunity for the writer to miss," she said. "Hence the hand delivery."

"It's a nasty thing to happen," Matthew commented. Rina was grateful that she'd had the chance for a proper chat with him before introducing the matter to the others. It had helped her shed some of the upset and tension so she could approach the matter now with at least the appearance of sanguinity.

"You need to speak to Mac," Bethany said.

"And I will. He and Andy have been called to Septon Hall and it looks like they'll be seconded to the investigation. I'll try and catch him later but Sergeant Baker is bound to tell him anyway."

"I just don't see what they hope to gain," Steven Montmorency said. "It's not as if they're blackmailing anyone, or at least not so far as we know. They're just causing upset and mischief."

"Which might be enough," Rina said. "Some people just enjoy inflicting pain and then standing back to watch how things unfold. I suppose it's a sort of power play."

"It's just spiteful," Eliza's tone was querulous and, Rina noted, she looked pale and unusually distressed. "Can you imagine how much worry this has caused for so many people? It's a horrid thing to do."

"It is," Rina agreed. "But I'm sure it will be dealt with in the end."

"Even Mac doesn't seem to be able to solve it," Eliza cut in as though Rina hadn't even spoken. "And if Mac can't, then where are we?"

Where indeed, Rina thought.

* * *

Anning's briefing was concise. They only had a preliminary report on the cause of death, the full post-mortem was due to take place the following morning. Death was presumed to have been caused by a single stab wound to the neck which had punctured the carotid. The fact that the fibula had remained in the wound had somewhat limited arterial bleeding — no sudden spurts of blood hitting the ceiling — but death would still have been rapid. Crime scene photographs showed a wide pool of blood spreading out from the wound around the head and the right side of the body.

Mac frowned, something suddenly occurring to him, but Anning was still speaking so he kept his thoughts to himself. Beside him, however, Andy Nevins shifted uncomfortably. "Why didn't he move?" he muttered. "It looks like he just lay there and let himself bleed to death."

Mac nodded. He was wondering the same thing. Phil Perry's hands were flat against the carpet, fingers spread at about the level of his hips. It was as though he had been pressing his hands against the threadbare rug that covered the floor of the room. In some of the photographs it was possible to see that one hand had interrupted the flow of blood as it had spread outwards from the body. In the image taken after the body had been moved there was a definite void where the pressing down of the palm of the right hand had prevented blood from flowing beneath.

Mac, half listening as Anning summarized Phil's movements on the night of his death and touched on his relationship with his colleagues, noted that there was no such void on the left, and, looking more closely, he realized that his first observation had been mistaken. Phil's left hand actually lay palm up on the carpet. The palm of that hand was bloodied as though it too had at some point been face down and in contact with the already spreading blood.

The back of the right hand was clean. But . . . Mac looked more closely.

"What's that mark on the back of his right hand?" he asked. "It looks like a bruise."

Anning paused and glared at Mac. "We don't know," he said. "It definitely looks like bruising, but the shape is odd. I was going to get to that, if you'd been good enough to give me a minute!"

Mac was about to apologize, but someone laughed and Anning turned his glare towards them, so Mac didn't bother.

Anning enlarged the image. "Semicircular or circular," he said, "pressed hard against the back of the hand, by the look of it. The bruising developed further after death, which would suggest it occurred around the time of death but obviously we'll have to wait for the post-mortem to verify. To me, it looks like the shoe from a walking stick. You've got an inner and outer circle in the rubber if you take a look underneath and the size looks about right, but the pathologist will be able to tell us more, I've no doubt."

Mac looked at the picture and was inclined to agree. "Does it match anything in the props room?"

Anning shook his head. "There were two sticks in the costume department, one with a silver ferrule, the other rubber, but the profile doesn't seem to match. We've bagged and tagged and sent them for examination, just in case, along with all the other sticks and canes we've rustled up about the place. That's the thing with country houses, lots of folk inclined to go walking and a load more inclined to carry a stick about, just to beat the nettles with."

"Or to go blackberry picking, guv," someone at the back of the room called out.

"Wrong bloody season," someone else told him.

"Well, I'm sure we can all think of plenty of uses," Anning's voice rose above the chatter. "But yes, it is suggestive of something. I'll avoid speculating as to what until we've got the PM report and I'd suggest the rest of you do too." But he exchanged a glance with Mac and Mac knew he was drawing the same conclusion as he was.

It was Andy who put it into words as they drifted back to their desk. "He was held down, wasn't he? There'll be marks on his body where someone most likely put their foot on his chest or on his belly, kept him in place, leaned the stick on to his hand with their weight on it. He wasn't a big man and he'd have gone into shock very quickly and then been too weak to fight back. Whoever it was stood over him and stopped him from moving while he bled out. They watched him die, Mac. I mean, sir."

"As Anning said, best not to speculate," Mac said quietly. But he mused, Andy was probably right.

* * *

The rest of the day passed quickly. Mac briefed the team on the poison pen letters and confirmed that the one Grace had received looked as though it had come from the same source. He made the point that many people could have seen the other letters and so it would not have been hard for someone to have copied the format.

Mac and Andy read through statements, bringing themselves up to speed on what had been said and, sometimes more importantly, what hadn't. No one had a bad word to say about Phil but, then again, no one had a really good one to say about him either.

As Anning had found when doing his own review, the comments about Phil were bland and non-specific. The impression Mac got was that Phil was pleasant enough, apart from those times when he was downright annoying. That he got along on a superficial level with most of the cast and crew but that he'd formed no deep friendships and had no particular allies. He would make no lasting impression upon anyone's life.

If any of this cohort of the Lydia Marchant cast should have happened to run into him in a few months from now, they'd perhaps even have had to take a moment to remember who he was. They'd probably then have been happy to nip off for a coffee with him, but Mac could not conceive of the reacquaintance leading to an invitation to come home and meet the significant other, or even a suggestion that they share a spot of lunch somewhere.

It was odd, Mac thought.

Because he knew her, he found himself comparing Rina's comments in her statement about Phil to conversations he'd had with her regarding other members of the cast. Seth, for instance, or even Alison. The observations she had made about Phil were generic, shallow, unspecific. She hadn't been interested in him. He had not, in any significant way, attracted her attention and that was unusual. Rina was curious, even to the state of outright nosiness, about practically everyone. Sit with Rina for five minutes and she'd have your life story out of you. He'd had first-hand experience of Rina Martin's powers of persuasion.

He commented on all of this to Andy.

"No one really knew him," Andy agreed. "He seems to have presented the same front to everyone and no one's bothered to look any deeper. No one was interested enough to. So . . . either he was a really shallow sort of person, or he was really good at making people think he was."

Mac nodded. "But he did something to annoy someone, enough that they wanted to kill him for it."

"Yes, but Phil Perry didn't know that, did he? He met them there or he went with them and he doesn't seem to have had an inkling."

No, Mac agreed. He didn't seem to have anticipated anything at all.

CHAPTER 14

The following morning Rina was first down as usual and was startled to find another hand delivered letter sitting on her mat. She picked it up and found that one of her worst fears had been fulfilled: the letter was addressed to Eliza.

This, she decided was just too much.

Not wanting to risk the possibility of Eliza seeing it — she occasionally came down early to join Rina for a morning cuppa — Rina took the letter up to her room and laid it on her bed. For a moment or two she stared at it and then slit it open with her finger and withdrew the single sheet of printer paper.

The message was carefully centred, as Rina's had been, the page folded into three, top and bottom folded over middle. Rina was careful to touch it only by the corners, just in case there might be fingerprints.

There was only one line on the sheet, but it chilled her.

What's it like, the sender enquired, *to know you're losing your mind?*

This was beyond the pale. Just what was the sender trying to do?

She photographed the letter with her phone and then, for the second time in two days, made her way to the police station at the end of the promenade, for a conference with Frank Baker.

* * *

Anning had asked for a review of CCTV camera footage and, in particular, any observations of the small door through the old laundry room. First thing on the Saturday morning, he sat with Sergeant Hurst reviewing the relevant footage.

"According to the house manager the general public have pretty much free access to the grounds and there are two historic public footpaths locals and visitors regularly use. One is through the woods at the back, which bypasses the house by a couple of hundred metres and then ends up at a stile close to the main gate. Going back the other way it leads to the village of Henbury and the nearest of the local pubs, The George. According to our canvass the landlord says he's seen quite a lot of the cast and crew in the past weeks. It's a nice pub," she added, "Olde worlde and used more by locals than tourists."

Anning nodded. He knew The George. He checked the map Hurst had laid open on the desk, marked with the two footpaths. "So, about a mile or slightly under if you walk from the house."

"About that, yes. It's not lit, but it's quite wide and smooth, be no bother if you'd got a decent torch."

"And the other footpath comes up to the folly, back side of the hill." Anning traced it with his finger. "If anyone came down from the folly towards the house, they'd be seen by anyone looking out a front window."

"Or be picked up on camera. The coverage isn't bad at the front of the house. It covers part of the drive, that front lawn and most of the hill."

"And anyone of interest?"

Hurst shrugged. "Grace Sweetman takes a regular morning constitutional, several other members of the cast and crew have taken the opportunity of a nice walk those few times it's stopped raining, but nothing particularly of note.

Coverage around the back is not so great but you can see anyone approaching that little back door through the laundry. I've got lots of footage of the catering staff coming and going through the main rear exit, and Seth Collins regularly nips out through the little door of an evening for a smoke. He likes an evening cigar."

"Figures," Anning said. Seth Collins struck him as a cigar man.

"A few of the cast and crew vape and the closed in bit near the door—"

"The old drying area?"

"I suppose so. Anyway, they congregate just there usually after lunch and in the evening. We've got footage of Seth Collins and Grace Sweetman coming in late the evening before Phil Perry was killed. That fits with their statements about having gone to the pub for dinner. A few other people coming and going, but no one that can't be identified or that can't account for their movements and nothing out of the ordinary from the night of the murder. Seth Collins smokes his cigar, three of the vapers come out together, and stand around talking for a bit, but that's about all."

Anning nodded. "And from the preliminary report on the fingerprints, that door is well used by just about everyone," he said. "Anything on that back stairwell?"

"Nothing yet."

"Well," Anning said. "It's worth taking another look at the outbuildings and storerooms. This house seems riddled with odd passageways and suchlike. It's not beyond the realms of possibility there's another way in that we've not spotted yet or that the estate manager hasn't thought to tell us about."

"I'll get someone on to it," Hurst said. "But there's still footage to go through."

Anning nodded. He was faintly disappointed that nothing interesting had emerged so far, but not entirely surprised. "Hopefully there'll be something more helpful on the rest."

* * *

On the way back home, Rina paused just before she got to Peverill Lodge and looked up and down the familiar street, wondering where the person who had delivered the two letters might have come from. Frank had confirmed that these had been the only two letters, so far as he knew, that had been delivered by hand, but from which direction?

Newell Street was quite a long road. At the top end it opened on to Victoria Road, a thoroughfare that ran parallel to the promenade. At the far end, down the hill was a cul de sac, the road effectively blocked off by the Alderman Calvin Trust, a sheltered housing and nursing home project that had been built on the site of an old school back in the 1970s. Footpaths led in several directions from there, one leading to some allotments and then back into town, another to what were locally known as the tin huts, in remembrance of when that was exactly what they had been. Nissen huts, left over from the Second World War and later turned into premises for small businesses. These had gradually been cleared and replaced by more permanent units and, more recently, a software company had bought some of the land adjacent and set up their headquarters for designing games and developing interactive training software. Clustered around the Trust were houses built around the same time and originally also owned by the Trust. Small and now quite shabby, they had always had a temporary air to them, though their recent takeover by a local housing association might improve things, given time.

At Rina's end of the street it was all Victorian houses, mostly three-storey villas, many of which had become B&Bs, though a few had recently reverted to family homes and two, down towards the crossroads, were houses of multiple occupancy. There had been a fair amount of grumbling about that, Rina remembered, about it not being suitable for the area but Peverill Lodge, she supposed, was not so very different.

About halfway down, Newell Street was bisected by a crossroads. Turn left and the road curved and eventually met up with Victoria Road on the edge of town. Turn right and in half a mile you'd reach the Jubilee Estate and eventually another crossroads, one arm of which went to the old airfield, recently restored and now operating pleasure flights and with the Art Deco buildings available for weddings and other functions. The main road went to Dorchester if you turned left and linked up with the coast road if you took a right.

When you added it all up, Rina thought, the purveyor of cruel letters could have come from any part of town or even beyond Frantham. No, she contradicted herself. Whoever it was, they lived close by. Close enough to know or at any rate observe their victims. The thought made her flesh crawl.

Diagonally across from Peverill Lodge was a similar house, a one-time boarding house that had recently been granted change of use back to a family home. The family had moved in the previous autumn, parents, a widowed grandmother and three adolescent children. Rina, though she could not claim to know them well, had enjoyed several conversations with the grandmother and the mother. More to the point, they had one of those doorbells that had a camera fitted.

Annoyed with herself that she had not thought of it before, Rina crossed the road and rang the bell.

CHAPTER 15

Mac and PC Andy Nevins had driven back towards the coast to interview Grace Sweetman.

"We're almost home," Andy commented. "We could nip into me mam's for a cuppa and a sandwich."

Mac's stomach rumbled at the thought and he was reminded that it was now two in the afternoon and he'd not eaten since an early breakfast. He liked Andy's mum. Single mother to her own brood of four and adopted mum to most of the kids in the street, she always seemed to have a houseful and, though Andy had moved out some time before, Mac knew his mum was the still the first person he would go to when he needed a bit of advice.

"Has she got any thoughts on this letter writer of ours?" Mac asked.

"Well, like most people I've talked to, she thinks it's a woman. She also thinks there must have been something happen to her, just before the letters started. Something to set her off. Something shocking or traumatic, like."

Mac nodded encouragingly.

"See," Andy went on, "the letters came out of nowhere. There's been nothing before and a sudden spate of them since last September. They don't target any group in particular so it's not like it falls into specific hate crime territory. It's not even like the letters accuse people of similar things. We've got cheating on partners, cheating on job applications, and that might be the start of a pattern, I suppose, but then you've got poisoned cats and leaving the scene of a road traffic incident — the hit and run. I think that's the most serious one so far, isn't it?"

"I'd say so. Now, if that had been the first, then we could assume the writer was someone directly affected by the accident," he said. "But that letter arrived just before Christmas and weeks after the RTI actually happened."

"And the first letter was about someone cheating on their CV," Andy said. "Which makes me wonder if the person writing those letters lost out on a job, or interviewed someone who turned out to have lied or something like that. But that excludes the youngest and the oldest recipients."

"And could also include a big chunk of the population who have not been targeted."

They had reached the crossroads that would have taken them back to Frantham — and tea and sandwiches. Reluctantly, Mac drove on, passing the old airfield and joining the coast road. He was oddly disturbed by the fact that Grace Sweetman lived so close by. He had not liked the woman on their previous encounter and had no great expectation of liking her any more now.

But did he think she had murdered Phil Perry? Instinctively, no. But he would reserve judgement until he met her again.

"The hit and run accusation," he said, returning to the subject of the letters. "That is one that stands out from the rest. Not only because it's the most serious but because the author of those letters made sure we knew about it. All the rest could have remained private. I know the team reinvestigating it is keeping in mind that the writer might have known the victim, but I don't think it's brought them any progress so far."

Andy nodded. A copy of the accusation, along with the name of the accused, had been sent to the local paper, who had then contacted the police and the person accused, a man called Robert Markham, who had no criminal record and seemed to have a solid alibi for the evening in question.

Family of the victim had gone to Markham's house and an ugly scene had ensued, which caused the police to be summoned and a very angry Markham to demand that charges should be brought.

None had. The family had been spoken to and sent home with threats of further action should they attempt to contact Markham again. And, despite the case being reopened, they were no closer to finding out who had killed their young relative.

He thought about a similar incident that he had become aware of just before the previous Christmas, of how many years that had taken to be cleared up and the violent consequences that had resulted from the truth eventually emerging.

They passed the Palisades Hotel, where this past December another murder investigation had taken place and where Mac and Rina's friend, Tim, performed his illusions three times a week. Five miles on and a turn on to a single-track road brought them to the hamlet of Sutton End and the home of Grace Sweetman.

"Well, it's all right for some," Andy commented, regarding what had once been a farmhouse. The old stone was bathed gold in the weak spring sunshine and the short driveway lined with staddle stones on either side opened out into a parking area that could have accommodated a dozen cars. Only one was in evidence, a vintage Volkswagen Beetle, pristine and shiny in powder blue.

"She's successful then," Andy commented.

Mac, who had done his research before coming out, nodded. "She was in Hollywood for a time when she was younger, apparently made her money then but her movie fame doesn't seem to have lasted and she returned to the UK. Since then it's been mostly television roles, I think. I know she's been married three times so presumably the divorce settlements also helped."

He was aware of Andy looking at him. "What?"

"You really don't like her, do you?"

Mac laughed, told himself that he really wasn't being fair. He had met the woman only briefly and that had been a long time ago. "I'll do my best to put my prejudices aside."

Grace Sweetman knew that they were coming but Mac had to knock three times before she answered the door. She seemed irritated by the fact that they had come at all and demanded to know if they were reinterviewing all the cast and crew or just persecuting her.

"We'll no doubt be speaking to most people again," Mac told her levelly. "May we come in?"

Reluctantly she stepped aside and led the way into one of two rooms that led off the hallway. There had been no indication that she recognized Mac, but then, he thought, why should she? Years had passed since her run-in with the law and they had both changed and in any case had met only briefly. It had been her arrogance and self-serving insistence that her celebrity should be recognized that had made her memorable.

She sat down and gestured for them to do the same. No sign of tea or coffee being offered. She wanted them out of there as soon as possible and clearly resented the intrusion into her personal space.

Mac produced his notebook though it would be Andy, prepped and sitting a little back from Grace and Mac, who would take the most detailed record.

"Tell me about your relationship with Phil Perry," Mac said.

"Relationship? I had none. I didn't even like the little shrimp."

"You argued, I believe, about a missed cue?"

Grace snorted. "Not the first time. Don't suppose it would have been the last. He was grossly unprofessional. That I had to work with someone so lacking in the basic craft skills was demeaning."

"He had a long career," Mac said. "His first role was in a soap, I believe, then at fourteen he was in a stage version of *Kes*. I found that quite impressive."

She narrowed her eyes at him then rummaged in a box on the table beside her and produced a lighter and a long black cigarette. She lit up without asking if they minded. Mac let it pass. If she thought this would make him uncomfortable, she was wrong. He recognized that Grace Sweetman wanted to keep her hands occupied more than she needed a cigarette. She took a token drag, did not inhale significantly and then waved her hand irritably through the smoke.

"You think someone is out to implicate you, according to your statement," he said.

"Damned right I do. Phil and I had a spat, not the first and it wouldn't have been the last. But that's all it was. I had insufficient interest in the man to want to murder him. Another week and we'd all be going our separate ways anyway. This was a job. I do my job to the best of my ability, and it irks me when others fail to do the same."

This last, Mac felt, was said with a sincerity and simplicity that surprised him. "And do you have any idea of who might have had sufficient interest in him to have wanted him dead? Anyone who might have borne a bigger grudge than you?"

"I didn't bear a grudge," she told him sharply. Angrily, she stubbed out the unsmoked cigarette in a cut-glass ashtray and gestured helplessness. "How should I know? Look, no one else will be honest enough to tell you, but Phil wound everyone up. He'd pick, pick, pick at everyone's nerves. Make what he called 'jokes' about people and their relationships or their fashion sense or their education or their background or . . . and he'd get on everyone's wick, then he'd laugh it off, say it was all a joke and he meant no harm.

"I'll tell you this, there was not one member of the cast who hadn't had it with him, who would not cheerfully have strangled the little shrimp at least once while we've been filming. He was like a terrier and the more you tried to shake him off the more he would rag you. Everyone might tell you he was popular and well liked because no one wants to stick their bloody head above the parapet and say that actually he was a pain in the arse and they couldn't stand him. And they won't say it because they all want to be seen to play nice with others because that's what gets most of them their next job."

"Not you, though."

"Me? No. I couldn't give a damn." She paused and then said in a much quieter and, Mac felt, more honest tone, "But then I'm fortunate enough not to have to. I can pick and choose my jobs and I'm financially well enough off that I don't have to stay on the treadmill. I work as much as I want to but no more and in our business that's a rare privilege."

"I imagine it is," Mac said. "So, what made you take this role?"

The blue eyes narrowed again, this time beneath a major frown.

"I know you have some history with Judith Tavener."

"No, I have some history with her ex-husband. I barely knew Judith." The harsh, overbearing tone was back again.

"It must have been awkward when you found out she intended to visit the set."

"For her, perhaps. I didn't give a damn. I happen to like the series and I had an appropriate gap in my schedule that I felt like filling. When my agent told me about the role I thought it might be interesting. Besides, Tony Emmerson is very much water under the bridge. He was fun for a while, then he wasn't. End of."

"You broke it off?" Mac asked. "From what I remember you don't generally take well to being the one who gets dumped."

He knew he was provoking her.

She reached for the cigarette box again. Thought better of it and asked, "What's that supposed to mean?"

"I'm just recalling an incident of criminal damage about fifteen years ago. You smashed up a car and burned your ex's possessions on a bonfire."

She frowned. "Old news. The charges were dropped."

"Your ex chose not to press and you agreed to accept a police caution," Mac said.

"And what? You think because I took a cricket bat to some loser's car, I went on to commit murder? You call yourself a detective?"

"It says to me you have a somewhat short fuse," Mac replied.

"A short fuse implies I act in the moment, without thinking. How does that square with me having a spat with Phil in the afternoon and then biding my time for hours, for a full day and more in fact, before I decide to do him in?"

Mac waited while she fumed. "The same could be said of anyone you claim he upset," he said. "Why murder him on that particular night? Miss Sweetman, did anything happen the day he died that was out of the ordinary? That might have triggered someone?"

"Triggered someone? Are they running courses for the police on current buzzwords? No, I don't remember anything 'triggering' having happened. The flow was somewhat interrupted by Judith's arrival — we were already behind schedule and of course she had to be introduced to everyone and their dog. But then we got on with things again and it was a normal enough day."

"And can you think of anyone who Phil might particularly have upset and who might be nursing a grudge? For that matter, can you think of anyone who might have been particularly upset with you? The attempt to implicate you might suggest that someone was."

"I already told that Sergeant Hurst all this. You're just wasting my time and yours asking these questions all over again."

"People often recall small details after they've made the initial statement," Mac said gently. "We usually follow up on interviews because of that. Incidents that seem small and insignificant can sometimes be crucial."

She sighed and leaned back. "I can't think of anything. I suppose I've been a tad more impatient than usual, but . . . well, that can be the nature of the business. You want to just get on with things, and there've been so many damned delays in this schedule. Technical issues and people falling ill and filming in that wreck of a place is enough to fray anyone's nerves. Sometimes I wonder if it's even safe!"

Something else is bothering her, Mac thought. But does it have anything to do with Phil? He waited.

Finally, with an impatient gesture, she got to her feet. "And the truth is, I suppose I've been on edge, if you must know."

"Oh, and why is that?" Mac added a seasoning of sympathy to his tone.

She crossed to the window, stood staring out at the garden beyond. Mac could glimpse roses not yet in bloom and lilac that most definitely was. He imagined the scent of it filling the space; he had a soft spot for lilac.

"I'm getting a divorce," she said at last. "But I'd appreciate it if you'd keep that to yourselves. No doubt the press will have a field day."

Marriage number four, Mac thought. He gave her his condolences.

"Trouble is," she said sadly, "I really thought I'd got it right this time. Shows how little I know, doesn't it?"

He asked her if she'd had any more thoughts about the poison pen letter, but she just grimaced and shook her head.

"Some people are just bastards," she said.

* * *

"So, what do you make of that?" Mac asked as they drove away.

"That she's not as tough or as confident as she makes out. That she had a good reason to be even grumpier than usual, I suppose. That, if she's to be believed, Phil wasn't the popular paragon everyone made him out to be, which does change the way we might look at him in the context of who else he upset. Do you think she might have done it?"

"Do you?"

"No," Andy said. "I don't think so. I mean, I think she's capable of lamping someone if she lost her rag, but I think it would be an in-the-moment kind of thing. She doesn't strike me as the premeditative type. More the impulsive, 'take your husband and think what to do with him later' type. It's funny, though, her wanting to be in a Lydia Marchant. You'd think she'd want to avoid anything to do with Judith Tavener, especially if she was being honest about being secure enough to pick and choose what parts she wants to play."

"Yes, *if* she's being honest about that," Mac said.

CHAPTER 16

The problem was she had been unable to resist and had wanted to see a reaction. Rina Martin, always at the centre of things, feted and admired, even if she was a busybody who thought she could do anything and know everything. The idea of having a secret, of being able to perhaps disturb the equilibrium of someone so confident and self-assured had been too much.

She had heard, of course, about the murder at the Palisades Hotel just before Christmas and had thought about sending one of her letters then. But an old friend had invited her to stay with them for a few days and by the time she got back it had seemed a little late for action.

It had, she reflected, felt good to get away from everything for a while and to refresh a friendship that she had allowed to grow stale. Her husband hadn't particularly liked Julia or approved of her. Julia was too loud, too assertive, had never married — was she a lesbian? Not that he had anything against lesbians . . . but people might gossip.

He had always been worried about what people would think, as though they actually thought anything most of the time. Marcia was fully aware that most people had enough of their own issues to deal with to be looking at what was happening to other people.

Oh, for sure, people liked a good gossip, but would anyone care that she had an unmarried friend? That seemed such a bizarre thing to worry about. But, of course, Marcia now knew that people did not like being talked about, not really, not if it was something that put them in a bad light. Even an imaginary bad light. Perhaps because she had always been so careful not to do anything that could attract anyone's approbation, that had clouded her judgement?

No, more likely it was because deep down she had despised her husband, his attitudes, his petty-mindedness, and so had decided he must be wrong.

No, she thought, being honest with herself — she'd been doing a lot of that lately — she hadn't thought any of those things. Marcia had been a 'go along to get along' sort of person all her married life and before that she'd been a 'do whatever they want so I won't be in trouble' sort of person. So when she'd found herself a nice, considerate, hard-working man, she'd not wanted to do anything to upset his particular apple cart. Well, that had gone well, hadn't it? He'd left her because he was bored. Because she was boring. Well, she wasn't being boring now. Marcia was upsetting a great many apple carts.

Was it bringing her any satisfaction?

Not as much, perhaps, as she'd have liked, this pulling against the traces and running amok. At first it had been like punishing her husband by proxy. Saying things to other people that she'd never have dreamed of saying while he'd been around and she was playing at being the good little wifey. But as time had gone on, it wasn't nearly as satisfying. She'd heard people talk about drug and alcohol addiction and that they needed more and more, over time, to get the same kind of hit. Was that what was happening to her? That she was somehow becoming addicted and that addiction would have to go further and deeper and become more extreme if she was to get satisfaction from it? She felt bad about the letter she had sent to Eliza in a way she'd not felt bad about the others. Eliza was a sweetheart who'd done no harm to anyone and was, so far as Marcia was aware, still fully compos mentis.

Marcia didn't know what had made her hit out at the woman. She blamed the way she felt about Rina. And she felt the way she did about Rina because Rina always made her feel so damned inadequate. Just like her husband had done.

She stood on the corner and watched Rina talking to the neighbour across the road from Peverill Lodge and then go inside. She had been pointing at their doorbell, asking something about it. Curious, now, she waited until she was certain Rina had gone inside and then walked past the house, glancing at the doorbell as she did so.

Marcia never swore but she was tempted now. Of course, that was what Rina wanted. The doorbell was one of those with a camera on it. A camera activated by movement. Had she got that right?

So, when she had posted those letters through Rina's door she must have been caught on camera.

Oh, Lord, would it have shown her face? She had been bundled up in coat and hood and scarf, so probably not, but it still gave her pause. How could she have been so stupid? She should have posted those letters, just like all the rest. Separated herself from them long before they arrived at their destination.

Shaken now, Marcia walked up to the promenade and then headed towards home.

* * *

The Peters sisters had gone out for the afternoon to a tea dance held at the marina. The Montmorencys would often go with them, but Rina had quietly asked if they would stay behind so she could talk to them, so Matthew had driven the sisters to the marina and then returned.

"Bethany's nose is twitching," he told Rina. "She's twigged our little conflab has to do with those letters, so I had to tell her that one had been sent to Eliza. She was terribly shocked and wanted to be party to any discussion we might have, but she saw the sense in keeping Eliza out of the way this afternoon. Rina, I think she's a little hurt you didn't confide in her. I suggested that there'd not been any opportunity without dear Eliza being around to overhear but while that's true, her feathers are still a tad ruffled."

Rina nodded. "I can understand that. And we can't keep things secret for ever. I'll take time to speak with Bethany when they get back and smooth things over and then, if she needs me to, I'll help her talk to Eliza about the letter." This was no time for disharmony, she thought.

"Was there anything on the doorbell camera?" Steven asked.

"Yes, but I don't know if it's useful. The doorbell camera is motion activated and the woman — I'm almost certain it was a woman — can be seen crossing the road close to the Greens' house. The camera catches her coming to our door, posting the letter and then going back the way she came. This was at two fifteen this morning and about the same time before. She seems to have come from the direction of the crossroads, but who knows what route she took before that? The fact that the time is almost the same on both occasions might mean something. She might be coming off shift, I suppose."

"From the OAP home?" Steven wondered, referring to the sheltered housing at the other end of the road. "There are a lot of shift workers employed there."

Rina shrugged. "It's possible. The Greens are sending the footage to Sergeant Baker. I think they were quite excited about it all," she added ruefully. "Though none of it's very clear. She's wearing a very distinctive long coat and a hat pulled down so her face is in shadow. The coat is one of those military-style ones, with the little cape bit at the back, and I caught a glimpse of polished metal buttons. The street lights were out by then but the Cavendishes have that motion-activated porch light. I think that must have been what shone on the buttons. It startled her when it came on. She jumped a bit and then seemed to collect herself and posted the letter very quickly before scurrying off."

Rina noted that her tone was slightly scathing. She'd not meant to sound like that, but she was still fuming; she couldn't get away from that fact.

"So, what do we do about this?" Matthew asked. "And I don't just mean about you and Eliza, I mean, what do we do? This has gone far enough and, due respect to Mac and co, but the police seem to be getting nowhere fast. No, we need to put our collective heads together as a community. If we can, we should get as many people as possible who have received these letters in one place. Get everyone talking, however uncomfortable that might be. Show this person a united front and that they can't go on persecuting people on a whim."

Rina nodded. She was a little surprised by Matthew's vehemence, but then two people he loved had been threatened, she supposed. And Matthew was very protective of the Peverill Lodge family and, lately, especially of Eliza.

"I agree," Steven said. "And if we can get Sergeant Baker involved in a public meeting, so much the better. He's the epitome of an old-fashioned community policeman. He knows everyone and everyone trusts him."

That was true, Rina thought. Born and bred locally, Frank Baker had his finger on the many pulses of community relations and was the closest thing to the *Dixon of Dock Green* image you were ever going to find.

"We could borrow the big hall at the airfield," she said. Being friends with the new owners, Rina was pretty certain she could get it for free for a couple of hours and they could all pitch in to get refreshments sorted. The big hall had been the check-in and waiting area when the airfield had been fully functional and the new owners had repurposed it as a function room with a mix of Deco and forties vibes, appropriate as the airfield had been opened in the thirties and commandeered by the RAF in the forties.

"So, how are we going to let people know this is happening? I suppose we can get the local press involved, post flyers through doors and that sort of thing. Sergeant Baker could spread the word," Matthew said. "And at least we'd be doing something."

Rina glanced at her watch. "I've got time to nip down and speak to Frank Baker before Bethany and Eliza get back. He's going to be key to the plans. Then we can have a family conference after dinner and firm up the details."

It felt better, Rina thought, to be grasping the nettle and taking action. Would people come to a public meeting? Would the right people come? As she walked back again to the police station, Rina thought they probably would. There would be recipients of the letters, hopefully, and no doubt also the merely curious as well as the handful of people who seemed to turn up for every public event because it was something to do and broke the monotony, as Rina's mother would have said. It might even bring anyone who had not yet admitted to receiving a letter out of the woodwork. That would be a good thing.

Would the writer of the letters also come along? Maybe out of pure curiosity, perhaps in irritation or, more likely, fear that if everyone communicated and exchanged information, she might be exposed. The most upsetting thing, Rina thought, was that undoubtedly at least some of the recipients would know the writer personally. Perhaps Rina did. Whoever it was must have a method of choosing their targets and that, like as not, included casual gossip. When all was out in the open, there would be a fair few hurt feelings to be dealt with and likely some righteous anger. It wasn't going to be pretty, that much was certain.

That thought in mind, Rina hesitated a moment before turning on to the promenade. So, was this the right thing to do?

Her hesitation passed. Yes, on balance it probably was. Too many people had been upset and that could not be allowed to go on. Mac was obviously going to be tied up with the murder at Septon Hall for a while and, while she was loath to judge her friend in any way, he hadn't seemed able to make much headway with the poison pen letters thus far.

No, this should also be a community effort. Frantham on Sea had been affected badly by one person's spite or ill will, or perhaps by that one person's pain — though Rina could not quite forgive the pain they had caused to others even if that was the case. It was time for the people of Frantham on Sea to get their collective act together and sort this business out and, as she pushed open the police station door, she decided that Frank Baker would have to either lead, follow or get out of the way.

CHAPTER 17

The post-mortem on Phil Perry was scheduled for 10 a.m. Mac met Anning at the mortuary. The pathologist, Doctor Morton, a cheerful woman with steel-grey hair cut in a chin-length bob, was not someone Mac knew well but Anning greeted her as an old friend, asking about her husband and her kids and the pet donkeys that she had apparently adopted. Seeing Anning in this casual, social mode surprised him. He'd always had Anning down as a curmudgeonly bugger.

"Before we start," Gwen Morton said, "I want you to have a good look at this man's chest and hand. Now we've got him undressed and the pre-mortem bruising has now fully developed, it's quite revealing and I particularly wanted you to see what I do."

She drew back the cover and revealed Phil Perry's body. What the pathologist wanted them to look at was immediately obvious. A dark bruise spread across the solar plexus and on to the ribs.

"A boot mark?" Anning asked, indicating the curve around the back of the heel, and fainter marks that may have indicated tread. "A man's foot?"

Gwen Morton was not keen to commit. "Most likely a boot, yes. The heel went in hard. I could speculate that it was almost like a heel kick, though the angle suggested by the bruising suggests our victim was already on the ground." She demonstrated, angling her own foot to indicate a heel being rammed into the soft tissue of the solar plexus, just below the ribs.

"The remainder of the foot was pressed down hard enough to cause bruising, and my feeling is that the killer put weight on the rest of the foot in order to keep the victim in place. That, together with whatever he used to pin the left hand to the floor." She indicated the marks Mac had noted on the photograph.

"We thought perhaps the ferrule of a walking stick," he said. "The rubber ones you can get that have an inner tube that fits over the stick end and a wider profile outside of that for better balance."

"I think that's a definite possibility. The other hand was unfettered, and there's blood all over the palm, perhaps where the victim pressed against the floor to try and gain some purchase, though you've got to remember he's bleeding out and getting weaker by the second. Interestingly, it looks as though the blood on the fingers has been smudged or even wiped. Perhaps he grabbed at his assailant's trousers or foot. I can't tell you exactly what happened, only what is suggested. We've photographed everything for you; make of it what you will."

"But you think a man's foot," Anning persisted.

"Probably. But it can be hard to tell with boots or even some trainers. A chunky trainer or a boot with a wide welt, that sort of feature can skew the observations. Some women have larger feet. The bruising at the toe end hasn't developed enough for me to get more than an approximate estimate as to size and you've also got to think about how the skin and muscle beneath is going to spread outwards as the pressure from the shoe or boot is shifted and changed. Imagine the first impact is hard, from the heel. Then the foot is flattened out and pressure brought to bear along the length of the foot."

Again, she paused to demonstrate. "That pressure is not going to be even or consistent and because of that the outline of the shoe print, if you like, is possibly going to be pushed outwards and its shape distorted."

That made sense, Mac thought. "So," he said, "our assailant stabs the victim in the throat, he goes down. Then he's pinned down hard by the killer and left to bleed out."

The pathologist nodded. "One more thing, though, that I suspect but won't know for certain until we start the PM — we removed the murder weapon, as requested, and it's gone for fingerprinting and further analysis. I have to say, it had gone in pretty deep, the pin was thicker than you'd find on a modern brooch, much thicker and appeared to be the same metal as the brooch itself. I'm told it's called a fibula?"

"Yes. A bronze replica of a Roman original," Anning said.

"Right, well, it did a lot of damage when it went in. It was thrust in with some force and, just on initial examination, I suspect it was twisted within the wound, presumably with the intent of doing maximum damage."

"So, whoever wanted Phil Perry dead, really wanted him dead," Anning said.

"They weren't playing about," Gwen Morton confirmed. "It looks to have been a deliberate and decisive blow, with full intent to incapacitate and kill. Essentially the brooch pin acted like a stiletto blade. Sharp point, a long enough reach to penetrate around three inches or seven to eight centimetres into the neck." She shrugged. "Obviously I have no insight into the killer's state of mind and when I eventually come to testify about this, it'll only be the facts, milord. But my sense is that whoever did this was angry, I mean properly enraged. Most people, in my experience, tend to strike out and then back off. A lot of the time they lose impetus after that. They're often shocked by what they've done and, I'm sure you'll have had the same experience, it's not uncommon for a killer to then drop the weapon and run. Consequences unconsidered. A few murders display what you might call frenzy, what our friends in law enforcement across the pond like to call overkill."

Mac nodded. "And this?"

"Was efficient. The killer knew what he or she wanted to achieve and went for it. This feels stone cold."

Mac and Anning retreated to the small, glass-fronted viewing room and watched the post-mortem, listening to the pathologist's running commentary. Internal bruising bore out her observations and conclusions from the external damage. The hole made by the original stab wound seemed to Mac to be unusually large, though he reminded himself that the edges of a wound shrink back after death so sometimes even the shape of the wound could become distorted. Even so, a lot of damage had been done with what was, when all was said and done, a piece of antiquated jewellery. Somehow, Mac thought, the banality of that made it even worse.

CHAPTER 18

Over the next few days Rina looked more deeply into the background of Phil Perry and the others involved in the tragedy at Septon Hall.

Conversations had been had with Bethany and Eliza and, much to everyone's relief, Eliza has been less disturbed by the letter than Rina had expected.

"When we were young and still performing in our skimpies, you couldn't go a night without somebody telling one of us we looked too fat, or too thin, or we were indecent or stupid or inciting men to sin or something of the sort. You got so that you ignored it all because if you didn't, you'd want to crawl into a corner and hide. I ignored all that and I shall ignore this."

If anything, Rina thought, the letter had stung Bethany far more. She loved her sister more than anyone else in the world and the thought that someone might deliberately set out to hurt Eliza, who was kind and gentle and a genuinely lovely person, was just too much. Rina had found her crying one day, sitting on the seat in the garden away from everyone as though hoping no one would see her tears. Rina would not be loath to admit that she had shed a few as well. Over the years her little family had been through so much and stuck together through thick and thin. They had welcomed others into their sanctuary with a generosity of spirit that Rina was fiercely proud of. She doubted Mac would have survived if they had not intervened and then there was George and Ursula, whom she had known since their early teens and who were now fine young adults and she knew it was not going too far to say that she and her Peverill Lodge cohort had played a part in that.

Knowing that she had cried, that she had been genuinely hurt and that Bethany had been caused great pain hardened her resolve. If *they* had felt the effects of these anonymous letters so personally, even though they had a support system around them, what would happen to anyone who received a letter and was isolated or, because they might perceive there to be some possible truth in the somewhat random accusation, was made to feel needlessly guilty? From those letters Rina knew about few had come up with definite, applicable wrongdoing. Mac had commented that it was like the cold calls you got from firms of solicitors specializing in compensation claims. That sooner or later the call would resonate with the recipient. She agreed with him that the letters were very much like that.

It made Rina angry.

She had spoken to Mac over the weekend when he and Miriam had come over for Sunday tea, as they often did. He had heard about her plans from Sergeant Baker and though he was a little reticent about them he understood her need to do something.

"Just be careful," he had said. "Sergeant Baker is a willing participant in this, he wants it cleared up as much as anyone, so make use of official channels and don't try to go it alone."

"As if I would," Rina had said, but she had promised Mac that they would be led by Frank Baker's undoubted experience. For all that, Rina was still convinced that this was going to be solved by community effort and not necessarily by bringing in the authorities. The action was too ephemeral, too random and, she felt, those involved too isolated from one another for a clear picture to have emerged via the police investigation.

In addition to this, even if the accusations had been hollow, for many there was still shame attached. Someone saw them as being guilty of something, had pointed the finger, and the victim found themselves stuck. If you defended yourself, did that not suggest that there was something to defend? If you remained silent, and the matter came to public attention, might that not suggest that you were hiding something? Perhaps bringing people together and bringing this matter out in the open would dilute those feelings and make them more manageable.

Rina hoped so.

She had asked Mac on the Sunday how the murder enquiry was going and how he was getting along with Anning. Somewhat to her surprise he had told her that they seemed to have developed a good working relationship and also that she should be hearing from the production company soon about the resumption of filming. Anning was releasing the scene. And, sure enough, Alison had called her that Sunday evening and told her that filming should be resuming on the Wednesday and hopefully there would be no more hitches.

When Alison called back on Monday morning to give official confirmation of this, Rina told her that she must be back in Frantham for the Wednesday evening but that she would be sure to return for an early start on the Thursday. Something in her tone told Alison that she would brook no contradiction to this. The public meeting was scheduled for the Wednesday, when hopefully many of those who had received letters would come together to exchange information and try and get the bottom of what was going on. It was, she thought, at least worth a try.

Meantime, Rina was keeping herself busy. She had read every news report she could find relating to the murder and followed up every hint in every article as to previous relationships, scandals and productions that people had been involved with, any scrap of information she might have missed during her first trawl.

The only new item she could find was the appearance of Phil Perry in a few gossip columns in the kind of magazines that Rina never actually read. Perhaps, she thought, she should start. There were rumours that Phil Perry and Grace Sweetman had once had a thing going. No one seemed to be willing to call it an all-out affair, but a couple of sources suggested 'a serious flirtation' — a very old-fashioned way of putting these things, Rina thought, seemingly at odds with most of the content in such modern and faintly scurrilous magazines.

This, she learned to her surprise, had happened about four years previously, when Grace had been between marriages. So far as Rina could make out, Phil had never had a long-term relationship. One of the sources she read had professed shock that Phil should be enamoured of Grace Sweetman. The writer of the article had always assumed that he must be gay. Digging a little deeper Rina discovered that the foundation for all this sudden interest in Phil Perry had come about because he had accompanied Grace to a rather posh charity ball.

"Who is this man?" seemed to summarize the thrust of most of the initial articles that had led to a brief journalistic frenzy — or at least what passed for one in the kind of gossip columns that specialized in who was bonking whom and whose husband someone else's wife had been seen with.

Interesting, Rina thought. She had never gained the impression that Phil and Grace were even friends, never mind that Grace might choose him to squire her to a public occasion. Even if the reason was as simple as Grace just not having a plus one for the evening, surely she would have had a whole host of men who at a moment's notice could be persuaded to don a tuxedo and play the escort. So why choose Phil Perry?

He was not bad looking, but he was not exactly the kind of eye candy that Grace Sweetman usually went for.

She was by now familiar with Grace's type and they were definitely tall, dark and handsome, and not shortish, slightish and sandy.

It also seemed very odd that the two of them should have seemed so hostile during the filming. There had been no hint that they'd even known each other before meeting on set and certainly no hint that they even liked each other, never mind knew each other well enough to attend an event together.

She wondered if Mac knew about this relationship or whatever you might call it.

Presumably he did, but then he did not have the time to go back and read obscure gossip columns or follow the kind of path that she had via major news items into more esoteric and ephemeral sources containing the minutiae of lesser celebrities' lives. She texted him with the information anyway. What harm could it do?

* * *

News arrived on the Monday morning about a walking stick that had been sent for forensic examination. It had traces of blood impacted into the rubber ferrule. The stick itself had been wiped clean of fingerprints and an attempt been made to clean away the blood but some still remained. It was group B, the same as Phil Perry's, and there was not much doubt in either Mac or Anning's mind that this was the stick that had been used to press the victim's hand against the ground so hard that it had broken bones.

"So where was the stick found?" Mac asked.

Andy, who seemed to have landed the job of assistant collator, consulted his list. "The stick stand in the hall, the one with the dragon on it."

Mac recalled the one he meant. It was a tall Chinese vase with coiling dragons on a blue background.

"It was among four sticks in that stand. There were a dozen in all taken from around the house, including the two in the props room," Andy told him.

A few minutes later Mac was consulting with Theresa Barnett as to the possibility that any other walking stick might have been in the props department. The assailant having taken a stick from the hall spoke of another level of premeditation. The stick itself was hefty, formed from root wood, with a heavy club-like handle. Perhaps the killer had meant to beat Phil Perry to death and then changed their mind.

He was, however, surprised at Theresa's response. "That's the one from wardrobe, it's Lord Ellsworthy's stick."

"Are you sure? This one is supposed to have been found in the dragon stick stand in the hall."

"Let me look at the image again," she said, and he could hear sounds of her tapping on the computer. "No, that's definitely the one Lord Ellsworthy was using. There are two very similar sticks but I chose this one because of the silver collar — it seemed like the kind of thing Lord Ellsworthy might use. The other stick, though it's still root wood and has a very similar look, is plain. I just thought Lord Ellsworthy might like a little bit of bling."

"Give me a minute," Mac said. With Andy's help he skimmed through the images of the other walking sticks photographed both in situ and side-by-side on the bench before being sent to Forensics. They had all been packed in clear plastic, carefully labelled, but even through the packaging he could see clearly enough that she was right. There were two very similar walking sticks with knobby tops and twisted root wood shafts, ending in rubber ferrules.

"This was definitely in the hall stand," he said. "It was photographed in situ before it was taken out to be sent to Forensics. The other stick, the one without the silver band, that one was in the wardrobe."

"Then someone changed them over," Theresa told him. "Lord Ellsworthy was using the silver-banded stick in a scene that we shot the day before. So, the day before Phil was killed. It was brought back to the props department and checked in. It would be in the book — everything is checked in and out. I would have noticed, any of us would have noticed the difference. If it didn't have the silver band, it wasn't the right stick. We have to be so careful for continuity."

"I'm sure you're right, thank you. And the last time that was used was when exactly?"

She paused for a moment before responding. "It was in the last scene that Judith Tavener watched. You'd have to check the book, and you'd have to cross-reference with Alison, who will be able to tell you when they finished shooting for the day, but I'm guessing it would have come back to wardrobe at around five o'clock on the Thursday, so the afternoon before . . . Before we found Phil dead the following morning."

Mac thanked her again and rang off. He took this new information to Anning.

"So that would suggest that the killer used the stick that was in the props room, took it away to clean it but then left it in the hall and took the other stick back to the props department. That seems like an odd thing to do. Why not just dispose of it? There's a lake not five minutes' walk from the house."

"Maybe they intended to later," Anning said.

"Maybe he didn't want to go stumbling about in the dark," Andy commented. "It might only be five minutes' walk, but it would have been pitch black out by the water. Or they might have been worried about the security lights coming on. This place is a bit limited for cameras, but there are security lights all around the building, all motion activated."

Mac nodded, good points. "Then why not clean the stick up and put it back in the props department. It looks as though the killer cleaned the stick, put it in the hall stand then took the other stick back to props and left it there, which would have meant going back into a scene where you've just killed someone. That's cool, that's downright cold."

"Perhaps when the killer cleaned the stick down and wiped the blood off it, it still looked stained and he thought it would be noticed. Perhaps he intended to swap it later or perhaps it never occurred to him that anyone would realize that the sticks had been changed over. I'm not sure I'd have paid any attention to the little silver collar, but obviously Theresa would have been intimately familiar with everything that went on in her department."

"Maybe they thought we wouldn't even realize a walking stick had been used, just the brooch," Andy put in.

Anning nodded. "Perhaps our killer knew nothing about how bruising can develop post-mortem," he said. "So, our killer is clever, but not that clever. They can be caught out."

Well, I suppose that's a small blessing, Mac thought. No bloodstained clothing had been found in the house or in the search of the grounds that had been carried out on the day the body had been found. But then, the murderer would have had hours in which to dispose of anything incriminating and, when asked by the police to produce the clothing they had been wearing the evening before, could easily have lied. So, where would they have disposed of evidence?

Anning's guess had been that it had been burned in the basement furnace that fuelled — however inadequately — the antiquated radiators. It wasn't difficult to get into the basement and the furnace door had a tool for opening it when it was running, so it could be refuelled.

They had spent a cold day waiting for it to burn out and cool down enough that the interior could be raked out. A clue, in the shape of an unusual belt buckle or a fragment of a trouser button, the sort of thing that Lydia Marchant might have discovered in one of her adventures, was disappointingly absent. They found nothing of interest.

So why not dispose of the stick in the furnace? Mac wondered. Was it because the killer knew it might be missed? He supposed that must be it — sooner or later it was likely someone would have realized that the stick in the props room wasn't the one being used by Lord Ellsworthy. The killer probably intended to get it back to where it belonged but for whatever reason hadn't had the opportunity. But, no, that wasn't right, was it? They'd gone back into props to leave the other stick, hadn't they?

Mac shook his head. That didn't make sense. But when did the actions of a murderer ever really add up? For most people this would be a one-time action, no rehearsals, no way of anticipating everything that might happen or everything they might feel or think or do. For most killers that would also be the last time. It was only in a very few and thankfully rare cases that murderers worked to refine their skills over subsequent killings and even then they eventually made mistakes.

A little later he was checking his phone and he saw Rina's message sent together with a link to the articles she had been reading. Mac handed it over to Andy to check out and ten minutes later Andy came back to him to say that Mrs Martin was of course right. There did seem to have been more to Grace Sweetman and Phil Perry's relationship than being mere colleagues on the shooting of the latest Lydia Marchant.

"Very interesting," Anning said. "Well done for finding that, Andy."

Mac could see Andy open his mouth in preparation for explaining where the intelligence had come from. He shook his head gently hoping Andy would see and that Andy would have the sense to shut up.

Fortunately, Andy had been well taught and closed his mouth before the explanation escaped. Rina wouldn't mind passing on the credit, but Anning would definitely mind knowing that this piece of evidence had been provided courtesy of his derided Mrs Martin.

Inspector Anning had a lot to learn, Mac thought.

CHAPTER 19

Rina had called Seth to ask if he'd had any knowledge of Grace and Phil's previous friendship . . . or relationship, or whatever it was.

Seth laughed. "I had no idea," he said. "And I'd never have guessed by the way the two of them kept sniping at each other. Though maybe that should have been a clue. You know how people reckon that folk who are secretly in love engage in misdirection. That they lead everyone to believe they hate the sight of each other, just as a ploy?"

"Does that really happen outside romantic novels?" Rina wondered.

"Well, it happens in TV and film as well, so . . . maybe?"

"I mean in real life," Rina argued.

"Rina, my dear, for the likes of us and particularly for the likes of Grace, TV and film are real life. That's where she lives and breathes, where we all do to a certain extent, I suppose."

Rina wasn't so sure that applied to her, but she took his point. "Would it have been out of character to have taken Phil to an occasion like that? I thought at first it was a straightforward awards ceremony but it was actually some kind of charity fundraising evening. She was dressed to the nines in the pictures and so was Phil. He looked very different."

"Grace used to support several charities," Seth said thoughtfully. "Organizations that support retired actors. Maybe she still does. She got involved during her brush with fame and fortune when she was in the USA. You know she was in Hollywood for a while and then in a couple of Broadway productions?"

"I did, yes."

"Well that certainly raised her profile. She was patron of something or other, I forget exactly. Some charity that provided funds for community youth theatre."

"That doesn't sound like Grace."

"Not the Grace you met, no. But I've told you, when she was younger and less cynical, she could be a lovely person to be around."

Rina noted the *could* but didn't comment on it. "But to take Phil along suggests that they knew each other well."

"Or that he was involved with the same charity. It might have been coincidence that they were photographed together and then the media tried to make a thing of it. I'll tell you something, that would really have put Grace's back up, linking her with someone she hardly knew. No, I really can't see it, Grace and Phil being friends and not mentioning it. You say this was what, four years ago?"

"About that, yes."

"Oh, well you can ask her yourself on Wednesday, can't you?" Seth joked. "When we get back to Septon Hall."

"I probably will." Rina could feel Seth's discomfort almost oozing though the phone.

* * *

Mac had been dispatched to speak to Grace Sweetman again. "Catch her on the hop" had been Anning's instructions. "Find out why she didn't tell us she had a previous relationship with the victim."

Mac had elected to leave that pleasure until the end of the day. Grace's house was only a small detour on his way home. She could be dealt with then and Mac could head back to the boathouse flat he shared with Miriam without unnecessary delay.

At five fifteen he was knocking again on Grace Sweetman's door. The door was heavy, solid wood with an equally solid brass doorknocker in the shape of an anchor. The sound echoed and he imagined the flagstones in the hall and the lime-plastered stone walls throwing the sound of it back and forth. She couldn't make the excuse that she'd not heard him knocking.

Even so, he knocked twice before she opened up. She frowned. "Inspector, what brings you here?"

Her tone said that whatever it was it wasn't excuse enough.

Mac had printed the article and the photograph of Phil and Grace, dressed for a smart night out, standing on the steps of the hotel that was hosting the ceremony. Grace, in a form-fitting blue dress had a gloved hand resting on Phil's arm. Phil Perry was grinning at the photographer. It was apparent in the image just how much younger than Grace he was. There was a ten-year age gap, Mac knew, but in the photograph it looked to be more, probably because Grace looked so unhappy in this image. No, he thought, not exactly unhappy. Grace's look was stern, uncompromising. He held up the photograph.

"What about it?" she asked.

"Why didn't you tell us that you knew Phil Perry well? That your relationship with him stretched back much further than the filming of this production?"

She shrugged. "So, I knew him before. What difference does that make? I still didn't like the man and I still viewed him as unprofessional. I expect better from my fellow actors."

"Miss Sweetman, I have to remind you that you are still a suspect in a murder enquiry."

"And I have to remind you that I didn't kill him. I didn't like the little shrimp, but I didn't dislike him enough to murder him! Now, if that's all."

She began to close the door. Mac put out a hand to stop her. "No, Miss Sweetman, it's not. Now your failure to declare a previous relationship may seem trivial to you but in a murder enquiry it's imperative that we have a complete understanding of anything in the victim's past that might be relevant. You believe someone is trying to frame you for the murder. You were keen to state that this was because of a spat you and Phil Perry had on set and which made you a convenient scapegoat. But, Miss Sweetman, if you and the victim had a shared past, we need to know about that. If there's even the slightest possibility that his death had something to do with that shared past, then that is evidence that you are withholding. That's obstruction, Miss Sweetman."

Mac knew he was overplaying his hand. So, Grace Sweetman and Phil Perry had been to the same event, possibly together — and it suddenly occurred to Mac that Phil might have invited Grace rather than the other way around. She certainly did not look too happy at being photographed with Phil's hand on her arm.

He asked, "Did you go with Mr Perry or did he go with you?"

She looked suddenly weary. "We went together."

"But who did the inviting? Were you his guest or was he yours?"

She closed her eyes. "Oh, for God's sake. What does it matter now?"

"It might be important. I've no way of knowing unless you give me details."

She sighed, opened the door a little wider and leaned back against the wall, but did not invite him inside. Mac waited her out.

"Ours is a very tight-knit industry," she said. "Everyone knows everyone or at least that's the way it feels sometimes. Our paths had crossed on a few occasions, we had mutual acquaintances, one of whom was supposed to be getting me an invite to this particular event. Jerry Casson, a Hollywood director, was going to be there. I knew that and I wanted the opportunity to speak with him. Professional reasons."

"Couldn't your agent have arranged a meeting or at least a conversation?"

She laughed harshly. "You don't know how these things work."

"So tell me." Mac wished he'd thought to put on his coat when getting out of the car. The wind was blowing in off the sea and had a cold edge to it as it often did this early in the year. April had been wet and dreary so far and the evening felt damp and chilly. Grace was dressed in jeans and a high-necked pullover and he realized now that she was leaning against a radiator and not just the wall.

"Talk to me and I'll get out of your hair," he said. "Or I can arrange for you to be interviewed at the local police station, if you'd prefer."

She laughed then. "What, that little box at the end of Frantham promenade? You'd not have the space."

"For you and your ego? Probably not."

She stared at him. Mac had not intended to say that out loud. The words had escaped in an unguarded moment, provoked by tiredness and cold and the feeling that this woman really was taking the piss. That was unprofessional, he told himself and then realized that he didn't really care. Let her complain if she wanted.

For a moment or two she glared at him, a look of pure malice in her gaze and then she sighed and it was as if all the fight had gone out of her. "You'd better come in."

Mac followed her into the house and this time down the corridor and into the kitchen. She gestured to him to sit down and he pulled out a chair set beside a scrubbed pine table. The classic country kitchen might have come from the pages of an interior design magazine but when she opened the fridge to take out the milk for their tea he noted that it was stocked with the kind of ingredients that people actually have to prepare. Meat and vegetables and various kinds of cheese. It reminded him that he was hungry.

The kettle had already been on the hob of the Aga so presumably she had been about to make herself a drink and had just set it to one side when the knock came at the door. It only took a short time to boil and she poured the water on to loose-leaf tea in a plump brown pot. It was a surprisingly homely thing to do and Mac began to reassess this woman.

She stood with her back to the Aga after giving him his tea and he got the impression that she had been rehearsing what to say to him.

"So what happened?" he said. "You wanted to go to this event. You'd been let down, Phil was available, is that it?"

She nodded. "Pretty much. The friend who had been going to get me a ticket was aware that I knew Phil slightly and was pretty certain he wouldn't have a date for the evening. Phil rarely had a date for anything. Not that he ever worried about it, he just didn't seem to be that much into relationships. There were always friends he could ask and someone would be glad to go with him because, most of the time, he was quite good company. He was funny, or at least he was funny if it wasn't you he was taking the piss out of. Then it got less funny. Then it got downright miserable."

"And so you contacted Phil Perry?"

"No, Jamie, our mutual friend, he did that. He said Phil leaped at the chance. Well, of course he did. I was much more high profile than he was, and was getting a lot of attention. I must admit, I probably hadn't thought it through. That's my problem sometimes, I don't think things through. I have an aim in mind and I go for it and I figure out the rest later. I've always been like it, ever since I was a kid. I drove my mother mad."

"And what was the aim that you had in mind on this occasion? Speak to this . . . what was his name?"

"Jerry Casson. Yes, that was the aim. I thought if I could talk to him again in person then . . . You see, some time before that he'd offered me a part in a big-budget film and the negotiations had gone ahead and I thought it was in the bag. So did my agent. It would have been my big breakthrough moment. I'd already made three films in Hollywood, I'd already got good reviews, I was well thought of, my career was going places. Then as often happens, it all fell apart. As any actor will tell you, it's a rollercoaster at the best of times.

That was about ten years ago. I came home, I made the best of it, I got decent parts, but it wasn't the same."

"I can imagine that must have been frustrating. So this Jerry Casson, he'd have been giving you a chance of getting back to the big time?"

She gestured angrily at him. "You make it sound so crass. This is my job, this is my life, this is what I do. I thought your friend Rina Martin would have made you understand that."

Mac wasn't sure that Rina had ever been quite so driven, but he could be wrong, he supposed. "So there was the possibility of a part. A major role."

She nodded, picked up her mug and came to sit down at the table. Mac chose to view that as progress. "Jerry and I had known each other back when I was in the US, but we met up quite by chance at a film festival. That was about six months before Phil went with me to the charity ball. It was nice, it was like we picked up where we left off and he happened to mention this role. He was looking for a European actor, and he said he wanted someone with classical training, which I'd had. And maturity." She grimaced. "You get to a certain age and really meaty roles are hard to come by. Anyway, I auditioned, it was all approved and the contract had been negotiated. All that remained to be done was to sign on the dotted line."

"And that didn't happen." Mac sipped his tea.

"No, no it did not. It was never sent to my agent. She tried, numerous times, to contact him, but it was very clear that he was ghosting us. Eventually I heard through the grapevine that he was considering someone else for the role. She was twenty years too young for the part, American, blonde and a complete airhead. So . . . so I was annoyed. And, as you can imagine, that's putting it mildly."

"I think you deserve to be incandescent," he said.

That earned him a smile. "So I thought maybe if I could talk to him . . . We got on so well I was certain that he was being pressured from above, but thought maybe if I talked to him again he would see that I really was right for the role and he would, well, resist the pressure. And, yes, I know that

147

was being very naive but I wanted this role, I wanted a second shot at being a big star and whether you think that shallow or not, I can't help it, it's what I wanted."

Mac nodded. He didn't actually think he was in any position to judge. It was not a world he understood, despite having known Rina for quite a while. He had long ago decided that Rina was not representative of the acting world. In fact, she probably wasn't particularly representative of anything. She was just Rina Martin. Kind, compassionate, no-nonsense and someone he definitely was happy to have had in his corner over the last few years.

"So you went to this event," he prompted.

"When I heard he was going to be there, it was like fate. I thought, this is my chance. I spoke to my agent about it and she told me just forget about it, that other things would come along. But I was not in a good place. I was getting divorced, I had lost good friends over that divorce or at least people I thought were good friends. This was the last straw. So when Phil told Jamie he was happy for me to go with him I accepted his invitation, put my glad rags on and off we went."

"And did you manage to talk to this producer?"

"Yes, we talked. He said, 'Yes, I remember you, didn't you audition for something or other?' And then he looked at me as though he was struggling to recall anything else about me. I was so ashamed, so embarrassed I was also more than a little drunk. I'm afraid I made a scene."

"It happens," Mac said. "I think we've all had too much to drink and done or said things we regret." There must have been something in his tone that made her look at him more closely. He smiled but did not elaborate. At that point in his life, when he had first come to Frantham, broken and not quite sure how he was going to survive, he had often drunk too much and it was pure good fortune that he'd not done so on duty. "I suppose Phil was there, witness to it all," he said.

She nodded. "Phil thought it was hilarious, to see Grace Sweetman brought so low. Oh, no, I'm being unfair, it wasn't because of who I was or what it was that I was hoping for

— Phil just found that kind of thing funny, when people made a public scene about anything. It was all grist to his mill. But I knew he'd repeat it. I mean, I know a lot of people saw what happened, but I managed to gather my dignity and I left and . . . And, the truth is, Grace Sweetman was not an important enough person for anybody to make a big fuss about what happened, not when there were real celebrities at the party. Some drunk woman made a scene, end of."

"It must have hurt," he said. "So you broke contact with Phil after that?"

"I suppose I did. I left without him anyway, hailed a cab and went home. He tried calling me the following day but I didn't take his call. I didn't take any of his calls. Jamie, our mutual friend, heard what had happened of course and he got in touch, all sympathy, but the kind of sympathy that just wants to know more detail, that just wants to gossip. Gossip is then disguised as well-meaning concern, but I suppose that was the last straw. I bought this house and I told myself that I would not be returning to anything like an acting career, not to anything public. I'd had enough. I sold my house in London and with what was left from that sale after I bought this and with some savings I had and decent investments I'd made I knew I had enough to live on for a while. I thought it was time to think about doing something else."

"And yet you went back to acting," Mac said.

"And yet I went back. The truth is after six months or so of blissful countryside living I was bored out of my skull. My agent managed to get me a couple of decent roles and I accepted them. And then of course Lydia Marchant came along. I thought it might be fun. Something light and cosy, even if it is all about murder. I didn't know Phil Perry was going to be cast, not until I had signed the contract but, anyway, I figured it was time just to bite the bullet. I made it plain to Phil that I didn't want the past brought up, not in any way, shape or form and as far as the rest of the cast was going to be concerned we were mere acquaintances at the most."

"And how did he react to that?"

"Surprisingly well. In fact he was surprisingly conciliatory, at least at the start. The trouble with Phil is he never knows when to let go. He never *knew* when to let go. But I didn't kill him, he was an irritation, that was all."

"And you are certain he wasn't more than an irritation to anyone else?"

"As certain as I can be. The trouble is, Phil can also be lovely and so it's hard to stay mad at him. Even I was having trouble with that. He was thoughtless rather than vindictive, he never really grew up and, as I say, he never really settled into a relationship, so I can't think he understood how it felt to be ragged and teased about something that was important to you. Genuinely, nothing seemed to be particularly important to Phil."

"Friends, family?"

"He seems to have broken contact with his family years ago. I know nothing about them and I don't think he has any siblings. As far as friends are concerned, yes, he has some. I can give you Jamie's contact and he'll probably be able to tell you better than I can. He and Phil were at school together. I take it you've contacted next of kin?"

"An aunt, who hadn't seen him since he was about five. His parents have both passed on and you're right, he has no siblings."

Grace looked thoughtful for a while and then said, "The thing is, in that moment, when he made fun of me for being so upset, I could have killed him. I could have picked up a bottle and bashed him over the head with it. He got me so angry that I think I would have been capable of anything. But the moment passed and I decided he wasn't worth my time. I decided I had to pick myself up and get over it. There is not an actor in the business who hasn't been through something similar, suffered the same kind of disappointment. You have to eventually be grown up about it."

Mac nodded. Perhaps that is what happened, he thought. Phil caught someone at the wrong moment, pushed too far and that someone could not hold back.

"And it never bothered you that there was a link to Judith Tavener?" he asked. "That as writer of the Lydia Marchant books, she might object to you having a role?"

"Yes, of course I wondered about that. When my agent suggested I go for it, I was dubious. I thought Judith was bound to object. I raised the question again just before the contract was signed and was assured that they'd run it by her and she wasn't bothered at all. It never occurred to me she'd turn up on set. She'd apparently shown no interest in doing so before. Naturally, I was concerned in case she'd waited until that point to make trouble for me, but the truth is, beyond saying 'hello' and 'how are you' when our producer was doing the rounds with her, we didn't really speak much. We had a brief conversation during a break in filming. Rina will attest to that."

"Not until you ran into her in the wardrobe department that evening."

Grace nodded. "I admit that made me uneasy. I'd not had the best of days, then the lining of my bloody coat had ripped all the way down the back and, I'll admit, I probably hadn't helped matters by fiddling with the tear when I took it off. Anyway, she turned up with Richard in tow, thick as thieves. I probably overreacted. Probably behaved like a silly ass. She always did throw me off balance, that woman."

Well, you did steal her husband, Mac thought. Or rather he did leave her for you. Not that it had lasted. "You've not seen her since . . ."

"Since her husband Tony left her? No. Though I'll tell you something, she'd never have been a success with him around. Talk about needy and narcissistic. He makes me look like Mother Theresa."

Mac, who had yet to meet Tony Emmerson, Judith Tavener's ex, made no comment.

He left Grace Sweetman not long after, convinced now that the woman had nothing to do with Phil Perry's death. Everyone, he thought, had known someone like Phil Perry. Someone who likes to pry and poke and tease and say that they're just having fun and don't mean any harm by it. It was the kind of behaviour that Mac abhorred because it made him feel deeply uncomfortable. He was at heart a very private person and he did not like his weaknesses being exposed to public view. But, he supposed, he was not alone in that. Everybody has embarrassing moments and no one welcomes the exposure of those embarrassing moments to the world in general. In time, and in the company of friends, those moments can become something to laugh about knowing that people are laughing with you, feeling for you, making you feel better about yourself. Those practice runs in the company of friends could even make it easier for those moments to be exposed in a wider sense.

But at that moment, when you are angry and hurt and embarrassed, the laughter of others is just painful and humiliating, and for someone to say they were just having fun and didn't mean it when they've had a laugh at your expense remains painful for a very long time. He could imagine someone lashing out in a moment like that, could imagine himself doing it, though probably verbally rather than physically.

As Grace Sweetman had said, Mac thought as he drove away, the moment passes and, for your own wellbeing, you decide that it doesn't matter as much as you initially felt it did. You slowly separate yourself from the humiliation and pain. And you hope that you are not so angry and so humiliated that you lash out and cause pain in return.

Or perhaps, in this case, you end up committing murder.

CHAPTER 20

The first day back at Septon Hall felt strange to Rina. The atmosphere was tense and somewhat febrile. It was, she acknowledged, good to be back but she also realized she would be happy when filming was finally over.

"What's up with Richard?" Seth asked. "He's been prowling about like a bear with a sore head all morning."

Rina moved her attention from her cake to the writer. He was deep in conversation with Alison, who was frowning. Richard Cartmell was waving his arms about as though trying to make a point. He thrust a piece of paper he was holding under Alison's nose, the movement so sudden and abrupt it caused her to step back. She took the paper from him and studied it, then gave it back. She didn't look particularly happy.

"Looks like a new draft for the script," Rina said and then added, "I suppose, with Phil being gone, they'll have had to change some of the scenes. They can get by with his still being the murder victim, I suppose, as most of his scenes were completed an age ago. But there are still a couple that will need changing. One with Grace and one I think with you?"

Seth nodded. "When Lord Ellsworthy and the game-keeper talk about specific arrangements for the shoot," he said. "No, you're right, Rina, there's information in that scene that directly leads to poor old Phil being in the right place at the right time for Lady Ellsworthy to do him in. All that will have to be changed or reshot with someone else. Hopefully Richard will have found a way to sort it out." He sighed deeply. "It feels wrong, you know, just getting on with work when Phil's lying dead in some mortuary. What do his family think about all this? He must have had someone."

"No one close, I don't think. Presumably they've given their permission or their blessing or what not."

"They must have. Which I suppose is for the best — everyone needs the work. I think most people are trying not to think it might be one of us that was responsible. I think most of us are intent on believing it was someone from outside. However uncomfortable that might be, it's not as bad as . . . well, you know. And I think we're all determined just to knuckle down and get on with it. Just get these last few scenes done. After all, we all need the series to continue, don't we?"

Rina nodded. This was not an industry where many people had permanent contracts. Loss of work meant loss of income and for the sake of all the cast and crew, who had come to look upon Lydia Marchant as a steady earner, Rina hoped that the series would not be dropped. Quite a few members of the team had now elected to stay off-site, and Rina had noticed that no one was keen on being alone. She had also noted the extra security cameras that had been hastily installed.

Rina thought about what Seth was saying about the series continuing. Of course, she hoped it would, if only for the work it provided for so many people. But did she really want to make more? Just now, she wasn't so sure. "They're going to be dedicating the episode to Phil," she said.

"What else could they do? You'll be going to the funeral?"

"Of course."

"Fancy buggering off somewhere else for dinner tonight?" Seth asked. "I think by the end of the day I'll be ready for a break."

She knew what he meant. Everyone seemed uneasy and fractious. Even Alison was impatient. "I can't," she said. "I'm heading back to Frantham, just until first thing tomorrow. The public meeting I told you about, that's tonight. I have to be there."

"Oh, the one about the poison pen letters. I'd forgotten that was this evening. Well, good luck with that one. Insidious things, allegations like that can be. Undermine trust all round."

Rina nodded.

"Oh, look out," Seth continued, catching sight of Richard Cartmell now bearing down upon them. "Any money this is the new scene. More lines to learn." He rolled his eyes and Rina smiled, knowing that in reality Seth would relish the challenge.

CHAPTER 21

Any doubts Rina may have had as to the turnout at the public meeting were dispelled in spades. She had arrived, with Matthew, just a few minutes before the meeting was due to start and was immensely gratified to see Andy and Sergeant Baker putting out extra chairs.

"Evening, Mrs Martin," Andy Nevins said. "It's a good showing."

"Good evening, Andy. It is indeed. There must be a hundred people here. I didn't know you were coming."

"Mam wanted to come so I said I'd bring her. She said if I was going to be here, I'd best wear my uniform."

Rina glimpsed Mrs Nevins two rows back from the front, chatting to Mrs Eames, her next-door neighbour. "Has she received anything?"

"The whole town would have heard about it if she had," Andy said. "The boss sends his apologies, he's going to try and get here but he'll probably be late."

Rina thanked him and she and Matthew went to find the seats that had been saved for them by the rest of the household. It occurred to Rina that she'd still not managed to get Andy to call her anything but Mrs Martin, despite the years she had known him. In his first year as a probationary officer, Rina knew she had scared the life out of him, but they had since become friends, and she had nothing but respect for the young officer.

Rina sat down, leaning her cheek to receive Bethany's kiss and then returned it. Eliza leaned across her sister to do the same.

"Isn't this exciting?" Eliza said. "All these people here. They can't all have received letters, surely. How would anyone find the time to write so many?"

"I imagine a lot have come just out of curiosity," Rina said. Glancing around the room she spotted Trixie Burns and her mother, Mrs Bluett and Mrs Majors — oh, it must have been hard for them to come, Rina thought — and a handful of others that she knew had received missives. A number of others, looking ill at ease and probably wondering if this had been a good idea, were also likely recipients.

She spotted the Greens, whose doorbell camera had captured the picture of the woman posting letters through the door at Peverill Lodge and her next-door neighbours, who waved enthusiastically. It was, Rina thought, a curiously upbeat affair, as though everyone was relieved to get this strange business out into the open and into the light.

Sergeant Frank Baker got up on to the small stage and tapped the microphone on the podium. It boomed ominously and a ripple of laughter spread through the room. Then the chatter stopped and all attention was on the uniformed figure standing on the stage, pages of his prepared speech laid out in front of him. A familiar figure, solid and reliable and, Rina noted, a lot greyer than when she had first met him some dozen years before. She supposed the same could be said of her. He must be close to retirement she thought, the idea taking her by surprise. Well, that wasn't right. Who could replace Frank Baker?

"Welcome," he was saying. "Thank you all for coming tonight. It's wonderful to see so many of you. It's especially wonderful to see so many people who I know have been seriously upset by what has been going on. Hopefully, now we're all getting together to exchange information and to reassure one another, we can get to the bottom of this business and get our little town back to normal again."

A soft murmur of agreement spread throughout the room and Rina was suddenly aware that someone in the audience had stood up.

Frank Baker turned to look at the young woman who suddenly had all eyes resting upon her. "Yes, Miss Burns, do you have something to say?"

He sounded avuncular, Rina thought, but a little stern at the same time; he would not be putting up with unnecessary interruptions but if anyone had anything useful to add, he'd accept their right to say it. Frank Baker was a man cut out for community policing, Rina thought.

"I wanted to say that I got one of those letters and that I took it to the police. But I'm not letting it get to me and neither should anyone else here. No one's done anything wrong apart from the person sending the letters. You've got nothing to be ashamed of if you've got one. So it's best, if you haven't reported it already, to do it tonight. Let's work together to stop all this and I hope whoever's doing it has come here tonight and can hear me say this. You should be ashamed! You really should." Trixie sat down, her performance greeted with a round of applause.

Frank waited for it to die down before thanking her for her input and adding that he agreed. "I would urge anyone who has not yet reported the receipt of a letter to come and speak to me or PC Nevins later on. Now let me tell you what we've been doing so far to try and get to the bottom of this business. And," he added, giving in to the inevitable, "if you've got questions, then I hope you'll ask them."

Brave man, Rina thought as the hands went up and Sergeant Baker moved his speech papers aside, knowing he'd not get to say any of it. Content for now to just be an observer, she settled in for an interesting evening.

About half an hour into the meeting, the outer door opened quietly. Rina glanced back and was astonished to see Grace Sweetman standing awkwardly at the back of the hall.

Rina slipped out of her seat and went to join her. Grace was examining the crowd intently, a troubled look on her face. Her late arrival had attracted a fair bit of attention and a few whispers as she was recognized. Rina took her arm and led her into a quiet corner, found two chairs and gestured to Grace to sit down. Somewhat to her surprise, Grace settled herself, her attention now focused on Sergeant Baker at the front of the room.

"There are a lot of people here," she whispered.

"Yes, we're all very pleased. It's best this gets flushed out into the open. Silence and secrecy are what give the writer power, don't you think?" She looked sideways at Grace, trying to gauge a reaction.

Grace nodded slowly. Once again she let her gaze travel around the room as though looking for someone specific. "They'll be here, don't you think?" she said. "They'll want to see what they've done."

"Quite possibly," Rina agreed. "But I don't imagine they'll give themselves away, at least not on purpose."

Grace sighed. "I'm not sure why I came. I just felt I needed to."

"I think the same will be true of most people here," Rina told her.

"People will know, won't they, that I got a letter. Otherwise why would I be here?" She sounded annoyed with herself as though she should have thought of this sooner.

"Possibly that's what they'll think," Rina said. "but not everyone who is here tonight will have received a letter. Some have just come to give support or because they are concerned about what's happening to our little community."

She turned her attention back to what Frank Baker was saying. He was urging, once again, for anyone who had been affected by the letter writing to come and speak to him or one of his colleagues. It was evident that this part of the meeting was coming to an end.

Grace stood. "I think I'll go. I think maybe I shouldn't have come."

She walked swiftly away before Rina could say anything.

That was odd, Rina thought as she watched the door close behind Grace. Maybe she had been more upset by this whole business than Rina would have guessed.

* * *

"Well, that went well," Matthew commented as they restacked the chairs.

"It's as well we're not paying for the hall," Rina said. They had overstayed their allotted time by more than an hour and, although many people had drifted away, judging by the number waiting to see Frank or Andy or, now he'd arrived, Mac, they were likely to need it for a while longer.

There had been aggrieved victims of the poison pen campaign, with sympathetic and not so sympathetic responses from those who had not. There were inevitable demands that the police should be doing more — Frank had very gently suggested they should define what they wanted doing and then countered with evidence that they already were — and reassurances that the matter had in fact been taken very seriously.

"It has to be someone we all know, someone in our community," Mrs Bluett had announced, and Rina had been terribly aware of everyone in the room looking at one another as though the impact of that had suddenly been brought home to them.

Rina had been surprised by the number of people who admitted to having been accused by the anonymous writer. Eliza's words came back to her: how had they found the time? It took serious commitment not just to write the letters but, presumably, to research the recipients sufficiently that there was some chance of the accusations hitting home. Not to mention the cost of postage over the past seven or eight months. It was almost as though the writing of the letters had become an addiction. They had started and now could not stop.

"Well, that was all very interesting," a familiar voice said.

Rina put the chair on the stack and turned around to look at the dark-haired woman, who was fastening her trench coat in preparation for going out into the rainy evening. She was younger than Rina. And taller and slimmer, but Rina wasn't about to hold that against her.

"Oh, hello, it's Marcia, isn't it?"

"That's right. We both got highjacked into helping with the school summer fete last June."

Rina laughed. "Yes. I don't remember volunteering but suddenly I was designated as bingo caller and handing out teddy bears left, right and centre."

"It was fun, though."

"It was. So, what brought you here tonight? Have you—"

"Had a letter? Oh no. Just curious, I suppose. This is happening in my community, and I wanted to know what was being done."

Rina nodded. "It was a very good turnout, all things considered."

"Oh, Rina, that went so well. Was that Grace Sweetman I saw you with?" Rina turned to the new speaker.

"Sandy, yes it did, didn't it? And yes it was. She couldn't stay, just wanted to show her support." After a brief chat, she reassured Sandra Brady from the chip shop that yes, she should have some decent foliage available for the church flowers, even if nothing much was in bloom.

"It's been such a late spring," Sandy complained as she headed off.

"Rina, how's the filming going? I heard about the murder. That must have been so distressing." The vicar's wife this time, attempting to arrange her face into a look of sympathy when Rina knew she was simply abuzz with curiosity.

By the time she escaped some half an hour later, Rina had spoken to three more women and a solitary man she knew from various committees or local activities she was either involved with or trying to avoid being.

"You really do know a lot of people," Matthew said as they left.

"I suppose I do. Occupational hazard of living in a small town."

"Occupational hazard of being famous and of being unable to say no."

"I often say no."

"You're getting better at it," Matthew conceded.

* * *

Marcia had walked home slowly. She felt oddly light-headed, the sense of dissociation from self returning forcibly. Who even was she these days?

It had been hard to pluck up courage to speak to Rina Martin — which was ridiculous, when you thought about it. She and Rina had been crossing paths for years. Rina was involved in everything. Marcia did her bit but she'd always had to work around *his* needs. Her husband's work, his constraints. She'd always felt constrained, anyway. She wondered now what would have happened had she said no to him more often and carried on with her own interests regardless. Would that have made her less boring?

She was also shaken by the strength of feeling she had encountered at the public meeting.

Imagine, a public meeting because of something you had done! That was both shocking and terrifying — and oddly exhilarating all at the same time. She was suddenly the focus of everyone's attention.

She couldn't help wishing it was for something else.

So, what now? She knew the police had been involved but seeing that involvement in action had disturbed her. Would she be arrested? Presumably she was breaking some law or other. She'd not really thought about it until now. What would happen if — when? — she was discovered.

Everyone would hate her.

Marcia stopped dead. Everyone would hate her. The strength of feeling at that meeting reinforced that. They would think she was worthless, evil. They would hate her.

Marcia could not recall the rest of her journey home. She vaguely remembered putting her key in the door and the way her hand shook so much she could hardly get it in the slot. She dropped her bag and coat on the hall floor and staggered through to the dining room, her legs barely able to hold her up any longer. She poured herself a glass of something from one of her husband's decanters, slugged it down without even noting the taste and then poured herself some more. Finally, she lowered herself into one of the dark wood, red-upholstered dining chairs that she had always disliked, put her head in her hands and wept, violently, angrily and eventually out of pure despair.

CHAPTER 22

The following morning Mac met early with Frank Baker to discuss what had come out of the public meeting. The sergeant told him he had a meeting later on with Matthew Montmorency so that they could discuss what was next on the agenda.

"Matthew?" Mac was momentarily taken aback and then remembered that Rina would be away now filming had resumed. "I fully expect Rina will also be expecting an update," he said.

"No doubt. My task, as I see it, is to collate the information we have, take another look at any crossovers we might have between victims and integrate that with the material have already collected. Frankly, I don't think it's going to get us very far."

"Oh and why is that?" Mac enquired. It wasn't like Sergeant Baker to be pessimistic.

"It's all well and good looking at who knows who and how," he replied, "but the problem you've got in a place like Frantham is that it's a small town that's more like a large village, if we are honest. Everyone crosses paths with everyone else at some point. The local weekly paper picks up all the stuff that's in the newsletters and republishes that alongside all the broader regional news. To my count there are at least a dozen newsletters, some of them still printed and the rest online, for everything up to and including the local branch of the Rotarian Society and the Women's Institute to a little group who send one another cat videos and then blog about it. Then there's the fossil hunters, theatre groups, Scouts and Guides, friends of the hospital, friends of various churches, each of whom have various subcommittees and most of which have something that resembles a newsletter or a round robin or some means of communicating which is semi-public. If our letter writer is local, and I think they must be, they have access to an absolute mountain of material on a daily basis from which to pick and choose their next victim. And the same names come up over and over again, because if you are interested in the Scouts, the likelihood is you're interested in the church because the Scouts meet in the church hall. When the vicar is on the lookout for volunteers — and I use the word advisedly — for the next fundraising activity, you are likely to find yourself volunteering, especially as a lot of the groups pool their resources so they can create a bigger event from which everybody benefits."

Mac nodded his understanding. "All you can do, Frank, is collate the material as far as possible and then pass it on up the chain. The team investigating the hit and run asked for any connected info we might have, so see if they want a heads up on this. And, of course, Anning will want a full report on the off-chance Grace Sweetman receiving a letter is more than just coincidence. I'll see if I can rustle up some assistance for you in the meantime."

"I won't hold my breath," Frank told him. "Thankfully it's not busy season yet, but if this goes on after Easter then all of the demands of the tourist season will kick in and yours truly will be a presence on the promenade most of the day."

The sergeant wasn't wrong there, Mac thought. After Easter everything in Frantham changed, the population more than doubling during the summer season.

Andy had already gone back to Septon Hall that morning so see if any memories could be jogged and if Mac would be rejoining Anning. "I've been giving some thought as to what they might charge the poison pen letter writer with," Mac said. "As far as we're aware there's been no attempt to blackmail, and when you look at them, they're not even real letters. More like the malicious trolling you get on the likes of Twitter, or X or whatever it's called this week."

"Yes, whatever happened to the lengthy missives written in copperplate you get in the typical Agatha Christie story?" Frank said. "With a nice threat of exposure thrown in and the demand for solid hard cash left in an envelope inside a tree stump or whatever. Still, it's a nasty business and the number of people that turned up last night indicates just how upset the community has been. Aside from the merely curious of course."

"Anybody stand out as odd?" Mac asked. Frank and indeed Andy would have been far more likely to notice as they had lived in the area all their lives and Mac was a relative newcomer, a blow-in.

"Not that immediately comes to mind. A few people I was surprised to see and a fair few strangers, oddly enough, people I could not immediately place. Like you say, the merely curious. One or two questions that made me wonder, maybe think the questioner knew a little more than they should have done. But talking to them after, it turned out they'd got connections with people who had received letters and who maybe didn't want to come forward, or they were guilty of no more than reading far too many crime novels. Still, I'll be following up. I'm surprised we didn't get more media. Andrew Barnes put in an appearance," he said, referring to a local journalist they both got along with surprisingly well. He was also a friend of Rina's, which probably accounted for a lot. "No media outsiders, but then I suppose it is a small and local matter in a small and not very famous seaside town."

"Yes, we had a quick chat," Mac said. He considered Barnes to be a reliable contact and an honest journalist.

"Me too. He's going to do a write-up, a summary of the story so far and urge people to come forward if they have not already done so. He did warn me that having a public meeting like this was inevitably going to attract some outside attention in the longer term, so we'll have to be aware of that. We got chatting about the murder too."

"Presumably he's going to be covering it."

"Reckons he's got some interest from a couple of the nationals. But he needs an angle. The TV production company put out statements and understandably no one else seems keen to say very much."

Mac glanced at his watch. "I'd best be off," he said. "I'm interviewing Tony Emmerson later on today, the ex-husband of Judith Tavener."

"Is he involved?" Sergeant Baker asked.

"On the face of it, no, but he's been in touch with Anning, apparently thinks he should fill in some background or some such. Someone would have got to him eventually, of course, because of his association with Grace Sweetman, however brief. But the fact that he's contacted us means someone's got to talk to the guy and that someone is lucky old me."

"A job for Uniform, surely? His association with Grace Sweetman was years ago — is he just the type that wants to be involved?"

Mac shrugged. "Who knows? No doubt I'll find out. Well, I'll leave you to your sorting and your collating."

"Thank you for that." Frank Baker laughed.

* * *

Matthew and Rina were also discussing the public meeting as he drove her back to Septon Hall.

"On the whole I think it went rather well," Matthew said. "I've heard back this morning form several individuals who were able to chat with our police officer friends last night and who now feel that they have actually been taken seriously."

"Well, that's a start," Rina said. "I do hate to feel that anyone thinks Mac has let them down but I've got to admit no one seems to have got very far with this."

"That nasty hit and run is being reinvestigated."

"Well, that's true. But it's the smaller, hateful stuff that impacts on the community."

"True, but that's also the stuff that's harder to act against. Something like that car accident, well that's a clear offence, isn't it? But these letters are harder to pin down, I suppose. I mean, how many of us have wondered if someone's husband is paying a bit too much attention to someone else's wife, or if someone is capable of killing a neighbour's cat, or that so-and-so didn't deserve to get that job because you just know they padded their qualifications, even if only ever so slightly. And there's not one of us who hasn't played up our roles a bit from time to time. We could all of us be accused of something. And that letter to Trixie proves how little this writer really knows about the people they are persecuting. The world and his wife know that Trix is living with her girlfriend."

He sounded slightly envious, Rina thought. Matthew and Steven were from a time when such openness had been all but impossible.

"But what about Mrs Majors? The details of how her husband had been found, lying on the kitchen floor."

"Known to everyone at the marina within days of him dying," Matthew said. "Sheila Bluett told us all what had happened, in great detail, only a few days after. She came to the committee meeting and apologized on Esme Majors' behalf that she wouldn't be available to run the tombola stall. We all knew already Mr Majors had died as we had a card and some flowers and such ready to send back with Sheila. Then there was something at one of the tea dances, I think, straight after the committee meeting. Lots of concerned people asking a myriad of questions, which Sheila answered. We all knew how ill he was and that the inevitable was, well, inevitable. We all felt for poor Esme and natural curiosity and natural sympathy combined meant everyone wanted to know exactly what had happened. We all felt for her."

Rina nodded. Of course, she thought, what looked like insider knowledge was going to be common knowledge in reality, and that knowledge would spread exponentially. She hadn't personally attended Christopher Majors' funeral — she didn't know Esme Majors all that well — but she knew people who had and was aware that in the crematorium there had been standing room only. It was obvious that a wide pool of people would have known exactly what had happened, and the tragic tale of the kind old man collapsing on the kitchen floor, his wife unable to do anything to help him, had sufficient pathos that it would have been sure to have done the rounds, even among mere acquaintances.

"You'll be seeing Sergeant Baker later?" she asked.

"Yes, we're going to go over what happened, all the information that was gathered last night and try and collate it into some kind of order. I believe Mac has arranged for all of that to be passed on to whoever is leading the investigation into the hit and run. *They* weren't there last night, of course. The man who got *that* letter has been keeping a very low profile."

"He claims to have an alibi."

"So I heard. But hark at us, Rina. Neither of us sound as though we believe it. We don't know the man from Adam. We've just heard the rumours and read about it in the local paper and we saw that bit on the television news when the family of the injured girl turned up at Mr Markham's house. But despite the reports that he has an alibi, despite the fact that the accusations are probably malicious, we're still using words like 'apparently', still doubting his innocence just because mud has been thrown and, unfortunately, mud sticks."

They were pulling into the driveway at Septon Hall now and Rina caught a glimpse through the window of Alison and Seth in conversation. "You're right," she said. "Doubt and suspicion are very rampant crops. You only have to scatter a small amount of seed." She turned her gaze back to him. "Were you surprised by who came last night?"

"Not especially. Many attendees were people we already knew had received letters. Then there were the usual interested parties from local community groups and the usual interested busybodies who turn up for everything just so they can keep up with the local gossip."

"You mean the vicar's wife, the newsagent's daughter and the landlady from The Railway Inn," Rina guessed.

"Among others. Not that I believe any of them would do harm. But a couple surprised me. I half-expected them to have something to say, but they both sat quietly and just observed."

"And who might they be?" Rina asked.

"Well, Marcia Trent, for one. Since she misplaced her husband last year, she's hardly been anywhere. Then there's Phyllis Steel. Well, you know how she is, wouldn't volunteer to make so much as a jam sandwich. Agrees with the ex-Iron Lady that there's no such thing as society. When did she start to attend public meetings about anything?"

Rina nodded and prepared to get out of the car. These two women had been surprising additions to the crowd. Phyllis Steel had been a librarian before she retired and had no doubt terrified several generations of children who were late returning their books. She had this way of peering over her glasses as though she was examining some exotic but quite disgusting specimen of slime. She could, however, as generations of children had also found, be won over very quickly if you asked her to recommend a book. Her younger and more approachable colleagues might have been less terrifying, but Phyllis Steel knew everything about anything when it came to her book hoard. But no, she was not exactly sociable, didn't give a toss about committees or public meetings or community affairs so far as Rina knew and certainly didn't give an even bigger toss about what people thought of her.

Saying goodbye to Matthew and walking towards the house, Rina speculated whether Phyllis Steel could be the letter writer. Somehow Rina couldn't see it. She liked Phyllis, despite her rather austere manner and general disregard for anyone or anything she didn't happen to find interesting. And that was it, wasn't it? Phyllis wouldn't have been interested enough to accuse people of random indiscretions. She simply wouldn't care who was sleeping with who . . . though she might be more concerned about people cheating on their job applications or killing cats. Rina happened to know she had two very spoilt moggies of her own. More importantly, if Phyllis wanted you to know how she felt about something, she'd damn well tell you and never mind the consequences.

So, what had she been doing at the meeting the night before? Rina found herself wishing she'd had time to ask. She made a mental note to do that the next time she was home but she supposed that even the Phyllis Steels of this world liked to exercise their curiosity.

And what about Marcia Trent?

A sudden thought struck Rina and she turned around and went back out on to the drive. Matthew was turning the car around. He pulled up beside her. "Something wrong?"

"I don't know yet. Just a thought. Matthew, could you come and pick me up this evening? There's something I need to do."

Back inside, Rina hung her coat on the rack in the hallway and made her way into the Grand Salon, said hello to Seth and Alison and then settled in for an hour or so of not doing very much. She wasn't due to shoot a scene until that afternoon but had felt she really ought to put in an appearance earlier than that, seeing as how she'd gone home the night before and, besides, there were rewrites to deal with now that Phil wasn't around to shoot his final scenes.

So, Marcia Trent. Yes, it was a little unusual for her to attend something like the public meeting, but that wasn't to say she wasn't community minded. She had been roped into a number of fundraising events in the past, as had Rina. The basic difference was that Marcia never did anything that called for regular involvement, such as the committees and boards Rina found herself co-opted to — once you'd agreed to one, it seemed, you were fair game for receiving invitations to partake of others.

Marcia had always had the excuse that her husband worked odd hours or something and didn't like her being out at night if he couldn't pick her up. Or she didn't really have the time to spare for a regular commitment, or . . . well, there had always been excuses. Rina had occasionally envied not just her ability to come up with them but also her ability to stand her ground and not be drawn, even when the weakness of her excuse was challenged.

Though, lately, Rina had noticed, Marcia had definitely been more willing to participate. Since last summer in fact, when, as Matthew had put it, she had mislaid her husband. She hadn't been very forthcoming as to the whys and wherefores, but it seemed that Mr Trent was no longer living with his wife.

She was distracted from her thoughts by the arrival of a rather harassed-looking Richard Cartmell. He was carrying a sheaf of paper and heading straight for Alison.

"That'll be the rewrites, I'm guessing," Seth said, coming over to join Rina. "Alison's just told me that it's looking a lot more complicated that we first thought."

Rina frowned. "No offence to the dead, but I don't see why. Phil had wrapped almost all of his scenes and I'm sure the rest can be rejigged without any problem. There's only one scene left with any significant dialogue, from what I remember, and that's just the gamekeeper making some point about staff for the shooting party."

"True, though that does lead straight into the bit where he tries to blackmail Lady Ellsworthy. Alison's a bit antsy about the actual murder now, the one in the novel being so similar to the way poor Phil actually died. I wouldn't be surprised if she's had Richard change the murder weapon or something and that would have quite a major impact on some of the pieces we've already shot. Would Lord Ellsworthy make quite such a big thing of showing Otis Finch the fibula, for instance?"

Rina thought about it. "I don't see why not. He'd be keen to show off his treasures no matter what, I reckon. It could be turned into a piece of misdirection quite easily."

"True. Oh, Alison doesn't look too happy."

"I don't think anyone's too happy," Rina said. "Whatever Richard's managed to pull out of the bag it's going to be disruptive and it's going to drift away from the original plot. You know how close the series has managed to keep to the original. Unusually close if you compare it to your average adaptation."

Seth nodded agreement. "Hello," he said. "What's this?"

The sound of a car engine drew their attention outside.

"Oh, that's young Andy Nevins," Rina said. "Mac said he was popping over today to see if anyone has recalled anything more about that night. Alison apparently has no objections so long as he keeps out of the way."

"He's a nice young man," Seth said. "Very polite."

His attention switched back to Alison, who still didn't look happy. She was speaking into a radio now and Rina knew she would be making sure the main gates to the estate were closed and there would be no more vehicles coming up the drive. Her gaze still rested irritably on Richard Cartmell.

What's he done? Rina wondered.

She glanced towards the door as Andy Nevins crept in and she patted the sofa. The young officer sat down gingerly as though afraid to make any noise. "It's all right," Rina told him. "They're still setting up."

"Ah, right, well, this is exciting, Mrs Martin."

She smiled at him. He'd be bored by lunchtime, she thought, but no doubt Andy would find it educational anyway.

Alison had beckoned Seth over to where Richard Cartmell was still fussing with his papers. He laid them out on a side table and turned to address Alison once more.

"She looks miffed," Andy said. "She's the director, isn't she?"

"Yes, she is and yes she does," Rina agreed.

Alison's voice carried across the room this time. "There's got to be a better solution, Rich. Reshooting that scene would put us back by at least a day. To say nothing about the time and money involved in getting those actors back. You've got to find another solution."

"There is no other solution, not if you want the murder weapon changed. You never heard of Chekhov's gun? You want the murder weapon changed then it has to be an integral part of the plot from the very beginning otherwise it's going to turn into amateur hour. And let's face it, we're not far off that, are we? This whole series is turning into a farce."

Alison moved closer to the writer, her body language spelling out her annoyance, her tone now lowered.

Rina frowned. Speak up, she thought, I want to hear. She noted Seth hadn't moved. He was clutching several sheets of paper that Richard Cartmell had handed to him and was following whatever was being said with great concentration.

"Chekhov's gun?" Andy asked.

"What he actually said was something like if you have a gun in scene one then it should be used in scene two, and if you weren't going to use it then it shouldn't be there. But the way most people interpret that is that if you want someone shot in scene three, then the gun has to have been revealed to the audience earlier, so they know it's likely to be used." She shrugged. "It's not a bad bit of advice but in reality it's ignored all the time. Sometimes the gun is just misdirection. In this case it's likely to be the fibula that becomes misdirection. Alison's unhappy about art imitating life now, feels it's going to come across as a bit insensitive."

"More like life imitating art," Andy said.

Wasn't that the truth, Rina thought. "Well, yes. Seth and I reckon the easiest thing would be to make the fibula into a bit of a red herring, replace it with another weapon in the murder scene. I mean, that's already been shot but with a bit of careful editing it would be easy enough to hide the actual murder weapon and, in the scene where the body is found, have it changed for something easily grabbable. A knife or something."

Andy nodded. "Has that scene been shot?"

"It has and it's likely it would have to be reworked somehow. I know Alison wanted the audience to see the face of the victim, just briefly and the murder weapon too. They'd have to either recut or even reshoot a part of that scene, using a stand-in for poor Phil and with a more oblique angle, so his face isn't in shot. But it could be done and with minimal changes."

"Looks like Mr Cartmell has different ideas," Andy said.

From the way the argument was continuing, Rina felt he must be correct. Seth took the opportunity to withdraw discreetly and plonked himself down at the other end of the sofa from Andy, crowding Rina a little.

"So, is Anning making any progress?" she asked. "And what's he like to work with? I imagine, seeing as we're all here and he's allowing filming to continue, he thinks the cast and crew are in the clear."

Andy chuckled. "You know I can't tell you anything, Mrs Martin."

"And you know I've got to ask," Rina told him.

"Actually," Andy said, "Inspector Anning is OK. Not as grumpy as I first thought and he and the boss are getting along fine."

"You sound relieved."

"I am," Andy admitted. "I know he gave the boss a bad time, but they seem OK now." He hesitated for a moment. "And I don't think he's ruled anything out, suspect-wise. I get the feeling he prefers to have everyone in the same place, just to see what shakes loose."

"Isn't that a risk? If one of our lot is the murderer?"

"Well, I think he figures that whoever killed Mr Perry did so for a very specific reason and isn't about to go on the rampage."

"Fair point," Rina said. "It doesn't stop everyone from feeling on edge, though."

"Well, no," Andy agreed.

"And I suppose you're the eyes and ears in case anything does get shaken loose," Seth said unexpectedly, looking up from his script.

"I suppose me and Mrs Martin both are," Andy agreed. "Only Mrs Martin would have to report it to Mac first, that or I'd have to pretend it was something I'd found out."

Rina laughed. She guessed he would.

Others had begun to drift in now. It was almost 10 a.m. and filming had been set to begin by then. Curious glances were being cast over to where the now heated discussion was taking place.

"Fine!" Richard Cartmell exploded and, seizing a bundle of paper from the side table, he stalked away.

Wearily, Alison rubbed at her face as though trying to clear away the stress.

"So, what's happening?" Rina demanded of Seth.

"Well, looks like Richard's losing the plot or at least he wants to write a different one. All Alison wanted was for him to rejig a couple of scenes to get around Phil's absence as simply as possible. He's gone and practically rewritten the entire script. Well, slight exaggeration, but he wants to change some key elements that have already gone to post-production. You know how much it would cost to reshoot."

Rina shook her head.

"Well, actually neither do I, but more than Alison is prepared to sanction. And it would delay everything by weeks and, frankly, I don't think anyone wants that."

"So what does he want to change?" Rina asked.

"He wants Phil written out altogether. Says it's disrespectful to keep him in now he's passed. He wants to change the identity of the blackmailer and so the murder victim altogether. Wants it to be the butler that did it, not the gamekeeper and while I agree that would be technically possible—"

"Practically, it certainly would not," Rina agreed. "It's not like Richard to be so difficult. He knows what we're up against." She was puzzled. What had got into the man? "So, what's happening now?"

"Well, she's sent him away with a flea in his ear and told him to keep to the brief. I've got some additional lines and it looks as though you will have too. I think we've got enough to get through the day, but if he's still not playing ball tomorrow, heaven knows. It's not looking good, Rina, that's all I can say."

CHAPTER 23

Mac and Anning had driven to Exeter to interview Judith Tavener's ex-husband, Tony Emmerson. Mac was not sure why it should take two senior officers to go and interview a man who was essentially an outlier in the drama, but he soon figured that this was more of a bonding exercise than one born of pure necessity.

"I've been doing a bit of what you might call research," Anning said, when they had been driving for a while. "Your career after coming down south has been what you might call eventful."

Mac agreed that it had been. Several murder investigations, kidnappings, some smuggling . . .

"And you finally got some closure on the Cara Evans murder."

Mac nodded. Her death had been what had broken him. Finding her killer had finally helped him move on. Properly move on.

"And it seems to me that I was half wrong. You are wasted in a dead end like Frantham on Sea. I can understand you've made the best of it, got yourself involved up to the neck in some messy business and come up smelling of roses. But my question is, how long will that be enough for you?

"I'll hold up my hands and say I didn't rate you. I mean, we're not exactly cut from the same cloth. I, like I daresay everyone else, expected you to do six months down here and then take medical retirement and no one could have blamed you. But you stuck it out and you saw it through and so I'll also hold up my hands now and say that I was wrong."

Big of you, Mac thought, but he held his peace, wondering where this was leading.

"Well, the fact is, and this is all hush hush at the moment, but I'm only a year or two off retirement, which means there'll be a position available. You'd be leading a bigger team, commensurate rise in salary, you'd be using your talents to the full. Your name's already come up in discussion so . . . the idea is you'd be seconded for a while at first, just to test out the fit, but long-term—"

He paused and Mac realized he was expected to respond. But respond how? He was happy where he was. Did he really want what Anning was offering? Aware that he had hesitated too long he said, "That's quite an offer. Not something I'd really thought about."

Anning nodded. "No, I don't suppose it is. But I hate to see talent go to waste. And I know a lot of us had written you off—"

"Thanks!"

"Well, let's face it, that's not exactly news, is it? But this would be a way back to the mainstream. Probably a fast-track promotion to go with it. All I'm saying is think about it. I just wanted to give you a heads up that your name is being mentioned. Favourably mentioned and this could be just the chance you've been waiting for."

Not quite knowing what to say, Mac thanked him and Anning seemed satisfied.

Was he waiting for a chance? Mac wondered. An opportunity to rejoin a greatly pressured environment at a potentially much more responsible level than he currently occupied? It would be more desk work and administration than he'd been accustomed to these past few years. Less hands on — probably more regular hours and a better salary. But would that suit him. The prospect had arisen so unexpectedly that Mac had no idea what to think.

The satnav told them they were almost at their destination and Mac turned his thoughts back to Tony Emmerson.

There had been no urgent reason to question the man that Mac could see. He had been out of the lives of both women obliquely involved in the Phil Perry murder for quite some time. Neither Grace Sweetman nor Judith Tavener had spoken to him in years, or so they said, and Mac had no reason to disbelieve them. But then out of the blue Emmerson had contacted Anning directly and suggested that he might have information pertinent to Phil Perry that the police should know. He had been vague on the phone and Anning would normally have sent a local uniformed officer to take a statement, but there had been so little movement on the case that Anning had made the decision that they may as well go and see what he had to say.

As a senior officer who should have delegated a lot more often than he did, Anning, Mac thought, still enjoyed being hands on. At least they had that in common. Perhaps taking over from Anning might offer the same accommodation to him.

"What's the betting this will be a wasted journey?" Anning said.

Mac shrugged. "If he can add any background, that might be helpful. So far, the only family we've been able to locate is an aunt who's not seen him since he was a child and a handful of friends he was at drama school with. In fact, according to the officers who did the interviews, they seem to be the only people he's consistently kept in touch with and none of them seems to have met up with him more than a few times in any given year. Everyone else seems to have been little more than an acquaintance. None of them could suggest the names of newer friends he might have mentioned."

"Unless he kept them in separate boxes," Anning suggested.

"Possible. Some people do compartmentalize. Anyway, looks like we're here."

Anning pulled their vehicle into the car park of a low-rise block of flats. Emmerson's was on the fourth floor of five. There was allocated visitors' parking in addition to what looked like one space per apartment. Mac got out and looked around. The block was well kept, built in the seventies or eighties, he guessed, though the windows looked to be of more recent vintage and the wide glass doors were equipped with digital cameras and a very new keypad entry. There were no names beside the row of buzzers and no space for names, only numbers for the apartments. Security conscious, Mac supposed. The logic probably went that if you were visiting or delivering you knew the apartment number. If you didn't then you probably had no reason to be there.

It all looked very clean and neat and, probably, expensive.

Tony Emmerson buzzed them in and told them they'd have to ring again at the inner door. Definitely security minded. The lobby was freshly tiled and a row of lockers lined one wall, presumably for post. Mac assumed that delivery drivers must be given a code to get in this far. A second set of doors led off to the left and Mac could see the stairs and a lift. Anning buzzed again and the door opened for them.

"Lift," Anning said. "I'll do stairs on the way down."

A man was waiting for them on the fourth-floor landing. Casually dressed in what Mac's mother would have referred to as slacks — a particular style of trouser that was difficult to define until you actually saw them — and a polo shirt. One hand in the trouser pocket spoke, Mac thought, of studied nonchalance.

This was definitely going to be a waste of time. He'd bet any money that Tony Emmerson just wanted to know what was going on and if there was any way he could benefit from it.

Impatiently, Mac told himself not to be so cynical, but ten minutes later he felt thoroughly vindicated in holding that view.

Tony Emmerson had freshly ground coffee waiting for them and that was probably the only redeeming factor in the visit.

"Of course," Tony Emmerson said, "I supported Judith while she was still trying to break into publishing. She'd not have had the chance if I'd not been earning decent money."

"I understood she was a full-time teacher," Anning said. "I know they've had reason to complain about pay, but my understanding is it's not bad. All credit to her, I'd say, holding down a demanding job and still finding time to put pen to paper."

"Well, yes. But she'd not have managed alone. She was always fragile, you know. When I left and — I know, I know, entirely my fault — she was bereft. She fell apart. She was never terribly stable, even when we were at our happiest. There was always something . . . missing. I suppose that's why I was so easily led astray. Grace seemed exciting. Of course, I soon realized I'd made a mistake. I was all for putting the past behind us and moving on, but Judith wouldn't have it."

"She seems to have done all right without you," Anning said bluntly.

"On the surface it must seem that way. But this will have been a great strain on her, I'm sure. I tried calling her, but I don't seem to have an up-to-date number." He looked expectantly at Anning.

"Well you won't be getting it from me, I'm afraid," Anning said. "But I'm sure you can find someone to pass your message on."

"You said you had information on Phil Perry that might be pertinent to the investigation," Mac said.

"Oh, yes. I suppose I did. Well about him and Richard Cartmell, really. You know there were rumours about the two of them?"

Mac waited, as did Anning.

"Well, you know about the two of them being an item a few years ago? I mean, I've no idea if that's true, but you know they collaborated on a couple of projects, one of which almost got commissioned? Then, of course, this Lydia Marchant thing came along and Cartmell focused on that. And on other things too, I suppose, and it came to nothing."

"You're talking about television," Mac asked. "They wrote a script?"

"Well, more of a treatment, I believe. That's like a proposal for a series, or for a one-off. I can't recall which this was. But they were apparently close until Lydia Marchant took off and then Phil was left out in the cold. I was very surprised to hear he was working on the series. It seemed very odd. And that Grace was involved too. Well, you'd think that would be uncomfortable for everyone. But then, Grace always was thick-skinned, and I doubt Judith would have had the nerve to say she didn't want Grace to be hired. Always a bit of a mouse was our Judith."

"I suppose it must have been difficult for you too," Mac said.

"I'm sorry?"

"You leave your wife for Grace Sweetman, that falls apart very quickly and, by all accounts, you're keen to come home but your wife wouldn't have you. Next thing you know she's a great success both with sales of her books and with the television series. If you'd felt you supported her, it must have been galling not to have benefited."

"She deserved her success," Tony Emmerson said stiffly. "And now, if that's all?"

* * *

"Subtle," Anning said as they returned to the car.

"I do my best. So, did that tell us much we didn't already know? Apart from the possibility that Phil Perry and Richard Cartmell may have written something together. Something that might have been commissioned if the Lydia Marchant TV series hadn't come along."

"Which would imply that Cartmell isn't capable of working on more than one project at a time, which I find unlikely. I've no doubt that writers are like plumbers or builders, always moving between jobs, three or four on the go at any given time. If it's fine next Friday I'll come and do a bit on your roof, if it's not I've got a first fix on an extension to see to."

Mac recalled that Anning's son and his family had recently come back to stay while their new home was being finished off. Last time they met, the project was taking longer than anyone had anticipated and he wondered if that was still ongoing.

"I suspect that anyone who freelances has to have several irons in the fire at any given time," he agreed, though he wasn't sure if plumbers and builders were exactly comparable to writers.

As they drove away Mac phoned Andy, asking him to speak to Richard Cartmell about the presumed collaboration.

"I'll have to give him a ring," Andy told Mac. "He was here but the director wasn't exactly happy with the revised script he'd come up with. I think he's been sent off to do better. He wasn't happy about it. He's not gone to his room in the house, so I'm not sure where he'll be."

Mac listened while Andy gave him a potted version of the morning's events. "Well, see if you can get hold of him," he said. "Ask the question. It might mean that he and Phil Perry were closer friends than he suggested. Tony Emmerson also suggested a romantic involvement, but I suspect he may just have been stirring the pot."

"If so, that might explain just how upset he seems to be, but I'll be careful how I ask," Andy told him.

Had he not been in Anning's company, Mac might have been tempted to get Andy to ask Rina to pose that particular question, but he supposed that would not be the height of professionalism. It occurred to him that if he pursued Anning's suggestion of once more climbing the career ladder, consulting Mrs Martin would become less of an option than it had been. The thought troubled him far more than it had any right to do.

"Before you go," Andy said, "I was about to give you a call about the security cameras anyway."

Andy sat on the stairs and gazed out through the main doors into the parkland beyond. The upper sections of the double doors were glazed, the glass old enough to have flowed downwards over time, consequently warping and rippling the view. It looked in the weak sunshine of the April day as though it was raining outside, heavy, sweeping rain that distorted the view of the hill and the folly beyond.

He had been speaking to the estate staff, reviewing once more what scant CCTV there was — surprisingly little, for a house and grounds of this size — and discussing ways of getting into the house without being seen on the cameras. As Anning had speculated, it was tricky but by no means impossible. The killer would have had to have known what angles the cameras covered.

They would have triggered the motion sensors on the security light set at intervals around the house but, according to the estate manager, so would random cats and foxes and, knowing that, he confessed that he took little notice anymore. No one else actually lived in. The rest of the staff simply went home at night. The lights and the cameras were there because the insurers demanded them, but as far as actual utility went, they served no real purpose.

Mac's call had come through when Andy had just returned to the house and settled on the broad, shallow-treaded stairs waiting for everyone to finish their filming and go to lunch which, Rina had assured him, would be around one fifteen. It was now just after one.

"I had another talk with Robbie, the estate manager," he told Mac now. "Something was nagging at me about the CCTV footage and the coverage, so I got him to walk the perimeter with me so I'd get a better idea of where the blind spots were."

"And?" Mac said.

"Two major blind spots where there's no coverage. The first isn't really relevant. It's as you turn the corner into the stable block. There's a section of wall that blocks the view of the yard but literally only for a few feet. The second dark area is more interesting. There's a small back door leading into what was the laundry. It's a bit of a squeeze because that whole block is used for storage and, from what I've seen, some of what's stored there goes back to the last ice age. Well, maybe the last dust age, anyway. But it's possible to get through from there into the narrow corridor at the back of the house that leads into the corridor at the rear of the kitchens. It was originally built so the house owners didn't have to see the staff coming and going with the laundry. The whole house is riddled with these little passageways and corridors. God forbid the owners should catch sight of the people working for them. Anyway, you go down some stairs and then along this really narrow passageway and then up a flight of steps and into a scullery. The door was locked but Robbie says there's several sets of spare keys to be found."

"And how come no one mentioned this before?" Mac asked.

"Oh, a couple of people did. DS Hurst and I went to look but we both assumed anyone going in would be picked up on CCTV but, I don't know, something was niggling at me. I took another look today and I just wasn't so sure the camera was as good as we thought. So, we ran some footage again from the night of the murder and then I walked up to that door from various angles just to see if I could get in undetected. Boss, you don't actually have to try very hard. The problem is, the camera's set quite high so it can record anything coming up the drive. But that means it misses a whole segment of path coming up to the door. It just adds to the ways and means of someone outside coming in. And it turns out they really wouldn't have had to try very hard at being invisible. Robbie's a mite pissed off," he added.

Ringing off, Andy checked his watch. Would Richard Cartmell come back to the house and go to the refectory for lunch? Or was he so annoyed with Alison that he would stay away? It was ten past one and there was no sign of anyone emerging from the Grand Salon, so Andy decided to give him a call.

Richard Cartmell was not happy to be disturbed. "I've just been asked to check a couple of things with you," Andy said. "It'll only take a moment." In the background he could hear voices and the chink of cutlery and glass. Had Cartmell taken himself off to a local café or, more likely, one of the local pubs?

"Well, ask then. But I'm busy. I don't have time for this, whatever it is."

Andy started with the question of collaboration.

Cartmell actually laughed. He sounded oddly relieved, Andy thought.

"Phil was always curious about the way people worked. He wanted to know how I put stories together, how I selected material when I did an adaptation, that sort of thing. We threw a few ideas around, just by way of explaining how I processed everything. I don't know, one or two of the ideas weren't bad so we played with them for a bit and even worked up a treatment for one. But that was it. Phil was busy, I was busy. It went no further. I've probably got what we produced on my computer somewhere, but it was years ago and neither of us was bothered enough to come back to it. Is that all?"

Funny that he didn't ask where I'd got my information from, Andy thought. He took a deep breath. "There have been suggestions that you and Mr Perry were in fact very close for a while. That you may have been in a relationship."

There was a beat or two of silence. Cartmell's tone was cold when he responded. "Grace tell you that, did she? Just the kind of thing she would say."

"And why is that, sir?"

"Because Grace is second only to Phil when it comes to mindless gossip. No, we did not have a relationship. Neither of us, to the best of my knowledge, is gay. Was gay, should I say. And Phil wasn't even a close friend."

"And yet you worked on some projects together."

"And you work on what might be termed 'projects' with other officers. Does that mean you're friends with them or have a relationship with them? They are colleagues. Phil wasn't even that. Now, I'm busy. If that's all." He seemed to assume that it was because he hung up.

Actually, Andy thought, many of those he worked with were friends. Valued friends. And one of them he did indeed have a relationship with. He and Yolanda, now a DC, had been living together for more than half a year.

The salon door opened and hungry cast and crew streamed out. Right, Andy thought, as he came down the stairs and fell into step with Rina Martin, he'd try and have another go at Richard Cartmell later but would do so in person. The writer was rattled — Andy was just not yet certain what about.

* * *

Richard Cartmell stared at his phone, a frown creasing between his eyes. What had that been about? He'd almost forgotten the script ideas that he and Phil had messed about with. It must be about five, six years before. They'd got into a conversation one night about the way stories were developed and the different roles of writers, actors and crew in making that story come to life. The way so much could be conveyed in a single shot. Richard recalled they were both slightly tipsy, happy drunk, uncomplicated, and that Phil had been one of a larger group of people all gathered in a pub, celebrating someone's birthday.

Must have been a mutual friend, but Richard would be hard pressed to remember who. There'd been a great many such celebrations over the years. Not that any of it mattered now.

Phil was dead. Whatever he'd done in the past was irrevocably lost.

Richard turned back to the script revisions he'd been working on. Unable to cope with the hothouse atmosphere of Septon Hall, he'd driven to the next village and was now ensconced in the more pleasant atmosphere of the Fox and Hounds. It was an old-fashioned sort of place, all beams and an inglenook fireplace, the traditional pub sign of a fox being chased to death replaced by one of a fox and foxhound sitting together in an imaginary Olde England landscape. He had discovered this place one night with Judith. They'd had a meal and a good long chat and he'd been back several times since. It had seemed like a better place in which to sort out his current conundrum than his dreary room at Septon Hall.

But Andy Nevins had interrupted his train of thought and, more importantly, interrupted his mood. He glared at the pages laid out on the table, one sheet slowly soaking up a little puddle of spilt beer and wondered if Alison was in fact correct. He was trying too hard, attempting to change too much. Worrying too hard about the absence of Phil from the current scenario.

Phil was gone. No longer a piece in play. He was just going to have to deal with that.

CHAPTER 24

Andy's partner, Yolanda, was one of those people who could start up a conversation with anyone, anywhere. Five minutes in a bus queue and she'd know what everyone did for a living and how many kids they had. Mrs Martin was the same, in a way, always able to worm relevant details out of people. The thing with Yolanda, though, was that she was genuinely interested just because she actually liked people, something her time as a police officer had done nothing to diminish. Andy knew a fair few officers whose view of humanity had been definitely skewed by their experience of the worst of it. Yolanda's certainly had not.

Andy had realized that he had absorbed at least some of Yolanda's technique. He'd been quite a shy teen and lacking in confidence even into his twenties. Being a police officer had helped him develop coping strategies, of course, but being with Yolanda had taught him to actually enjoy people in all their infinite variety and he put that experience to work now.

He had walked into the dining room with Rina and Seth and exchanged a quick conversation, but when he got his lunch he carried his tray to a larger table and asked politely if those seated there minded him joining them. He was soon chatting to half a dozen of the technical crew, asking questions about what they did and how they did it.

Reticent at first, Andy's strategy of showing interest in a subject close to all their hearts warmed the conversation up and by the time everyone had reached dessert, he had a sound working knowledge of what everyone at the table did. Sound man, runner, cameraman, assistant cameraman and two of Theresa's assistants, Kylie and May, who Andy had already met.

"So how is all of this affecting you on a practical level?" Andy said. "Are you having to go back and film scenes again or anything?"

Dave, one of the cameramen, laughed. "Well, you saw Ritchie Cartmell storming off just after you arrived?"

Andy nodded. "He didn't look best pleased."

"No, the silly sod wanted to do a massive rewrite, said it was more respectful of Phil's memory than the idea we just carry on and patch new material in as and when we had to. Well, Alison wasn't having any of it. We're all on deadlines, some of us have other work to move on to and we've only got this place for another five days. After that they've got a conference or something and then weddings all through the summer."

"I hadn't thought of any of that," Andy said honestly. "So, of course the production company only hires the house for a period of time. I didn't know people got married here," he added. "Not sure I'd fancy it. Not sure my fiancée would either."

"Planning a wedding, are you?" Dave asked.

"No, not really. We've been living together about six months and our mothers are both making noises about making plans but we're neither of us keen on big weddings. Costs too much for a start. Yolanda's more an 'elope to Vegas and get married by an Elvis impersonator' type of girl anyway."

Dave laughed.

"Not the posh frock type," Kelly, who had told him she was a runner, asked.

"Not really, no."

"And if she changes her mind?"

Andy shrugged. "Then we buy a posh frock. But I don't think this place would appeal to her very much. We'd probably book the Palisades."

"That's the Art Deco place on the coast?"

Andy nodded. "Has Mr Cartmell got to come up with something else now, then?"

Dave laughed. "So Alison told him. He is not a happy chappy, that's for sure. But I think we'll all be glad to be shot of this. It's not been right from the start."

"You've been involved in other Lydia Marchants?"

"The last three and usually it's a very happy and very efficient setup. Everyone gets on. No dramas. Ritchie can be a bit temperamental, but I suppose that's writers for you."

"He tends to make a big thing about knowing Judith Tavener," someone else commented. "Like that makes a difference."

"Doesn't it?" Andy would have thought it might.

"Well, I'm sure it's nice to have input," Dave said but he sounded dubious. "Thing is, a lot of authors aren't comfortable with the amount of messing about with timelines and even characters that it takes to adapt a screenplay from a book. I'd always assumed Miss Tavener liked to keep her distance, if I'm honest. A few of us were really surprised when she wanted to visit the set. I know Alison wasn't best pleased. We'd had enough delays at it was. Then when the request came out of the blue like it did, well."

"Oh, so it wasn't something that had been planned?"

"First anyone heard about it was about a week before. I mean, she's always sent good wishes to us when we start filming and there's always congratulations and that when we finish. Always sends chocolates and sweets and all sorts of treats when we're ready to wrap. She's always been very sweet about it all. Just never wanted to come and watch before."

"From what I heard she really enjoyed it."

Dave nodded. "I think she did. I'm not sure Richard was so taken with the idea. He put a brave face on it, but I heard him talking to Alison and got the impression he felt his toes were being trampled on. For all that he likes telling everyone he knows the author and values her input, I got the distinct impression he wished she'd do what she usually does and butt out of what he sees as his business." He glanced at the wall clock. "Time to go, folks. Nice meeting you, Andy."

Andy sat for a little longer, watching as tables cleared and people wandered off in chattering groups. Rina came over to him.

"How's it going?" she asked.

"Interesting," Andy said. "Mrs Martin, how well do you know Mr Cartmell?"

"I've been asking myself the same question," she said. "Oh, not just about Richard but about all of the usual crew and players. I've come to the conclusion that it's not as well as I thought I did. We've got used to one another, you could say. The first series when we all got together I suppose we told one another enough to be sure we could all get along. Some of us have formed deeper friendships, at least when we're on set, but if you asked me how many of us actually get together outside the Lydia Marchant experience, well, I'd say it's a pretty low number."

Andy nodded. He took his tray back to the lunch counter and cleared his plates, threw his rubbish away and followed Rina back towards the Grand Salon, but he didn't go inside. Instead, he tried to call Richard Cartmell again, intent on arranging a face-to-face meeting. The phone rang out.

* * *

Rina returned to Frantham that evening with a lot on her mind. After supper with the family she retreated to her sanctuary, the small front room in which her computer was set up, and reviewed the doorbell footage again.

She could not be certain, but the tall figure in the military-style coat was definitely familiar. The coat, the height, even the way the woman moved. It seemed to Rina that she was trying to make herself look small. Rina was almost certain.

What should she do?

Nothing tonight, Rina decided. She needed a little thinking time first. Needed to work out how to approach this before making an accusation. But tomorrow she'd get Matthew to bring her home and then she would go and confront Marcia Trent and give her a chance to explain herself.

CHAPTER 25

Matthew dropped Rina back at Septon Hall early. She was hanging up her coat when Grace Sweetman came in from her morning constitutional. They had not really spoken about Grace's appearance at the public meeting. Rina had got the impression that she regretted her impulse and didn't want to be reminded.

Grace nodded a good morning and Rina said, "Let's hope we have a less fraught day than we did yesterday. Richard was not in a good mood."

Grace shrugged. "He did seem very put out," she said. "Though I think everyone is on edge and I suppose it can't be easy, having to write around someone who's not there anymore."

"I imagine it's not," Rina agreed. "But he does seem to be making a meal of it. I don't think there's a lot to change, not really. He just seems to be taking it all very personally. I suppose he's got a lot invested in the series, professionally speaking."

"I suppose he does. You know, there were rumours about the books," Grace said. "Of course, there are often rumours about successful women," she added bitterly. "How they couldn't possibly have been that successful without a man involved."

"No," Rina told her, "I didn't know." Which is extremely annoying, she thought.

Grace shrugged. She seemed suddenly to be regretting having said anything. "It's probably nothing," she said. "Like I said, you get a successful woman, and people get bitchy." She smiled ruefully. "Yes, I know, I can be a right bitch too."

Rina didn't comment on that. "Rumours about her books and Richard?" she guessed.

"Well, yes. She was in a bad place when she wrote this one. My fault, I suppose. Richard was her friend even back then and it's possible he helped her finish the book. I mean, it's certainly likely he gave her some moral support at least, kept her on track or whatever. But she really was a mess at the time. It's a wonder she could string a sentence together."

Grace looked suddenly very regretful. "Thing is, she really was better off without Tony Emmerson. I knew them both, well before Tony and I had our little fling. He was one of *those* men. Charming on the surface, a total bastard when no one was looking. Well, I've known controlling, self-centred men, I'm sure we all have. All sweetness until you want to do something for yourself, something that takes the attention away from them, so I'm afraid I soon got rid."

I thought he dumped you, Rina thought. Maybe she had been wrong. "And Judith wouldn't have him back?"

"No. I think that was the most sensible thing she's ever done in her entire adult life and I've got to say I think it was Richard who helped her stand her ground."

Rina was still reflecting on this after breakfast. She took a chance on Richard keeping to his usual habit of arriving in the shooting location ahead of everyone else, usually so he'd have a chance to speak to Alison ahead of the day's business. Today they were in the main dining room, a spacious barn of a place with an oval extending table in polished walnut that could at a pinch seat twenty-four.

"How are you?" she asked him as he glanced up on hearing her come through the door.

"Oh, I'm OK, it's just all been a bit of a strain. But I suppose it has been for all of us." He managed an unconvincing half-smile.

Rina nodded. Aware that they might have only minutes before everyone else arrived, she got straight to the point. "You were close to Judith when her husband left? I hear you helped her finish the book?"

He paused in his shuffling of the papers. Looked across at her, a frown creasing his forehead. "Who told you that? But, yes, she was my friend," he said. "I cared about her. She had a deadline and she had bills to pay. When the marriage imploded she just fell apart so, yes, I helped.

"Their marriage had not been happy for years. They had a short holiday here. Back then they had some self-catering accommodation in one of the wings. I think they thought a break might help things. They were even talking about having children, as though that would fix anything. It never does, does it? Just adds to the misery. For the kids, at least."

"It certainly adds to the stress, I think," Rina agreed. "Not that I'm one to judge. I never had children."

Cartmell looked as though he was wondering whether or not to apologize for some unintended insensitivity, but then he carried on. "Instead of repairing the damage, being here, Tony used the occasion to announce that he was leaving her. I can only imagine what it must have been like for her, finding out they were filming this series in a place that had brought her nothing but misery. I think that's why she wanted to come and visit the set. It was like a test for her. Had she really recovered? I think she realized that she had not. That maybe she never would."

Was that what she'd discovered? Rina wondered. This might have been a challenging place to visit, given the history, and it must have taken some nerve to have come back but Judith had seemed quite happy as far as Rina had seen. True, she had seemed a little distracted when they had watched the scene with Lord Ellsworthy and the brooch, but she had recovered quickly enough. This was a woman facing up to her past and doing so with admirable equanimity. Rina held her peace and let him carry on.

"Anyway, Tony left her and she fell apart. I went over one day because she called me, sounding absolutely desolate. When I got there she'd taken pills and drunk a shedload of alcohol. She was sick as a dog. I helped her get cleaned up, and we sat down and talked. She told me she had no idea how she was going to finish the book. That she was at the end of her tether. So of course I helped. I helped my friend. Anyone would have done the same."

He turned to look intently at Rina as though expecting contradiction.

"Of course they would," she said soothingly.

He looked away again, his hands fiddling with the shooting scripts laid out on the table.

"When the series got picked up for television, it seemed like the answer to her prayers, but then she had to produce more books and, frankly, she was still a broken woman. So, yes, I helped her again. You could say I ghost-wrote the next two for her. Not that I ever got any credit or expected any. She got me the scriptwriting gig and for that I'm grateful. You know what it's like, trying to get a steady income in this business. It can make a world of difference when you get something fairly reliable. And I'll do everything I can to make sure this series is a successful as the others have been. That's my job."

The door opened and people began to wander in, ready for the work of the day.

What to make of all that? Rina wondered. How much was true? How much was the way Richard wanted it to be?

What would Mac make of it when she told him later?

* * *

At 9 p.m. Rina left Peverill Lodge, a woman on a mission. Marcia Trent's house was only a few streets away. Rina had been there once, delivering leaflets that they had both been persuaded to post around the town and she recalled it as being an ordinary semi with a nice front garden, defined by a low privet hedge.

Her memory of the place turned out to be accurate though, she noted when Marcia's security light flicked on, the grass had not yet been cut this year — too much rain, Rina thought — and the hedge had grown leggy. For Rina, that just emphasized how out of sorts Marcia must be feeling.

She rang the bell.

"Rina. This is a surprise. What can I do for you?"

It really had been a surprise, Rina thought. Although Marcia had recovered well, she had been unable to conceal the instant of shock when she realized who her visitor was.

"May I come in?"

Marcia hesitated. "It is rather late."

"I know. But what I have to say is important. I promise you it won't take long."

Marcia relented and stepped back from the door. She showed Rina into the smaller of the two reception rooms, with a bay window facing on to the garden. It was a tidy room, with two sofas at right angles to one another, facing a coffee table that was set in front of a gas fire. Tidy, but somewhat soulless, lacking in photographs or ornaments. Even the bookshelves on either side of the fireplace were almost empty.

Marcia must have been aware of her scrutiny. "I don't use this room much," she said. "I suppose I should. It's a nice room. But I've never liked the wallpaper, or the furniture for that matter."

"Those things are easily changed," Rina said. "You can please yourself now."

"Now he's gone, you mean. The books were all his. He sent for them. I was tempted to burn the lot, but that would have felt wrong."

A mix of emotions chased across Marcia's face — pain, anger, relief perhaps. Rina felt sorry for her. She had clearly been hurt and was still hurting a lot. But did that excuse her hurting others?

"I'll come straight to the point," Rina said. "I think you already know why I'm here. Both I and Eliza have received letters. Unpleasant letters."

"Like the ones they talked about at the meeting." Marcia straightened in her chair, lifted her chin and squared her shoulders as though preparing for battle.

She's going to deny everything, Rina thought. But of course she is. "The woman who hand delivered them was caught on a doorbell camera. I think that woman was you, Marcia."

For a moment Marcia Trent froze. Then she laughed. "Oh, Rina, what an accusation! How could you possibly think such a thing? Why would I do a thing like that?"

Rina shook her head. "I can't know what's going on in your mind," she said. "Or why you're doing this, but I think you've been deeply hurt and I think you may just be lashing out. But it won't do, Marcia, it won't do at all."

"Rina, what on earth makes you think I had anything to do with this? You say a woman was caught on camera. Well, I can assure you it wasn't me."

She was wearing a coat like yours, Rina wanted to say. She looked like you, she was tall and slim . . . and she realized just how flimsy that sounded. But she was here now, so she ploughed on. "Marcia, I can show you the footage if you like. I really do believe you posted those letters through my door and I really do believe you sent the rest. I don't know why you'd want to do this, why you'd want to hurt so many people, but—"

"Perhaps some of them deserved it," Marcia fired back and just for a moment Rina thought she had broken through the other woman's armour. That she'd get her to confess.

Instead, Marcia seemed to collect her thoughts. She sighed as though deeply disappointed in Rina. "I think you should go. Look, Rina, I know you're used to carrying out your little investigations and I've no doubt that you've done a lot of good for this community, but you've really overstepped the mark this time. You can't go around accusing people of things they didn't do. That sort of accusation, the sort of gossip it starts, can tear a community apart, as I'm sure you'd realize if you'd stopped to think."

Rina was taken aback.

"I'm sure you've been under a lot of strain lately, with work and with that terrible murder and now you say you've received unpleasant letters. Believe me, I know how stress can knock you for six. When . . . when my husband left, I really didn't know how to handle it, what to do with myself. But really, Rina, there's no excuse for this."

"Marcia, I have you on the recording. Your coat, the way you—"

"Rina, if you definitively had me on that recording you'd have gone to the police. And what about my coat? I don't suppose my coat is so different from the coats lots of women wear."

She took a deep breath, sighed her disappointment again and then stood. "Please go before you say anything else you might regret. I promise I'll let this slide and put it down to a moment of, well, madness, I suppose. I think you should take some time off, I really do. Have a holiday, perhaps."

She smiled kindly and ushered Rina to the door.

"Hope to see you soon, under better circumstances," Marcia said and closed her front door.

A little dazed, Rina began to walk back home. She took the long way round, along the promenade, hoping to collect her thoughts. Well, that had not gone well.

But then, what had she really expected? Yes, there had been a moment when she'd thought Marcia was going to spill the beans, but it had passed so quickly it might never have happened. And, of course, she had drawn exactly the right conclusion — Rina had suspicions but she had no actual proof. So long as she denied everything, she might well stay in the clear. Rina had forgotten that she was dealing with an intelligent woman, albeit one who was behaving in a most inapposite way, and that woman had well and truly called her bluff.

What would Marcia Trent do now? Would she at least take the hint that if Rina suspected her, others might too and so stop her activities? Or would she double down?

What if, Rina wondered, she really had got things wrong?

She dismissed that thought almost as soon as it arose. No, it had been Marcia caught on the door-cam, she was even more certain of that now.

Saddened and worried and with Mac away, contactable only by phone and a murder on his plate, she would have to confide in Sergeant Baker and trust that he could fix things better than she had been able to do.

CHAPTER 26

How often, Mac wondered, was it a dog walker who found a body? This particular dog walker was just sixteen years old, walking the family dog before school because his mum had flu and was too ill to do it.

He had, to his credit, behaved in an exemplary fashion. Checking to see that the woman he had found really was dead and then calling both police and ambulance, just to be sure. Only when he had done that, he told Mac, had he staggered over to some nearby bushes and lost his breakfast.

The ambulance crew had arrived first and, realizing there was nothing to do for the woman lying at the bottom of the tower known locally as 'the folly', had turned their attention towards the lad. When Mac arrived he'd been wrapped in a blanket and given water and was sitting on the tailgate of the ambulance looking cold and scared. His canine companion, middle sized and brownish, nuzzled him anxiously and, as Mac walked over to them both, climbed on to the boy's lap and glared protectively at this newcomer.

"I think she must have jumped. Jumped or fallen," Josh Morelli said. "You think she did? Her head . . . it's all . . . smashed in."

"We'll find out what happened to her," Mac told him gently.

"And you'll let me know? Please. I think I just need to know."

Mac regarded him thoughtfully and decided that Josh was just trying to make sense of the situation. He beckoned Andy Nevins over and asked him to drive the boy home and take his statement.

"What's your dog called?" he asked, stroking the mutt's head and soft, floppy ears.

"Mostly he's called Theo," Josh said.

"Mostly?"

"My little sister calls him Pip. She watched *Great Expectations* on the telly." He hugged the dog close. "I don't think he cares as long as he gets fuss. He was a rescue," he added. "He was just skin and bone, scars on his nose and back. But he's a great dog."

"I'm sure he is." Theo or Pip nuzzled Mac's hand and he saw what Josh meant about the scars, the fur not quite covering what must have been deep wounds.

"This is Andy," he said. "He's going to take you and Theo home and explain everything to your family. Then, if you're up to it, he'll get you to make a statement about what happened. That OK?"

Josh Morelli nodded. A scientific support van was driving up the steep hill. It stopped just behind the ambulance. There was no proper access up to the folly for vehicles. The footpath had allowed the ambulance and now the SOCOs' vehicle to get to within a couple of hundred metres, one set of wheels on the path and the other on the ridged and tussocky grass verge. Andy led Josh down to where he had left his car and the ambulance prepared to turn around and head off to the next emergency.

Mac stood and watched for a moment while the driver did a multi-point turn and then, with the two scene-of-crime officers, he returned to the body.

"Judith Tavener," he said when the lead SOCO asked if they had an identification. "Her name was Judith Tavener."

CHAPTER 27

Later that morning, Mac made his way down the hill towards Septon Hall. The commotion of the ambulance and police arriving would not, he realized, have been visible from the house. Although the folly seemed to dominate the landscape, it sat, in fact, in a shallow dip at the top of the hill. The side of the hill facing the house rose slightly, enough to hide the pathway and the activity from the view of anyone in the house. On the other side of the folly the hill fell away sharply, giving way to bracken and scrub and a copse of deciduous trees. The slow, cold spring meant they were only just starting to green.

Mac took the second path down, towards the house but following the curve of the hill. Today there seemed to be no activity in the Grand Salon so he guessed that filming must be taking place elsewhere in the building.

When, Mac wondered, had Judith gone up to the folly? It could not have been in the daytime or she would have been found much sooner. Dog walkers and people just enjoying the parkland were a commonplace up near the folly. The parkland was open to the public, the estate benefiting from a pay-and-display car park at the foot of the hill, though locals just tended to walk there from the village. They'd had to turn at least a dozen people away just that morning — if Judith had gone straight there yesterday and jumped or fallen from the tower, someone would have found her before now. Mac wondered if the car park might have CCTV. He doubted it.

When the body had been briefly examined at the scene, they had noted that her clothing was damp. A light rain had fallen just before 6 a.m. but hadn't lasted long. The ground beneath her was dry. There had been no rain the night before. Other SOCO and police officers had turned up and the forensic examination of the folly itself had begun.

Andy Nevins had returned, bringing sandwiches and coffee, for which Mac had been very grateful. They had sat in Andy's car for a while and Andy had shown Mac the statement he had taken from young Josh Morelli. It didn't tell them much. He had come upon the body when Theo, running on ahead, had started barking. Josh had gone to see what had upset the dog and discovered a very agitated animal and a very dead woman.

No, there had been no one else around. It was still not fully light and Josh had been scared in case the killer came back. He was glad he'd had the dog with him.

"You ever thought about having a dog?" Andy had asked.

"I don't think I've got the lifestyle for it."

"True. I talked about it with Yolanda and with Mum. She says if we want one it could be half hers. Stay with her in the daytime and come back to us at night. A kind of dog share."

Mac laughed. "I can see how that would work," he said. Any animal looked after by Andy's mum would be just fine, so long as it could get along with kids, the elderly folk Mrs Nevins went to clean and cook for, and the leafleting stints she did to bring in a bit of extra cash. It would certainly get walked.

He thought about the conversation now, as he approached Septon Hall wondering vaguely if Rina had ever thought of having a dog. He imagined there would be competition in the Martin household over who could give it the most treats.

His phone rang. Mac paused to answer it. It was Andy.

"There's a note," he said. "On the parapet, held in place by a bit of brick. It looks like a suicide note."

"Looks like?"

He heard Andy hesitate. "Want me to read it?"

Mac did.

"*I'm sorry, this is all too much, I should not have come back here.*"

"That's it?"

"Yes. It's handwritten on what looks like a page pulled out of a small notebook. Well, I say handwritten, it's more of a scrawl, as though whoever wrote it was distressed and not really concentrating. Or whoever wrote it wanted it to look that way. It's actually pretty hard even to make out the words."

"Well, it sounds vaguely plausible. But it also sounds very convenient, doesn't it? No, Andy, I'll go with the 'looks like' too, for now."

"She does have history," Andy said slowly. "Or, at least, Mr Cartmell and Mr Emmerson tell us she had history."

"Being upset your husband has gone off. Resorting to pills and booze and a drunken phone call. That feels different to jumping off a tower." Mac sighed. "We need collaboration of that first incident. Find out who her GP is, see if she was taking antidepressants. Do we know where she was staying?"

"I know where the film company booked her in. It's likely she just extended her stay there. It's a country house hotel called Laurel Vale, about three miles up the road."

"Let's follow it up. Is Anning there?"

"No, not yet. I spoke to him. DS Hurst is on her way over but he said he was sure we could handle it without him looking over our shoulders."

Mac laughed. "Better prove him right then."

* * *

Andy Nevins had waited until DS Hurst arrived and he had briefed her, then, with her blessing, he drove to Laurel Vale. A quick phone call had confirmed that this was where Judith had been staying. He had acquired an appointment with the manager.

Laurel Vale, Andy thought, sounded like the kind of genteel old people's home that featured in British sitcoms and his first view of the place just confirmed that opinion. The hotel had been a very large Victorian house, with a more modern extension forming an additional wing on the left-hand side as he approached. The building was stone, imposing and possessed three Gothic-looking towers too small to actually function as anything but decoration. The extension had a seventies look to it, though the row of mullioned windows gave the impression of the architect attempting to emulate a Victorian greenhouse or orangery. It hadn't quite come off. At some point a decision had been made to hide most of the blocky wing under a cover of Virginia creeper, which, Andy thought, might look spectacular for a few weeks in autumn but was currently straggly and in need of a prune.

A turning circle at the front of the house also provided parking. Where, Andy wondered, was Judith Tavener's car? The car park at the foot of Folly Hill had been checked but nothing registered to her had been found there. Had someone picked her up from here? A quick glance told him that Judith's Saab was not parked in front of the hotel.

He went inside and asked to speak to the manager.

* * *

Mac had asked that everyone be gathered in the dining room and now a couple of dozen people eyed him warily as he broke the news about Judith Tavener.

"You're saying she killed herself?" Seth demanded.

"I can't yet say what happened," Mac told him.

"Was there a note? Did she explain why she did it?" Seth had one idea fixed in his head and couldn't let it go.

"As I've said, we don't yet know what happened. Only that her body was found just before seven this morning."

"Who found her?" This from Richard Cartmell. He looked pale, Mac thought. Drawn.

"A dog walker," Mac told him.

He was aware of Rina watching him carefully, of Alison gnawing at her fingernails.

"I don't mean to sound crass, but does this mean we have to stop filming?" she asked.

"I see no reason why you can't continue — the scene is a long way from the house. But please keep to the building and don't go wandering around the grounds today in case we have to extend our perimeter. In case we have to conduct a search," he clarified.

He was aware of Rina's reaction as she took in the implications of this but it was Seth who said, "You think she was murdered?"

"As I've said, we're looking at all possibilities just now."

He stood, preparing to leave. "I know this has been a terrible shock, especially on top of Phil Perry's murder. I'll keep you all informed of developments."

"Are we in any danger here?" someone demanded.

Mac looked towards the speaker, a young woman. He recalled she was called Kelly or Kerry and was some kind of assistant.

"I don't believe so," he said.

"No? Well Phil Perry probably didn't think he was in any danger either." She stood. "No job's worth this. I'm sorry, Alison. But I'm off." Then to Mac, "You've got my address if you want to talk to me but I'm not stopping here."

Mac made no move to contradict.

"If anyone else feels they want to leave," Alison said wearily, "then please do so now. I can assure you I will understand."

Looks were exchanged. Two others stood and headed towards the door, heads down. They looked a little shamefaced, but Mac didn't believe anyone would blame them. They were among the younger members of the crew, Mac noted, presumably those with the least to lose. Everyone else, uneasy though they obviously were, stayed put.

Mac assured those remaining that he would ensure regular patrols of the area and then left a few minutes later Alison caught up with him in the hall.

"Are we in any danger?" she asked. "I mean, just what is going on here?"

"It's difficult to say," Mac told her.

"Did she kill Phil? Did she throw herself off the bloody folly because she killed him? My God, this is terrible. I don't know how to handle something like this."

Mac waited while she drew a deep breath and regrouped.

"Right, I know you can't tell me anything, I understand that," she said. "I've just got to get everyone through the next couple of days. Keep it simple, get on with the job, right?"

Mac nodded and watched as she turned on her heel and returned to the dining room.

Keep it simple and get on with the job, he thought. When it came down to it, that was all any of them could do.

* * *

Judith Tavener had been booked in for two nights, paid for by the production company. She had then extended her stay. She had mentioned, the manager told Andy, that it had been a long time since she had been in the area and had enjoyed it more than she had expected.

They'd chatted for a while, the manager told Andy, and Ms Tavener had mentioned that the last time she had been to Dorset her marriage had been ending. Bad memories had kept her away but now that she had finally come back, she felt like she'd been laying ghosts to rest and wished she'd done it years before.

"That's quite a personal thing to tell a stranger," Andy commented.

The manager nodded. "Hotel staff are a bit like hairdressers," she said. "I suppose people tell them random things."

He thought of Trixie Burns and her mother and all the gossip they must accumulate. For a brief moment he considered that Trixie would be in the perfect position to be the poison pen writer, but dismissed it as soon as the thought arose. Andy had been at school with Trixie and knew from experience that if she had anything to say, she'd say it to your face.

He thought about the suicide note, though he really couldn't believe that's what it was. It was an unsigned scribble. Would there be examples of Judith Tavener's signature in her room?

"She was lucky," the manager continued. "Another couple of weeks and we're booked solid. I'm so sorry for what happened to her, she was a very nice woman. Very polite, friendly to the staff."

Andy nodded. "I noticed that you have a security camera looking out into the car park," he said. "If I could look at the recording, I could verify what time she left the hotel. Can guests let themselves in and out at any time?"

The manager nodded. "We have a night porter from eleven until six. It's rare they have to do much but occasionally guests book in late or leave early." She checked her computer. "Sally Tring has been on for the past three nights. Pauly Cooper the nights before. They're both students. We get most of our night staff from UniTemps. I suppose you'll want to speak to them?" She sighed. "OK, I'll get you set up with the CCTV recordings and get someone to bring you some tea or coffee."

The setup at the hotel was more sophisticated than Andy had expected. There were three cameras in all, one pointing into the car park, a fish-eye lens allowing a wide view of the area. The second was in the main reception. A third covered the staff entrance and the door marked 'deliveries' next to the kitchen door.

The system was digital and accurately time coded, to Andy's relief, as that made it possible for him to select specific times and it was possible to view all three feeds on a split screen.

He began with the previous evening, initially preparing to have to run through the entire night. However, he was in luck. The manager returned with tea and biscuits and a phone number for Sally Tring. "If you catch her in the next half hour, she's between lectures. I just called her to see if she was available. Turns out Judith Tavener left around one o'clock this morning, Sally saw her go. Spoke to her."

Andy thanked her. He would have preferred a cold call and not one that had been pre-empted, but you worked with what you had. Moments later, Sally Tring was confirming what the manager had said.

"And how did she seem?" Andy asked.

"Oh, she seemed cheerful. She was a nice lady, friendly, you know. What happened, did she have an accident or something? I was a bit worried about her when she didn't come back but, you know, guests do what they want, don't they?"

"Did she say where she was going or why?"

"No, not where. She said she had insomnia and some-times the only way she could deal with it was to go out for a drive. She said there was nothing more miserable than sitting in bed trying to sleep."

"And she left around one a.m.?"

"Around then, yes. Look, I've got a lecture in a few min-utes, then I'll be going home to get some sleep."

"Are you working a shift tonight?"

"No, three days at a time. We've got a little bed in the back room so we can nap but I don't usually bother. I catch up with my work and watch stuff on my tablet. Then grab a couple of hours before I come in to uni. I work Monday, Tuesday and Wednesday, usually. No lectures Tuesday, so that's good. By the time Wednesday's done I'm knackered, but it's OK. Easier than bar work. I took an extra shift this week because someone was off sick, otherwise I'd not have been on last night. Poor woman, she was ever so nice."

Andy agreed that the night portering was probably easier than bar work and that it was a real shame about Ms Tavener, then settled down to watch the video feed. At one fifteen that morning Judith Tavener appeared in the lobby, exchanged a few minutes' worth of conversation with Sally and then left. The next camera picked her up going to her car.

Sally was right, Andy thought — she'd seemed cheerful. The two women had been laughing at something and Judith was still smiling as she opened the outer door and waved back at the girl in reception.

Her head was up and her movements relaxed and confident as she went to her car. The Saab reversed out of its space and headed down the drive towards the main road. Would she have been picked up on any ANPR cameras? Andy wondered. That really depended on which way she turned. Cameras were few and far between near the hotel, the roads being predominantly country lanes that led to small villages around the locale.

So, the night Phil Perry had been killed . . . had she left the hotel that night?

Andy backtracked to the week before. A young man in reception that evening dealt politely with a couple with a late check-in, just after 11 p.m. Someone came down to speak to him and then left. Andy fast-forwarded, watching the screen intently. Nothing until just before 2 a.m., when Judith Tavener appeared in the lobby.

She looked unsettled, Andy thought. Agitated, even, and exchanged only a few words with the young man. He watched her go as though he too had registered some unease.

She got in her car and drove away and again was lost to view as the drive curved towards the main road.

"So what time did you come back?" He watched some more. Only an hour passed before she was back at the hotel. Was that long enough to have driven to the hotel and killed Phil Perry, then driven back again? She had been wearing a cream-coloured jacket when she left and she was wearing it now. No sign of blood, but then, would you really kill someone while you were wearing a cream jacket?

Andy smiled at the randomness of that thought. No, you'd take it off. The clothes beneath were dark. What if she had blood on them? Though the time of her leaving didn't really chime with when the pathologist estimated Phil had died. She had put it closer to midnight . . . though Andy knew these judgements were often more educated guesses than precisely accurate.

Curious, he ran the recordings for subsequent nights. On three more occasions, Judith left the hotel and went for a drive. Similar times and similar lengths of time for her absence. Maybe driving did just help her insomnia. Maybe she did intend to just go for a drive and come back last night. Maybe she hadn't intended to go to the folly. Maybe someone who knew her habits had summoned her there.

Judith Tavener had been alive and seemingly happy at one fifteen in the morning. By seven a.m. she was dead and, from what Andy had observed and from initial body temp readings, had been dead for a while. Maybe several hours.

He would time his drive back, see how long it would have taken her to get from the hotel to the car park at the foot of Folly Hill. Except, he reminded himself, the Saab was not parked there.

He went in search of the manager and asked to be let into Judith Tavener's room. SOCO would probably be along later, so Andy did not intend to examine much but he should check for a note — a second note, he reminded himself, seeing as one had been found at the folly — and he wanted a look at that jacket.

Judith's room was neat and tidy, clothes put away and the bed made. The cream jacket hung in the wardrobe, not a trace of blood or anything else on it besides a faint whiff of a floral perfume. A diary and a notebook sat on the bedside table. Andy glanced at them before he bagged and tagged them and prepared to take them away. The handwriting in both was neat and almost childishly rounded, as though it had not changed since Judith's schooldays. Could the same person have written the note found at the folly? Possibly, he supposed, if they were violently distressed. But where had the pen and paper come from? There had been no sign of either on Judith Tavener's body nor on the tower and the notepaper used was totally different to the smooth white pages lined in pale blue common to both the diary and the notebook. The note had been written on cream paper lined in grey.

If she'd written it here — and where then was the grey-lined notebook? — how come she had looked so happy and relaxed when she'd gone down to reception? It didn't fit.

A quick examination of the bedside drawer revealed nothing of interest. Andy prepared to leave.

The manager stood in the doorway. "What happens now?"

"Well, as is routine with this sort of thing, it will be treated as a suspicious death unless or until we find out otherwise. So, my boss will likely send someone to do a proper examination of Miss Tavener's room."

"Is that really necessary?"

"I'm afraid so. If you could just keep the room locked in the meantime. And thank you. You've been very helpful."

The manager grimaced, clearly wishing she hadn't needed to be.

Andy drove away, convinced now that Judith Tavener had definitely not jumped from the folly tower. Convinced too that she'd had nothing to do with Phil Perry's death.

Whoever had killed her was someone she knew and trusted. Trusted enough to meet in such a remote place in the middle of the night. That, Andy felt, definitely narrowed the field of suspects.

CHAPTER 28

Rina had felt the need to go home. Work had continued that afternoon but the mood was grim. Everyone just wanted to get through the next few days and then get away.

She had tried to speak to Richard Cartmell to give her condolences for the loss of a friend and collaborator, but he had been short with her — short with everyone, in fact — and had disappeared back to his room to work on the remaining revisions to the script.

She had told this to Alison when the director had come looking for the writer. Alison had frowned. "He's done all the bloody revisions. We don't need any more."

It was unlike her to swear, Rina thought. Alison had headed towards the stairs as though preparing to beard Cartmell in his lair. Then she had turned abruptly away and shouted "Reset", ready to run the scene they were filming for, everyone hoped, the final time. It was a minor scene, Lydia Marchant wanting a word with the gamekeeper about the positions, or pegs, everyone had occupied during a pheasant shoot. Phil no longer being available, the task of replying had been given to Lord Ellsworthy. It should have been a simple fix but everyone was out of sorts and even Rina had fluffed her lines.

By the end of the day Rina had well and truly had enough and was relieved when Matthew arrived.

"You're welcome to come too," she told Seth.

He thanked her. "But no. I've got an invite to the local pub with some of the other crew. We all need a compete change of scene. We'll all be walking down there."

The George was about a mile from Septon Hall, close enough that no one need be the designated driver. She nodded sympathetically, thinking it might be nice to crack open a bottle of wine when she got home. Or maybe two. After all, she would be sharing.

In the car she tried calling Mac. She had tried to contact him mid-afternoon, when she'd taken the opportunity to speak with Matthew and arrange a lift, but the call had gone to voicemail. He answered now but it was clear from his tone that he was up to his ears.

"She didn't kill herself, did she?" Rina asked.

"I can't say for certain, but it seems not. We'll know more after the post-mortem. Look, I've got to go. I'll try and call you later, but if I don't manage it—"

"I'll quite understand."

"This is a bad business," Matthew said.

"It is indeed. Three people quit this afternoon. No one wants to be around another unfortunate death. Everyone is genuinely upset and most are scared."

"Won't that be breach of contract? It won't do them any good when they apply for other jobs."

"I think Alison will try and smooth things over for them. I think she came very close to walking today. I've never seen her so upset and I don't think it was just the news about Judith. The situation with Richard Cartmell is getting very fraught and no one's turning in their best work just now. Whoever declared that the show must go on no matter what never had a double murder to contend with."

"So, Mac is sure she didn't kill herself? On the lunchtime news they implied suicide and that she had a history of mental illness." He paused. "I didn't catch the whole bulletin, but Steven told me someone had interviewed her ex-husband."

"Oh, Mac will be delighted about that. So will DI Anning," Rina said. "It's a real mess, Matthew. I can't see there being a next series, not after this."

He nodded his leonine head. "And how do you feel about that?" he asked.

"Hard to say just now. I feel like I got a second chance at something I thought was history. I'm grateful for that. I feel very sorry for all the cast and crew who'd got used to having a regular gig for the last four springs, but they're all used to things coming to an end. I just wish it hadn't come to this kind of an end. I mean, it's the last book in the original Lydia Marchant sequence, and it didn't get filmed the first time round so it's nice that it got its chance this time. But, frankly, the whole thing is now so sour I feel I'd as soon finish and walk away."

"I can understand that," Mathew said. "In other news, Sergeant Baker says he believes our little efforts with the public meeting have been very helpful. Connections have been made — and I'm quoting him now — that were not evident before. He won't, of course, say what those connections are, but I'm guessing you spoke to him about Marcia Trent?"

Rina nodded. She had confided in Matthew when she had returned home from her failed mission and the two of them had looked at the door-cam footage again. Matthew didn't know Marcia well, but he agreed that she was a possible match.

"I slept on it, as you know, but I managed a quick telephone conversation after you dropped me off this morning. I still feel I handled things badly, but I also think I'm right about her."

"Well, it looked as though Frank Baker now has things in hand, so best leave it to him."

Rina nodded. It rankled, but Matthew was right. "She's done a fair bit of harm," she said.

"So she has and I think a fair bit of harm must have been done to her. Something set her on this path. If she'd suddenly started drinking no one would have thought much about it. Someone might have cared enough to get her to get her to an AA meeting. Turning to alcohol when you're in crisis is almost socially acceptable. Becoming addicted to writing nasty little notes less so. But when you think in terms of harm, how many are killed by drunk drivers every year? How many instances of domestic violence can be directly attributed to alcohol?"

"It's a valid point of view," Rina said.

"Steven has, as requested, opened a bottle of your favourite wine so it can breathe," Matthew said. "It should be perfect by the time we get home."

CHAPTER 29

The CCTV footage from the hotel had been sent to Anning and his team and Andy had supplied the time codes for Judith Tavener's various excursions. On the way back to Septon Hall he had driven various alternate routes to see if he could track down her car but without success. It was possible she had parked her Saab somewhere and been picked up by whoever she was meeting. An alert had been put out, and Andy was content to think that it would turn up before long. He returned to the folly to find Anning had joined DS Hurst and they were about to ascend the tower.

"Your boss has gone back to Frantham," Anning told him. "Sergeant Baker reckons he has a break on that poison pen letter business. I've told him to go and deal with it and then get his backside back here as soon as." He indicated the folly. "Don't get vertigo, I hope?"

"I don't think so, sir."

"Well, you're about to find out."

Andy led the way and was at the top of the tower well ahead of Anning. DS Hurst brought up the rear, looking somewhat impatient, Andy thought. Anning had made hard work of the ascent.

Andy stood by the parapet looking down at the place Judith's body had been found. It was a hell of a long way down. He thought about the way her body had landed and felt even more certain that she had been pushed or thrown over the low parapet and not jumped. The parapet was not high, not even hip height on Andy, the folly having been built before health and safety regulations relating to such matters were put in place. Judith Tavener was shorter. Jumping would have necessitated her climbing up on the narrow ledge. Something he had not been able to see when he'd been on the ground was the fact that the parapet was not only crenellated but topped with angled ridge stones. Not, he thought, an easy ask for anyone, though he supposed if someone was desperate enough it could be done.

But it wasn't right.

"So," DS Hurst asked, "what do you reckon happened?"

"I don't think she jumped. I mean, full disclosure, I didn't think she'd jumped even before I came up here. I saw her on the CCTV. And I've seen the note. Neither that nor the jumping make much sense."

"We'll come back to that," Anning said. "Put it all aside for the moment and concentrate on the scene."

Andy nodded. It was the kind of thing Mac would have said. He took his time formulating his reply. "If she'd climbed up on the parapet it would have been hard to balance, especially in the dark. And it's likely it was dark. It would take a lot of nerve or real desperation not only to climb up here," he patted the ridge stones, "but then to launch yourself off. She'd not have any real sense of how far down. That . . . that would have been hard, even for someone really determined. At least, I imagine it would."

"And imagination aside?"

"Oh, then if she'd jumped, she'd have landed a lot further out. Her body was right at the foot of the tower as if someone had pitched her over and, I think, they'd have had to do that rather than push her. She's shorter than me." He glanced at Anning and Hurst. "She was shorter than any of us, so pushing her probably wouldn't have sent her over. But she was really little — I mean not tall and very slightly built. It wouldn't have been that hard to grab hold of her and pitch her over the edge, would it?"

"No," Anning agreed, "I don't suppose it would. The SOCOs came to the same conclusion. Hard to be definitive, but it's certainly looking as though she came up here with her killer and he threw her off. And I'm going with it being a he, for the moment. Law of averages and all that."

Andy nodded. "She must have been terrified," he said quietly. "There must have been a moment when she realized what he was going to do and then she was falling."

"There you go with that imagination again," Anning said, but he clapped Andy on the shoulder before descending the tower and DS Hurst smiled at him. Andy didn't think either of them were displeased.

CHAPTER 30

"I have to agree with Rina, it could well be Marcia Trent in the door-cam footage and that certainly adds to my own conclusions. Do I have definitive proof? No," Frank Baker said. "We'd have to get a warrant, seize her computer and her printer and see what comes out, and with what we've got so far, I'm not convinced that's on the cards. However, I'm as certain as I can be that she's our writer. We could bring her in for questioning but if I've got this wrong, it will stir up as much unrest as the accusations about the hit and run driver, and I feel we can do without that. My gut says she's the one, the evidence points that way, but . . ."

Mac nodded and, reviewing Frank's evidence, he was inclined to agree. "She has links, either primary or secondary, to everyone we know of who's received a letter," he said. "But that could well be true of other people on our general list of interested parties."

"Of at least three others I've found the same, including, as it happens, our Mrs Martin and Trixie Burns. But Mrs Trent is also known not only to have undergone what you might call a trauma before the letters started, when her husband walked out on her. She's also been known to be involved in very public disagreements with the alleged cat poisoner, two of the errant husbands, and various other recipients, including Mrs Majors. The Majors' garden backs on to Mrs Trent's. Christopher Majors was a keen gardener right up until his death and Mrs Trent had grown that mile-a-minute vine — I forget its proper name — all along her fence. It was smothering his clematis and his climbing roses and, yes, I know it doesn't sound like a major crime, but the man was sick and easily upset and he went round her house one day to complain and then wrote letters to the council to try and get something done."

"From what I've heard, Mrs Trent was not best pleased," said Mac.

"Young Trixie may not be aware that she'd done anything to upset Mrs Trent, but it seems she did. Marcia Trent accused Trixie of laughing at her and maybe she did, but I suspect she was just laughing at the absurdity of the scene. I got this from the alleged cat poisoner, who lives about a hundred yards from Marcia Trent. It seems Mrs Trent came out to watch when he and his cat-owning neighbour were having a bit of a set-to. Cat poisoner — sorry, alleged cat poisoner — not unnaturally assumed that cat owner was the one accusing him in the letter and went to have it out with them. Marcia Trent and a couple of other neighbours went outside, ostensibly to see what all the fuss was about. Trixie was visiting her mum, who lives in the same street, and saw the scene unfolding. Apparently, it all got very dramatic and Trixie thought the whole thing was over the top and tried to get the participants to see how it all looked from the outside. Cat owner admitted to me it probably was getting a little over the top and that Trixie was trying to calm things down. Well, Marcia Trent tried to stoke the fires again, encouraging cat owner to dial the nines and report what was going on and Trixie apparently said something to her about not being so ridiculous. Now, I don't have anything verbatim. You've got to imagine me at that public meeting, listening to a half-dozen people telling me their version of the same incident and none of them pausing to draw breath. Well, you were there the other night, you know how passionate it all became."

Mac nodded again. "And all of your evidence, all of your connections are of a similar nature?"

"I'm afraid they are. Look, I know it's not enough to trigger anything official. We'd not get a warrant to seize anything on the strength of hearsay like this and even if we managed to firm things up a bit, the CPS would chuck it back at us. So, what I thought was we might pay the lady a nice informal visit, make the conversation all hypothetical like, and see what she has to say. We might at least scare her off. She's obviously troubled, but we can't let this go on — but we can't really deal with it by arresting her either, not on the strength of what we've got."

"She may well have been right about the hit and run," Mac said. "Any more on that?"

"Turns out to have been a non-starter. The man she accused is definitely alibied."

"I thought he was having trouble accounting for his time."

"He was, but the landlord of the pub he was drinking at was certain he was still there when the RTI happened. He and some of the other patrons managed to put a timeline together. Turns out the guy was playing darts around the time of the accident. He couldn't recall much about the night because he'd been celebrating getting a new job. Anyway, he hadn't even had his car with him. He walked home. Trouble was his wife was away and there was no one to say what time he got in or to vouch for him that he hadn't got in his car later and gone out drunk. Apparently, the whole accusation fell apart very quickly once our colleagues started digging and they've now got someone else in the frame for it."

"Would have been nice to have known that before," Mac grumbled.

"It would, but when I spoke to the SIO after the public meeting, about passing on any other info we had about the letter, he was just surprised we were even still considering the possibility of a link. To us it was important, to them just one more bit of random paperwork that had been checked out and dismissed."

"Well, isn't that nice?" Mac's tone was sour. He sighed. "OK, so we go and pay the lady a visit and see what reaction we get. When did you want to do that?"

"No time like the present," Frank Baker said.

Marcia Trent's house was just a ten-minute walk from the police station. There was not much, Mac reflected, that was significantly more than that distance in the whole of Frantham. You could stroll from one side to the other in less than twenty minutes. It was already dark because, as often seemed to happen at this time of year, the sky over towards the horizon was somewhat lighter than the heavy cloud settled above the town. They walked together down the promenade, deserted at this time of the evening, and it always seemed odd to Mac how loud their footfalls sounded when the shops had closed for the day. It would all be different by the end of the month, when the tourist season began properly.

At the end of the promenade they crossed the road and headed inland. It was all 1930s detached and semi-detached houses at this end of town and Marcia Trent's house was set back from the road behind a straggly privet hedge and a pocket handkerchief lawn. A light was visible in the front room and a decorative coach lamp came on as they approached the porch. Mac rang the bell.

Ten minutes later, after the formalities of tea, discussion of how she'd seen them at the public meeting and the inconvenience of the wet spring, Frank Baker slowly drew the conversation to the point.

"Obviously," he said, "you know all about these nasty letters that have been sent. Now the Inspector and I have had a talk about this and we've come up with a strategy, and to make our strategy work, we really need members of the public to help out. You see, we suspect that whoever is writing these letters may now feel as though they've painted themselves into a corner, so to speak. That maybe they're finding it hard to stop."

"And what does that have to do with me?" Her tone was frosty now and, Mac noted, her body tense as though waiting for a metaphorical blow.

"I'm not saying that it does have anything to do with you," Frank Baker said. "As I said, the Inspector and me, we've had a chat and we think, hypothetically speaking, you understand, that if the person writing these letters carries on, then sooner or later we or their neighbours or someone who's received a letter will work out who's been sending them. They will eventually give themselves away. That, we feel, could lead to all sorts of drama. If word could be got to the person doing the writing that if they don't stop then the consequences could be very serious indeed, we think that would be a public service. So, we're putting the word out, hoping that the person doing this will stop of their own accord before this turns even nastier than it is."

"Perhaps the people receiving the letters deserve to be upset, have you thought of that?"

"That's not for me to say, nor is it the business of whoever is writing these letters to make that decision, you understand me? It's not for them to act like this. What starts with anonymous accusations can lead to anger, even violence and people taking the law into their own hands, and I don't think anyone in this town wants to be a part of that, do you?"

"And whoever is doing this is committing a serious offence," Mac said quietly. "The Malicious Communications Act of 1988 makes it illegal to 'send or deliver letters or other articles for the purpose of causing stress or anxiety', so anyone responsible for the sending of those letters has committed this offence many times over."

"And you can't possibly think that I have done anything of the kind!" she snapped back at him. "I suppose that Rina Martin has been making her accusations? She came here, you know, all full of herself, accusing me of terrible things. That woman is a pest, can't keep her nose out of anything. And you lot listen to her like she was some great oracle."

"This has nothing to do with Mrs Martin," Frank Baker said. "This has to do with evidence. Mrs Trent, all we are doing is making a number of people aware that this is an offence and it is being taken very seriously. We figure that if we spread that information widely enough within the community then that message will eventually get back to whoever is responsible."

"You said this at the public meeting. Why do you have to come and say it to me?"

"I did," Frank Baker agreed. "And I plan to go on saying it until this business stops."

"So, hypothetically speaking," Mac continued, "if the person responsible should happen to hear about this, should be given the opportunity to think about what they are doing and the possible consequences both for themselves and others, then they might take this to heart and desist. If this person were to stop or, better still, if this person were to come to us and confess, then we could all move on and the incident would soon be forgotten.

"You see, we believe that whoever is doing this, perhaps something happened to deeply upset them. They reacted by lashing out and somehow the whole thing escalated and now is a bit out of control," he added.

Marcia Trent glared at him. "I still don't understand why you've come to me. I think I'd like you to leave now."

"Of course," Mac said, getting up. "Thank you for your time. Mrs Trent, we'll be speaking to several people in the same vein, so please don't think you've been singled out. Our main concern is to put a stop to this business before it gets even more out of hand. These letters have already caused pain and distress and distrust, to say nothing for the potential for ruined relationships and reputations. This needs to end before someone really gets hurt, because if that happens then the time for friendly warnings will be long gone and the time for search warrants and the seizing of printers and computers will begin. Do you have a computer and a printer, Mrs Trent?"

"Of course I do. Who doesn't these days? But this matter is none of my business."

"And yet you came to the public meeting. You must have felt some concern."

"Perhaps I was just sick of these four walls and wanted some company, have you thought of that?"

As they left the house, Mac glimpsed through the door of the dining room a laptop and printer set up on a flat-pack desk. It was at odds with the look of the rest of the furniture, which looked more eighties than contemporary melamine. He made certain that Marcia Trent had observed his taking note. "Thank you for your time," Mac said.

She had closed the door before they reached the front gate.

"You think she'll take notice?" Frank Baker asked.

"I think she'll either cease and desist or one or the other of us will be getting a nasty letter through the post. I think we're both a bit too far out of central Frantham for her to hand deliver." Mac lived in a converted boathouse and Frank had what had once been a farm cottage some three miles from town and down a single-lane track.

"I'll keep an eye on the post," Frank said.

* * *

Marcia Trent was enraged. Her first instinct was to hit out at the two men who had invaded her home and threatened her with police action. She had done nothing wrong! She had merely sought to prick the conscience of those who damn well needed it pricking. All that talk about innocent parties and hurting those who couldn't defend themselves. If there were consequences, then those people probably deserved them. Who were the likes of Frank Baker and that incomer of an Inspector to tell her she was wrong, threaten her with the law?

Eventually, after ten minutes or so of pacing the hall and telling herself that she was justified, she calmed down enough to switch on her computer and look up the law that Inspector MacGregor had informed her she was breaking. She couldn't recall exactly what he'd said but a little bit of searching soon brought it to light.

It was stupid, she thought. Wasn't it just a law against free speech? Against making your opinion of someone known? Wasn't it just telling the truth as you saw it?

She splashed spirits into a glass from one of the decanters on the sideboard, not taking much note of what it was. The brandy caught in her throat and make her cough. She wasn't used to spirits. Her usual tipple was a nice glass of wine.

She knocked it back anyway and slumped miserably in her swivel chair, staring at the computer screen, reason slowly taking hold.

They had come to warn her off, she realized, just as Rina had done, and despite their protests to the contrary she was certain Rina Martin would have spoken to her friends in the police. And, Marcia thought bleakly, she had only herself to blame for that. What had she been thinking, hand delivering those two letters? She knew CCTV in Frantham was patchy and so had never really thought about it as a problem, but she had completely disregarded the doorbell cameras, which now seemed ubiquitous.

She comforted herself with the idea that they didn't have enough evidence for an arrest and they were just bluffing. Was Sergeant Baker telling the truth and they were visiting several people who had been at that public meeting? Maybe they didn't know about her — maybe she was just on a whole list of suspects. Once again she allowed her anger to take hold. She opened her documents folder and her finger hovered for a moment over the template she had set up, so that what she wrote would be positioned neatly in the centre of the page. Both edges of the paper could then be folded across the middle and the missive would not be seen until the recipient had completely unfolded the paper, to be faced with her accusations.

She let her hands drop into her lap.

"You stupid woman," she said aloud. "You've not even covered your tracks."

There it was, in her documents file, the folder that contained everything she had so far committed to sending and a few more besides. She'd taken so many pains to create messages that might be useful, that might be appropriate. That might one day find a recipient. That she could make use of in a hurry, as and when the opportunity arose.

And all for what? All because of what? Because some worthless man she could not get at had caused her to feel worthless in turn.

Suddenly deflated, Marcia Trent felt like an absolute fool.

She got up and crossed to the sideboard and took two letters from a drawer. The first was the note he had written her, telling her how bored he was and that he was leaving but that she could keep the house. It was signed and dated, because he was meticulous like that. He signed and dated everything. It was scarred, of course from where she had slashed it with the knife but, to be frank, her aim hadn't been very precise. The table had borne the brunt of her anger. The letter was only lightly scarred, considering the rage she had been in.

The second had arrived a couple of days ago, from his solicitor. Divorce proceedings had begun and her husband wanted to discuss division of joint property, namely the house.

"Oh, no you won't be getting this place," Marcia snarled. She would make an appointment with a solicitor of her own, show them the letter, dated and signed and oh so cruel. But, more importantly, telling her that he did not want what had been their marital home had stung her deeply. She would fight him tooth and nail and, she decided, she would win.

Returning to her computer, Marcia began to delete her files.

CHAPTER 31

Everyone was subdued and miserable. They went through the motions, turning in reasonable enough performances, but Rina could see her own exhaustion and discontent reflected in the eyes of other cast and crew and it did not make for a good atmosphere.

No real surprise, she supposed. Surely it was only cult, schlocky horror films that were supposed to have murders and mysterious deaths associated with them, not cosy murder mystery dramas.

Rina had seen enough loss and pain in the past few years to last for several lifetimes, but somehow these two murders seemed almost the worst. The deaths of Phil Perry and Judith Tavener had invaded a part of her life that had been only positive and happy up until now.

There were journalists camped at the end of the drive, fortunately out of sight of the house, the sweep of the road-way making it impossible to either see or be seen at Septon Hall. Of course, someone enterprising would eventually make their way through the woods. Mac had told her that they had patrols in case anyone should take that into their head, but she was under no illusions. The grounds of Septon

Hall were extensive, the boundaries porous, comprising a mix of scalable walls, hedges, woodland and not a lot else.

Still, she supposed everyone must just keep on keeping on. Two more brief scenes to go and they could wrap everything up. Or so she thought.

Trouble, not entirely surprisingly, came with the arrival of Richard Cartmell. That morning, at the scheduled start time for filming, he had still not delivered the tweaks required for the purposes of continuity. Rina reckoned she could have made them for everyone involved in those scenes given ten minutes and a red pen and had said as much to Seth, who heartily agreed with her. Alison had practically been chewing the carpet. Rina had rarely seen her more agitated. The cast, eager to be done, was restless. Rina was about to request a red biro and put her suggestion to Alison, if only to get a possible laugh and relieve the tension, when the writer stormed into the room.

"Well, I've made the changes," he said. "Been up half the night. You're going to have to reshoot scene six with Lady Ellsworthy and there are other small changes needing to be done, but you'll see what I mean when you do the read-through."

"When we do what?" Alison's face was red. Fury emanated from every single pore. Alison was not tall, neither was she broad, but in that moment she seemed almost to tower over Richard Cartmell. "Richard, you had three or four lines to change. In the existing script! The existing script, Richard. That was all. No rewrites, no stopping up all night to do unnecessary work. Just three or four lines. Now if you can't do that, I'll damned well find someone who can."

"Give me a red pen," Rina muttered, glancing at Seth. She saw his mouth twitch but he was trying very hard not to smile. This was certainly not the moment for it.

"I beg your pardon." Richard Cartmell was equally incandescent. "If you think this job is as easy as shifting a few words about then you're even more stupid than I thought."

A collective gasp from cast and crew. Rina's eyebrows raised.

"*I'm* responsible for bringing Judith's vision to the screen. Not you, not them. *I* know what her intention was. I know what she wanted me to do. If you don't like that—" He tossed the rewrites on to the floor and stood there, breathing hard, head forward as though about to charge.

Alison, whose personal space he looked about to invade, took a step back. "OK, let's all calm down. Now, look, Judith always said how much she loved the scripts and, yes, that's down to you. But bringing that script to life is a team effort and right now we have the entire team ready to go. Time is money, Richard. We are over time and over budget and we are not reshooting or reworking anything. Now, I'm sure if you take five minutes we can get this business sorted out. Make those little revisions, to the original script, and then we can run the scene. After which we can all go to lunch and know we've got just one more effort to make before we can all go home."

"Those little revisions. Little revisions! You have no idea, do you? You think it's so easy, do it your fricking self."

He turned from Alison, stormed from the room and out of the house.

The company released a collective breath. Alison stood with closed eyes trying to restore her equilibrium.

"Well that was . . . not helpful," Seth murmured.

"No, no it was not."

Rina stepped into the hall and looked out through the upper glazed panels of the oversized front doors. Richard's car stood in the drive, just within view, but he had not gone to it. Instead, he was striding up the hill towards the folly head still down, arms swinging, the rage pouring from him leaving an almost visible trail, like a heat haze in the air behind him. Rina was genuinely concerned.

She ducked back into the formal dining room to retrieve her bag. Several people were now gathered around Alison and seemed to be indulging in a mix of comforting and practical discussions. Dave, the cameraman, always a source of calm, had a hand on Alison's shoulder. Someone else had picked up the papers Richard had dropped and tossed them into a nearby box of leads and sockets. Seth and Grace were glancing through the original script and exchanging thoughts on what could be swiftly improvised. Rina grabbed her bag from beneath the table, took out her phone and went over to join them.

"Richard's heading for the folly," she said. "I think I should follow him. He seems very distressed."

"If he wants to jump off, let him," Grace told her. "No, you know I don't mean that, it's just—"

Rina nodded. "I know. Look, I'm not needed at the moment. Alison needs support and I know the two of you can sort out those few lines between you. I'm worried that Richard is going to do something foolish. Judith's death really does seem to have knocked him off-kilter."

"Are you sure that's wise?" Seth asked. "He's off his rocker if you ask me. Who knows what the man will do? You want me to come with you?"

Rina shook her head. "No, I'll be fine. You see if you can sort things out this end and I'll be back soon."

On the way out she paused in the lobby and, sitting on the stairs as Andy Nevins had done a few scant days before, she called Mac and told him what had occurred. She wasn't sure what he should do about it — Cartmell had not threatened anyone or committed any crime. Had he?

Hesitantly, she confided her worries to Mac, suddenly not sure what she could usefully do if he was heading up to the tower. She knew she'd welcome company up at the folly, whatever Richard had in mind.

"Stay put," he told her. "I've got Andy with me and we've just got to find somewhere to turn around and then we'll be on our way."

"I'm worried about him, Mac. He's dreadfully upset. I don't know what he'll do."

"Please, Rina, just wait until we're there. We'll go up and advise him that the folly is still a crime scene, talk to him, see what's on his mind."

"Is there anyone on guard?" she asked hopefully.

"No, I think not since last evening."

"All right, I'm heading up to the folly as well," she said. "I'll meet you there. I've known Richard for a long time. I might be able to get through to him and calm him down."

She retrieved her coat from the stand in the hall, tucked the phone into her pocket and left Septon Hall. Well, she thought, it had been fun while it lasted. She had no doubt this would be the end of the Lydia Marchant Investigates series. Who would have any appetite for it after all this?

* * *

"What to make of that?" Andy said. "His behaviour's become more erratic over the past few days, I know that. When I was there a couple of days ago, everyone was talking about it. Apparently, he's normally really easy-going. Everyone just assumed he was upset over Phil's death, but what if it's more than that?"

"There's a farm gate just up there," Mac said. "I should be able to swing around. What did you make of him?"

"I don't know. Angry, irritable, but the whole company was fractious and no real surprise about that. I got the feeling he was used to getting his own way and that was because he was good at what he did, rather than him just being an awkward sod. From what people said, Judith really rated him and everyone thought he'd done a good job on the scripts. Maybe he is just upset. Maybe he just needs to sit down with someone and talk it through." Andy sounded doubtful even as the words formed.

"You don't believe that, do you?" Mac said.

"I spent time with everyone the other day. The impression I got was that people genuinely liked one another. That Phil was annoying at times, but that he was fine, in a general sense. No one could really understand how or why he'd been killed. I wasn't there when you came to tell them Miss Tavener was dead, but they'd have been shocked, I'm sure.

235

Several people said how nice she was and I got the impression everyone liked working on the series." He shrugged. "Cast and crew were a bit jumpy. That was understandable. They were looking after one another, checking in on one another. But Mr Cartmell seemed sort of separate from that. Everyone's different though, aren't they? And he and Judith Tavener seem to have had a very long history."

Mac, having executed the awkward turn, agreed that they were. "I wasn't present when Cartmell was interviewed," he said. "Were you?"

Andy shook his head. "No, and I only spoke to him a few times and at least two of those was on the phone. He was irritated, said he was busy, and I'm sure he was. Most people will go out of their way to make a good impression on a police officer. Apart from the habitual arrestees, of course, who don't give a damn — it's all part of their everyday life. But most members of the public only have to talk to us when things go badly wrong and usually they want to make the right impression, the 'it's nothing to do with me, Officer' impression. They tend to try too hard to be whatever they constitute as normal, or think we'd constitute as normal. I got the feeling he didn't really care."

Mac nodded and put his foot down.

* * *

Folly Hill was hard work. Septon Hall was in a dip where the landscape flattened out, spreading behind the house into formal gardens and then parkland and wood. The hill, at the front and slightly to the east, sheltered the hall from the prevailing winds that cut across the scrubby moorland landscape beyond. Not that it had made much difference in a spring where the rain had lashed down with equal vehemence wherever you happened to be.

The path up the hill rose gradually at first and then, as it began to loop around the hill, grew steeper and more challenging. Rina, walking quickly, wished she'd grabbed one of the walking sticks from the dragon vase in the lobby and then remembered that they were no longer there. They had all been taken by Forensics.

She trudged on, pausing occasionally to catch her breath and to look up ahead to try and see where her quarry had gone. He'd not had much of a head start on her, but he was younger, fitter and taller, with a much longer stride, and she had lost sight of him before the path began to curve around the hill. Her assumption had been that he was heading towards the folly, but what if she was wrong?

As the top of the hill came into view, Rina paused again. The folly rose above her, a round tower, windowless and austere, crowned by a crenellated parapet. She'd been in it once and knew that there was a room at the bottom, large enough for a small table and a couple of chairs. She had heard suggestions that it had originally been used for picnics and tea parties, but Rina really couldn't see that. Small and gloomy, even a tête-à-tête would have been cramped and dark.

The police tape across the door had been ripped away and the door was open.

A spiral staircase led upward and a hatch gave access to the flagstoned area at the top. The views were impressive, Rina would allow that, but she wasn't so keen on what she felt was a far too insubstantial parapet. On Rina it had been about waist-level, and she doubted it would even come up to Richard Cartmell's hips.

Notices in the lower room and on the parapet warned visitors that they entered the place at their own risk. She'd been surprised to find that it was open to the public at all but Robbie, the estate manager, had explained that public access to the parkland, the folly and the so-called temple by what had once been a walled garden, had been agreed with the local council in return for the estate receiving various grants and revenue from the car park at the foot of the hill. She had wondered if the cost of public liability insurance wiped out any profits that it might generate, but she'd not bothered to ask.

Looking up at the tower she saw a figure leaning on the parapet, braced on straight arms and looking down at her.

"I'm coming up," she told him, tilting her head back in an attempt to read the expression on his face. Taking the absence of response for consent and knowing Mac was going to disapprove, she began to climb the winding stairs to the top.

She arrived to find Richard Cartmell still standing where she had seen him, staring down at the ground.

"I'd feel much happier if you stepped away from there," Rina told him. "I've no great head for heights and you're making me feel queasy."

He laughed. "I didn't think you had any weaknesses. Not the great Rina Martin." He smiled, as though to show he meant no offence, and he also pushed away from the parapet and turned to face her.

"Oh, you'd be surprised how many I've got," she told him. Though vertigo was not actually one of them. "Don't we all? Richard, I'm worried about you. Are you all right?"

"Am I all right? Well, I suppose that's the question, isn't it? You know, Rina, I'm not sure I am."

"Come back with me now, we'll have a chat with Alison. Get things back on an even keel. She's upset that you argued, you know."

"Is she? I doubt that, Rina. But at least I know where I stand now. I did want to think she valued me, that she trusted me to do a good job, but it seems not. Hours, I spent, coming up with a solution. More or less a complete rewrite of some of the scenes. And I get it all thrown back in my face."

"Alison has to keep to budget," Rina said. "It doesn't matter that she might want to go with what you've done, you know she can't. She'd lose her job and you would too and then where would we all be?"

"Well, I think I've well and truly lost mine, so what does it matter now?"

"And if you come back with me, we can find a way to fix things. To sort it all out."

He sighed, looked beyond her to where the house lay hidden in the valley. "I think I've gone way beyond anything that could be fixed by tea and polite conversation," he said. "I think you know that's true as well as I do."

"Perhaps," Rina acknowledged. This, she felt suddenly, was nothing to do with Alison or the scripts or Lydia Marchant. "Perhaps we can avoid things getting any worse," she said cautiously. "Richard, did you have something to do with Judith's death? Did you have something to do with Phil's?"

Richard was silent for a few moments and she got the impression that he was considering her words. Eventually, he said, "We talk about moments of madness like they're happening to someone else or at least to some other part of ourselves. About being unmoored, dissociated, lost. We talk about not being ourselves when something we do seems like it's out of character. But is it? Is it really?"

For a moment he just stared at her. "I was worried about her coming here," he said. "I told her, 'Grace is going to be here, this is a place full of bad memories, just don't come. Wait until we're filming somewhere else. Visit the set then, it'll be a more positive experience.' I was worried she'd have another breakdown. I genuinely thought it would be too much for her."

"I have to say, she seemed fine to me," Rina said.

"Seemed fine, yes. Do you really think she was? She told me that was the point. She wanted to confront the past, she wanted to prove to herself and to me that she wasn't the broken woman she'd been when Tony left, that she was stronger than that."

He stepped away from her, looked out over the open countryside and she wondered what was going on in his mind.

"Richard," she said, but he just shook his head, seeming unable to respond.

* * *

"I'm fine, Richard," she'd told him. "I feel good. That woman, well she's just another actor playing a role in one of my books."

"One of my adaptations of one of your books." He'd laughed, but he'd actually felt hurt by her implied lack of inclusion. She may have written the book, but he'd brought it to life on screen. "Besides — it wasn't exactly your book, was it?" he'd said softly. "You couldn't finish it. I wrote the final third for you."

He remembered her gentle but painful rejoinder. "You helped me, Richard, and you know how grateful I am for that. But I wrote the book. The book is wholly mine and you know that as well as I do."

"She seemed fine to me," Rina told him again, breaking painfully into his thoughts. "I think she did the right thing, coming here, confronting the past, making peace with it. It took courage, but she did it."

"No . . . no she didn't," he insisted. "I could see she was breaking up inside even if no one else could. I could see it was all deceit. She was fooling herself, Rina, and I knew she'd fall apart again and I'd have to be there to pick up the pieces."

"Perhaps that's what you wanted," she said and in that moment Richard hated her as he'd never hated anyone.

How could she say that? How could she accuse him of that?

He dipped his hand into his pocket, removed the folding knife he kept there and opened the longest blade, waved the weapon in Rina's direction. He was gratified to note her surprise, to see her take a step away from him. It wasn't a formidable weapon, he knew that. Just a multiblade utility knife complete with two blades, scissors and a small screwdriver, but it got his point across.

"I cared about her. I helped her. Even when she never acknowledged that, I went on helping her. You know I wrote this book. Or practically did. She'd never have finished it if it hadn't been for me. And then the next two. She was still sick, still unable to get by on her own. She'd talk to me every day before she started writing and I'd check on her every night. She couldn't have done it without me."

"That's not the same as writing the book," Rina told him, her tone sharp. "That's a friend being a friend. Keeping a close eye on someone you care about because you know they are struggling. All credit to you for being a good friend, and all credit to you for turning these stories into very fine scripts, but you can't claim more than that. The books were Judith's."

He felt his anger rise up, so powerfully it almost choked him. That was what Judith had said. That was what had enraged him so much. He thought back to the conversation they'd had in the props department on that fateful night before Phil had stuck his nose in.

"You helped me so much and I've always been grateful, you know that. It was good to have someone to read my day's work, to bounce ideas off. To keep me on track, but, Richard, you didn't write my books. Not ever. Not even *Murder at the Folly*. You're right that I'd not have delivered on time if you hadn't been there to keep me at it, but I'd have got there eventually."

"And the next book? You used at least two of my plot points in that one."

"I used a couple of ideas we'd discussed, yes. But, Richard, think about what you're saying. You teach workshops, we've both of us done that many times. If you throw an idea out there and a student runs with it, makes something of it, that piece of writing becomes theirs, no matter where the original idea came from. Look, I've done masterclasses where I've given an opening paragraph to fifteen different people, so they all start in the same place. By the time they've all written the next paragraph, they're all off and running in different directions and the outcome of every piece of work will be unique. That's what's so special about it. About the process. You'd not claim to own any of their stories just because they'd riffed on an idea you'd put out there, any more than I would."

"This was different, you know it was."

"I know I'm grateful and I've shown that gratitude over and over again this past decade and a half. I wanted you

241

on this project and I fought hard to get you. It wasn't easy, Richard. They had other, much more experienced screenwriters on their shortlist. I've always said how good a job I think you've done. What more can I do?"

He closed his eyes, remembering what had happened next.

* * *

Rina watched the man standing opposite her on the tower, the pocket knife clutched in his hand. A strange thought entered her head that somehow it would be embarrassing to be stabbed by a knock-off Swiss army knife. But a knife was a knife and she had no illusions about what damage it could do in the hands of a man who was definitely unhinged. Though, on balance, she was more concerned about the parapet at the top of the tower. She had no doubt in her mind now that Richard had been responsible for Judith's fall, either intentionally or by some accident that Rina could not quite visualize. She had no doubt too he could do the same to her, the only difference being she doubted Judith would have even considered the possibility when she came up here with him.

Unhinged, she repeated to herself. That was yet another way of saying you were separated from where you should have been. He was right about that. Unmoored, untethered, unhinged, dislocated, cut loose . . .

More usefully, as far as Rina was concerned, Richard seemed momentarily to have absented himself, his thoughts having turned inward, away from Rina.

She began to move slowly, inching towards the hatch.

"Stay where you are!"

Rina sighed. So much for that idea. The sound of a car engine cut through the quiet, broken only by birdsong and the sound of the wind in the trees. Was that a car in the car park at the bottom of the hill? Had the stiff breeze carried the noise? Rina didn't think so. She allowed herself to hope. The noise of the engine ceased and Rina remembered that whoever was driving would only be able to get so far up the hill before the terrain became too uneven. The rest of the journey would have to be made on foot. It must be Mac. What did he plan to do?

She put the possibility of rescue to the back of her mind. It was her job to stay alive until help got there and hopefully talk Richard Cartmell back to himself.

"Did you kill Phil Perry?" she asked.

Cartmell looked sharply at her, then nodded miserably. "Stupid idiot could never leave well alone. You know that second door, the one blocked off by those big shelves?"

"Yes. I think it was the door to the housekeeper's parlour."

"Probably. Whatever. Anyway, he told me that he'd opened that so he could listen. He'd spotted me going in there with Judith and was curious. Of course he was — when was Phil not sticking his nose into someone's business? Apparently, the bookcase blocks the door so no one can go through but it's not right up close to it. There's a tiny gap. He opened the door and he listened. I mean, only Phil would have discovered that, wouldn't he? That was really the kind of mindless thing he'd find out. Well that got him killed if you must know, because after Judith had gone he waltzed in and he was laughing. He said something like, 'Well she really put you in your place, didn't she?'"

He remembered how furious he'd been. How humiliated he'd felt that this little nobody of an actor should actually laugh in his face. Should have witnessed his humiliation. Had Phil not arrived he'd probably have followed Judith, had things out with her for good and all. They would have shouted at each other for a while, perhaps, but they would have come to an agreement. It would all have been fine.

"Judith had been playing with that damned brooch. Fiddling with it, opening and closing it like she couldn't keep her hands still."

"Like someone clicking a pen," Rina asked.

"Yes, exactly that. I just can't stand it when people do that. I took it off her. I'd been about to put it back in its proper place after she'd gone but suddenly he was there. That little idiot — and he was just so pleased with himself. He'd got a secret. He'd found something out. I just knew he'd be spreading it all over by morning. I started to go towards the door. I told him to stop. I told him I was going to my room. I managed to get past him, but he wouldn't let up."

He's rehearsed this story, Rina thought. He knows he's going to have to tell it to the authorities at some point. He wants to be word-perfect for when he does. He's trying, in his own mind at least, to make this Phil's fault.

"And then what happened?" Rina asked. She had again edged a few inches closer towards the hatch and this time Cartmell did not seem to have noticed.

"The fool was practically wetting himself, he was so happy. Dancing on the spot. Laughing in my face. Before I knew what I was doing I lashed out at him and before I realized what had happened, he was on the floor, the pin in his throat and I just couldn't believe what I'd done."

"He'd fallen backwards in the doorway to the props room," Rina said. That was where she had seen Phil's body but suddenly it was important to have all the details clear in her head.

He nodded. "He was on the ground, thrashing about. You know what, he reminded me of some big fat beetle that had got stuck on its back and was thrashing its legs around trying to turn over. You know, Rina, I just couldn't bear it. The thrashing and the flailing, I just wanted it to stop. So I made it stop."

Rina swallowed, the taste of bile rising in her throat, making her want to vomit. She shifted closer to the hatch. Could she make a run for it? "So what did you do?"

"I reached around the doorway into the props room and I took a walking stick off the shelf. I rammed my foot down hard on his chest and I pinned one of his hands to the floor with the end of the stick. But I couldn't do anything about his other hand. He was grabbing at my trouser leg, grabbing at my shoe. It seemed to take for ever for him to stop."

Rina closed her eyes, just for an instant. In all likelihood it would only have taken minutes for Phil to have bled out, but it probably felt like much longer for both of them. For the man choking on his own blood and for the man waiting for him to die.

"And then what?" Her voice was shaking now and there was nothing she could do about it.

"I tried not to walk through any blood and I left. Then I realized I was still holding the walking stick. I was in the hall by then and so I wiped it down with a tissue and put it in the stick stand. Then I went down into the basement and I burned the tissue and my shoes and trousers in the furnace. I'd even cut out the zip so there'd be nothing left for anyone to find. I dropped it in the rubbish bin in the pub toilets the following day. I just hoped no one would see me as I went back to my room. No one did. But then I realized I'd left the stick in the stand and it would be needed for the next scene we were shooting. I had to go back down and take the stick back to the props room. I had to be so careful to avoid the blood when I reached over his body to put it back on the rack."

"What made you think we'd still be filming the day after a murder?" Rina asked, surprised that he should believe that.

Richard shrugged. "I don't suppose I was thinking by then, not really."

Rina sighed. "You know you put the wrong stick back."

"I did what?"

"The wrong stick. There was one in the stick stand, very similar to the one in the props room. You put the wrong one back."

A short bark of laughter burst from him. "I even fucked that up," he said. "Even something as simple as that."

For a moment they both fell silent, Rina straining to listen for any clue that the car she had heard a few minutes before really had heralded Mac's arrival.

"Did you kill Judith?" Was it wise to ask? Probably not, but she could no longer avoid the question. Wrong move.

Cartmell lunged for her. Rina jumped back. She'd made it to the top of the stairs before he grabbed her wrist with his free hand and dragged her across to the furthest side of the tower platform.

He then stepped back, holding the knife towards her, maintaining his grip on her arm. "Just stay put and shut up."

She could see in his eyes that he did not really know what to do next, but that he would kill her if he had to. After all, he had killed twice already. She didn't think the knife would be his weapon as he was waving the little blade around aimlessly. If he wounded her, it would most likely be by accident. But he had pitched Judith from the tower, she was certain of that, and there was nothing to stop him doing the same to her.

To her surprise, anger had now largely replaced fear. Anger at the stupidity of this man, at his description of Phil as some kind of helpless beetle, of his simple incompetence when it came to not even noticing which walking stick he'd used to pin his victim to the floor. Absurd thoughts, she knew, but better than giving in to fear. She could see that Richard Cartmell was dealing with some inner struggle of his own and was suffering from a kind of indecision. He had come up here to do what? To kill himself? Maybe that thought had crossed his mind but Rina thought it more likely that he had simply been drawn back to the place where he had killed his friend.

Gently and as calmly as she could, Rina freed her arm from Cartmell's grip and took a step back. She was close to the parapet now, too close for comfort, but she felt she now had a little room for manoeuvre should he lunge for her, something she'd not had while he'd had hold of her arm.

The fact that he'd allowed her to step away, had allowed her to peel his fingers from her wrist, made her feel like she'd also gained some more important distance than just a few feet of space between them.

Come on, Mac, Rina thought. I need you here, now.

* * *

246

Mac and Andy had driven as far as they could towards the folly before increasingly rough terrain had threatened to ground the car and they'd had to get out and walk. They circled slowly, keeping out of sight of anyone on the top of the tower, using trees and shrubs and the line of the hill for cover.

From his position tucked into the treeline, Mac could now see both Rina and Richard Cartmell. He seemed to have hold of her arm, gripping her tightly while his other hand waved wildly, agitatedly. Was he holding something? At this distance, Mac could not be sure.

"Doesn't look good," Andy said. "What do we do now?"

They watched as Rina freed herself from Cartmell's grip and moved a few feet away. Mac willed her to move further but guessed she felt she could not without reigniting Cartmell's ire.

"I'm going to move around to the front and get inside," Mac said. "Backup is on the way, but I don't think we've got time to wait. This could escalate quickly."

"And what do I do?"

Mac pointed to a spot at the opposite site to the entrance. "You stand over there and you create a distraction. Try to get him talking. Anything to stop him seeing me when I come through the hatch at the top. Once I'm up there, I should be OK, but I don't fancy getting shoved back down those bloody stairs."

Mac had never been to the folly but Andy had. He'd described the steep and narrow ascent and what Mac was likely to see when he got to the top in as much detail as he could, just in case his boss should have to go up. They had both recognized the possibility and now it had become a reality.

Mac had called in backup while they had still been en route, but that would have to arrive, would have to tackle the hill, would have to ascend the final stage on foot and all of that would take time.

Rina seemed to be talking to Cartmell now and the man seemed to be listening. Mac slipped back into the woodland so he could circle round without being seen while Andy moved out on to the hill, taking up position where Mac had indicated. A moment or so later, he started shouting up at the man on the tower.

Mac took the opportunity to make a run for the doorway and dashed inside.

* * *

"Mr Cartmell, Mrs Martin, Alison said I might find you up here!"

Both Rina and Richard Cartmell looked down in surprise. The young police officer was standing a few yards from the foot of the tower and waving excitedly.

"I bet it's a great view from up there," Andy shouted up. "Look, I came to ask a few more questions but everyone's busy. I thought I'd come up and find you both and we could all walk back together. It'll be lunchtime by the time we get there. I don't mind admitting I'm ravenous after the climb up that hill."

"You're always ravenous," Rina shouted back. She cast a look at a very confused-looking Richard Cartmell. "I don't know where you put it all."

"That's what my mum says," Andy responded cheerfully. "You all right coming down, Mrs Martin? It's a bit steep."

"Cheeky young beggar," Rina said. "I'm quite capable, thank you, Andy." Though she had to admit, the climb up had not been fun. So, Andy was here and was presumably providing a distraction for whatever Mac was doing. Mac had told her that the two of them were together in the car. Rina's hope soared that this would all soon be over.

"Shall we go down?" Rina asked.

Richard Cartmell glared at her as though she'd gone mad. "Down? No! What's going on?"

It was dawning on him, Rina realized, that there was more to this scenario than a friendly young police officer suggesting they all go and get some lunch.

"What's he playing at?" Cartmell growled. He swung around and made a grab for Rina but she was ready for him this time. She knocked his hand aside then retreated rapidly towards the hatch. She had no illusions about being able to get to the stairs and close the hatch behind her, there was far too little room for manoeuvre up there on the roof and Cartmell would never be more than a couple of bold steps away.

"He's just talking, Richard. He's just being friendly. Andy's always friendly. He's a lovely lad."

"He's a police officer," Cartmell yelled at her. "You brought him here, didn't you? You knew what I'd done and you brought him here."

"If I'd known what you'd done, would I have come up here?" Rina protested. "Richard, see sense. I knew nothing. I came up here because I was worried about you."

He lunged for her again and Rina backed away, horribly aware that she really had nowhere to go. Andy was still calling to them, trying to keep his distraction going. Mac, Rina thought, where the hell are you?

In the distance the sound of sirens interrupted her thoughts and, more to the point, interrupted Richard Cartmell in the act of reaching for her again. And then, as he turned his head in the direction of this new and threatening noise, Mac appeared at the top of the steps and charged at the other man. Rina, only a pace behind, grabbed Cartmell's arm and shook the knife from his grip even as Mac brought him down.

"Tell Andy to get up here," Mac shouted, but it seemed Andy had pre-empted his boss. Rina could hear him thundering up the stairs.

Cartmell lay on the flagstones, face down. Mac knelt on his back, pulled Cartmell's arms tight against his body and pinned him down. The knife he had been waving at Rina now lay close to the parapet wall. Rina found herself standing guard over it, as though concerned its owner would find a way to free himself and seize the rather ineffective little weapon again.

Andy knelt down and helped Mac get their suspect back on to his feet, cuffing his wrists firmly behind his back.

"What were you thinking, Richard?" Rina said. "Just how did it get to this?"

But he hadn't been thinking, had he, she realized. Something had happened that had not been under his control and he had reacted. A man had died and after that his course had been set.

EPILOGUE

A few weeks later a skeleton crew reconvened at Septon Hall to film the final scene of *Murder at the Folly*. Rina was glad when it was over. The mood had been sombre and even though the weather throughout May had been perfectly pleasant, on that day the sky was suitably grey.

"I'm guessing this is the end of things," she said to Alison as they sat drinking a last coffee together.

"No reason why it should be," Alison said. "I mean, you've seen the news coverage of all this. It's been crazy. You know what they say about publicity, and it looks like there are moves to recommission. Of course, they'll need another scriptwriter and permission from Judith's estate, but I can see it going ahead."

"I'm not sure I want that," Rina said. "But there's a new Lydia Marchant, I hear?"

"Nothing's been decided yet," Alison said. "Nothing may happen. But there's talk about taking the stories back from the 1950s and putting a spin on Lydia when she was young. Maybe back in the twenties? Apparently, it was something Judith thought about at one time. Her ex-husband found a few outlines among her possessions and—"

"What was her ex doing, firkling among her possessions?" Rina asked.

"Well, it seems, when they separated he accidentally took a box of her old papers with him. He claims to have asked her if she wanted them back and she said no, so he just put them in storage."

"Convenient for him," Rina growled. "But it would be hard to prove otherwise. I suppose her heirs could challenge him."

"They could, but he's spoken to the solicitor and in principle an agreement's been drawn up. Everyone would profit." Alison looked away, sipped her coffee. "In the end it's not just convenient for him," she said reluctantly. "The production company is talking about a reboot. Still Lydia Marchant but separated a bit from all this. It may not happen, Rina."

"Oh, I'm sure it will." Rina said. She felt bereft at losing all of this again . . . and more than a little relieved that she could walk away with no sense of responsibility remaining. Whatever happened next, if it all fell apart, it would be nothing to do with her. If it succeeded, it would be a completely new cast and writer and crew that would make it work. It was no longer her concern.

"I hope you're involved," she said to Alison. "You've always done a proper job."

Later that same evening Mac came to see her. He had been speaking to Judith's solicitor about the contents of her will and various contracts and business papers she had lodged with him.

"It seems that she was grateful enough to Cartmell that she ensured he received a percentage of the royalties and residuals from the TV show," he said. "Even for the books he absolutely had no hand in. And, of course, he and Judith drafted new plots together to fill in the years the books didn't cover, but she never claimed any income he derived from anything he did with that material. Judith went out of her way to make sure he was adequately compensated for everything he did and he would also have received a bequest in her will. The only thing she dug her heels in on was her individual rights of authorship on the books."

"Understandable. From what he told me, he provided a listening ear and emotional support, but she did the writing."

"I suppose we'll never know the truth of it," Mac said. "He's now insisting that he wrote most of *Murder at the Folly* and the subsequent two. Did you know that he and Judith were an item for a while?"

"For real, or is this just another Richard Cartmell claim?"

"No, apparently for real. I've seen photographs of them together when they were all much younger and Tony Emmerson reckons he was the reason they split up. Then, of course, he eventually left her for Grace and Richard came back on the scene. Though just as a friend, even though he may have wanted more. Emmerson's at pains to point out that Judith and Cartmell's relationship was never serious, though. It seems important to him for us to know that she had better taste."

"Hmm," Rina said. "Well, I think we'll beg to differ on that one. But it does mean that Richard was rejected in two ways, doesn't it? Both personally and professionally. It must really have stung, especially when he stepped up each time she needed him. He must have been carrying a torch for her all these years, maybe hoped that one day she'd start seeing him as more than a good friend and a shoulder to cry on again.

"Do we know how she came to be up there with him?" she asked. "For that matter, do we know how she came to meet him in the wardrobe room that night? Did she come back to Septon Hall later on?"

"According to Cartmell, she didn't actually leave when you thought she did. She visited the wardrobe room, when you were there, but later, she and Richard sat in his room for a while, talking through plans for the next series. She decided to leave around 11.30, which we know from other witnesses, which is around the time Phil finished playing pool and left the billiard room. Cartmell came down with her to walk her back to her car. It was dark by then, and he brought up the whole 'give me credit for co-writing your books' argument again. Anyway, the discussion very quickly got heated. They were passing the wardrobe department on the way out and he persuaded Judith to go where it was quiet and discuss things further or, as he put it, to give them both space to calm down before she drove off. He seemed to have been genuinely worried that if she drove off, still upset, she might not drive well. He insists she had no idea Phil was eavesdropping."

"What about when she met Richard at the folly?"

"That wasn't just something she did the night she died. It had become a favourite place of theirs. He says she liked to look at the stars and if you've got a decent torch the path up is not too bad. She'd met him there before, apparently. At night. You know she suffered from insomnia?"

Rina nodded.

"Well, that last time, it seems he confessed to her that he had killed Phil Perry. He told her it was an accident but he didn't think she believed him. I imagine that led to an argument and then to her death. CCTV at the hotel matches when Cartmell claims they met previously and also on the night she died. We finally tracked down her Saab. He'd moved it from the car park the night she died and driven it a couple of miles away, down a farm track and into a copse, then walked back. He wasn't certain of the location, said he'd got lost walking back to Septon Hall, but we located it eventually. Not that it adds much to the story."

"I imagine when she realized he had killed Phil that she wanted him to go to the police."

"Exactly that. They argued and he says she fell. The post-mortem doesn't support that, but the jury might give him the benefit of the doubt. He says he panicked and wrote the suicide note just after she fell. He's a writer — I suppose he'd always have a notebook and pen to hand.

"We'll certainly get him for Phil Perry and with luck the jury will see through his story about Judith Tavener."

Rina nodded. "I'm being traded in for a younger model," she told Mac.

"I'm sorry? What?"

Laughing, Rina told him about the proposed Lydia Marchant reboot.

"And how do you feel about that?"

"I think I'm all right," Rina said. "I think I can manage without her now. All things end and it would have been hard to go back, after two deaths and all the pain that will have caused."

When Mac left Rina collected her secateurs and wandered out into the twilit garden. Life, like gardens, needed pruning to keep it healthy, she thought. There would be new adventures ahead of her and when they arrived, Rina would be ready for them.

THE END

ACKNOWLEDGEMENTS

September 2025 marks thirty years as a published novelist, which seems very strange. In that time there have been a vast number of people who have answered my questions, pointed me in the right direction when it came to research and listened to the frustrations of a writer who couldn't get the plotlines to come together.

In particular, grateful thanks to KF and RC for technical advice. To Stuart Hill and Martyn Carey for coffee and writerly company and for listening to the occasional rant. To David A who was there at the very beginning and insisted that I treat my writing professionally, right from the start — and who called me once a week to check on my word count and submissions.

To the wonderful editorial team at Joffe Books; your endless enthusiasm and insight have been invaluable.

Special thanks to the amazing readers who have, in particular, taken Rina and her friends to their hearts.

And most of all, thanks to Julian and Katie who put up with having a writer in the house.

ALSO BY JANE ADAMS

NAOMI BLAKE MYSTERIES
Book 1: Two Little Blonde Girls
Book 2: The Camera Never Lies
Book 3: Let the Woman Go
Book 4: Killing a Stranger
Book 5: Legacy of Lies
Book 6: What Lies Beneath
Book 7: Dead Silence
Book 8: Darkest Secrets
Book 9: Out for Blood
Book 10: Without a Trace
Book 11: A Murderous Mind
Book 12: Fakes and Lies

MERROW & CLARKE SERIES
Book 1: Safe
Book 2: Kidnap

DETECTIVE MIKE CROFT SERIES
Book 1: The Greenway
Book 2: The Secrets
Book 3: Their Final Moments
Book 4: The Liar
Book 5: The Nail

DETECTIVE RAY FLOWERS SERIES
Book 1: The Apothecary's Daughter
Book 2: The Unwilling Son
Book 3: The Drowning Men
Book 4: The Sister's Twin
Book 5: The Lost Daughter

STANDALONES
Bury Me Deep
The Other Woman
The Woman in the Painting
Then She Was Dead

THE JOFFE BOOKS STORY

We began in 2014 when Jasper agreed to publish his mum's much-rejected romance novel and it became a bestseller.

Since then we've grown into the largest independent publisher in the UK. We're extremely proud to publish some of the very best writers in the world, including Joy Ellis, Faith Martin, Caro Ramsay, Helen Forrester, Simon Brett and Robert Goddard. Everyone at Joffe Books loves reading and we never forget that it all begins with the magic of an author telling a story.

We are proud to publish talented first-time authors, as well as established writers whose books we love introducing to a new generation of readers.

We won Trade Publisher of the Year at the Independent Publishing Awards in 2023 and Best Publisher Award in 2024 at the People's Book Prize. We have been shortlisted for Independent Publisher of the Year at the British Book Awards for the last five years, and were shortlisted for the Diversity and Inclusivity Award at the 2022 Independent Publishing Awards. In 2023 we were shortlisted for Publisher of the Year at the RNA Industry Awards, and in 2024 we were shortlisted at the CWA Daggers for the Best Crime and Mystery Publisher.

We built this company with your help, and we love to hear from you, so please email us about absolutely anything bookish at feedback@joffebooks.com.

If you want to receive free books every Friday and hear about all our new releases, join our mailing list here: www.joffebooks.com/freebooks.

And when you tell your friends about us, just remember: it's pronounced Joffe as in coffee or toffee!